MW01256826

Love at First ROAR

CELIA KYLE

NEW YORK TIMES BESTSELLING AUTHOR

What happens when a half-blind weremole girl falls for a scarred werebear guy? A match made in furry, dirt-caked heaven. Mostly.

Weremole Kira Kolanowski has spent twenty-nine-ish years of her life half-blind and occasionally half-dead. (Her family isn't exactly loving.) In an effort to remain fully alive, she moves to Grayslake, Georgia, with her poor excuse for a guide dog—a guide dog who decides to lift his leg and relieve himself on sexy-smelling werebear Isaac Abrams' belongings. And when he roars…well, it makes her heart go pitter-patter and other parts go "ooh baby, ooh baby." Just when she thinks she might have found happiness, a raving she-bitch werebear chick tries to kill her with the same poison that scarred Isaac to hell and back. The poison that Kira's family happens to manufacture…

Isaac Abrams is leaving Grayslake. He's tried, lord how he's tried, to settle into life in Grayslake after the birth of his niece, but it's not happening. He's been home for a year, and it's been 365 plus days of women looking past him and flat-out pretending he doesn't exist. The battle with the hyenas didn't just ruin his face, it ruined his chances at finding a mate in his hometown. So, he's leaving. Or he was leaving until one day a lush, curvaceous weremole wanders into his half-packed house with that damned peeing dog of hers…it's a good thing she's so gorgeous.

Maybe he will stay—stay and keep Kira Kolanowski all to himself. Well, once he kills everyone who's trying to kill her.

chapter one

Isaac understood the definition of "brittle smile." It was an expression he'd held all day, and he didn't imagine it would disappear any time soon. It'd been in place from the moment he climbed out of his SUV. It'd remained as he was met by his toddling niece, Sophia, and rapidly growing nephew, Parker. It'd grown shakier when he leaned over his sister-in-law Lauren's shoulder and stroked her baby daughter's cheek. It expanded when the rest of the werebear clan showed up for little Sophia's first birthday party.

Werebear after werebear parked in front of the clan den. Men and women he'd known his entire life quickly made their way to the back of the house. Since his brother Ty was the clan's Itan—werebear leader—his daughter's birthday was celebrated by one and all, as it should be. Ty was a good Itan and a better father. If anyone deserved happiness, it was Isaac's eldest brother.

Isaac just didn't want to witness it. Not when it burned a hole in his heart. He remembered easing Sophia into the world as he helped Mia—the clan's Itana and Ty's mate—with the birth.

1

He remembered Mia's tears and the shininess of Ty's eyes. He remembered their wonder and—

The heavy tread of someone approaching drew him from his heaping ball of self-pity and back to the rapidly growing party around him. He did what he always did—tucked himself against the house, in the shadows, away from the crowd. It hadn't always been this way, but after… well, after, he wasn't inclined to make a spectacle of himself.

Isaac brought his glass to his lips, tipping it back and swallowing the sweet tea infused with berries. Mia knew he didn't really drink—a Healer always had to be ready to help—and the woman made sure he got his dose of sugar that soothed his bear. Saint Mia…

Those stomps drew closer, and he swiveled his head toward the source. Ash, a big-ass bruiser of a bear and one of the family's most trusted guards, came his way with a woman in tow. Isaac sighed and lowered the cup. They really needed to stop doing this. It was becoming tedious.

Becoming? Hell, it already was. Over a year and a half had passed since the battle with the hyenas. A lot had happened that day, including Isaac acquiring a ton of scars—some more obvious than others. He gently traced the edge of one that ended near his chin. If women hadn't approached him before now, it wasn't going to change.

He turned toward the duo and pasted his semblance of a smile on his face. It wasn't wide and welcoming, not anymore. The scar that bisected his cheek kept him flashing a grimace rather than the intended grin.

"Isaac," Ash reached him, thumping his arm in welcome. "How are ya, man?"

2

God, no more patting his back. *Please.*

"Good, good. Busy as always." He kept himself busy on purpose. Everyone knew that, even if the words weren't voiced. Focusing on work meant he didn't have time to be lonely.

"Yeah, yeah. I hear you." Ash nodded and an uncomfortable silence surrounded them.

It was always this way. Isaac should stop him now before things got worse. Unfortunately, when he opened his mouth to end the farce, Ash pushed on.

"Oh, you remember my sister Eliza? She's rejoining the clan. She decided to finish her degree up the road but will be staying with me." Ash leaned close. "She wants to be close but can't stand our parents."

The woman in question rolled her eyes. "*Ash.*"

"What?" The male feigned innocence, adopting a look Isaac saw often at the clan den. He really enjoyed feeding Sophia and Parker sugar. When Mia caught them, he proclaimed he was nowhere *near* the raw cookie dough, and even if he was, it wasn't like raw eggs could hurt big strong werebears. "I didn't do anything." Ash paused. "Or say anything that wasn't true."

Isaac rolled his eyes and shook his head, which brought the man's attention back to him. Not only Ash's but Eliza's as well.

And she, like many other women in the clan, met his eyes for a moment—recognition in her gaze—before shifting to the deep, wide scar that marred his face. The mirth filling her bright green orbs quickly died and her attention shifted to his other

3

cheek. The clean one, the one not marred by evidence of his battle with the hyenas.

More silence enveloped them and he fought to fill the quiet. It wasn't her fault his disfigurement distressed her. It bothered many women. Not the men, they saw it as proof he'd fought for the clan and then put his fellow bears' recovery before his own. They looked at him with pride, thrilled to have a Healer of his skill and selflessness in their ranks.

The women pretended he didn't exist.

Which was fine. *Fine*. He wasn't sounding like some pussy-whining bear.

"Nice to meet you again, Eliza. I'm not sure when you left us, but Ty bought more land surrounding Grayslake recently. There are plenty of new beautiful spots along the water to hike and do some fishing." Her gaze didn't waver from Isaac's unblemished cheek. He supposed she needed to stare at some part of his face. Steeling himself for what was to come, he played his part in Ash's matchmaking scheme. "If you'd like me to show you around, just say the word. I spend a lot of time at my office, but I always have evenings free."

Ash smiled widely, obviously thrilled with Isaac's invitation.

Not so fast.

He'd become adept at reading expressions and noticing body language. He knew what her response would be even before she said the words.

"I-I-I… um, Ash promised to take me on a tour of the town and stuff." Ash's expression turned to a thunderous glare at

4

Eliza. He almost stepped in, but he knew there was more. "Brother-sister time, you know? Maybe some other time."

The smile was fake, but he had to hand it to her. At least she tried.

"Of course," he nodded, ignoring the stinging scent of Ash's rage, the strength managing to overwhelm the flavors of berries and tea that filled his nose. "Some other time."

Like never.

"If you'll excuse me," he let his gaze scan the crowd, hunting for a reason to leave the two siblings. When his attention finally landed on his brother, he refocused on the duo. "I need to talk to Ty real quick." He gave Eliza another tight-lipped smile. "It was nice to meet you."

Isaac escaped as Ash and Eliza said their goodbyes, striding away before he caught Eliza's relieved sigh. At least he assumed there would be one. Every other female shoved before him reacted the same way. Hushed whispers followed him, Ash's overshadowing Eliza's, and he was glad when they were out of earshot.

That encounter rounded out an even three dozen similar meetings and he was… done. He thought time away from Grayslake after the fight would make a difference. But he'd been proven wrong, hadn't he? Even strangers shied from his scarring. He wished…

No, he didn't wish anything. Looking across the yard, at the men he'd saved, at those he'd healed, he would take the pain again and again rather than push it on another. Rather than lose another.

Shaking his head, he kept on his path, finding his brother by following Sophia's high-pitched squeals and Parker's playful growls. He rounded a group of men, taking a few thumps and pats on his back as he passed. Those who didn't touch him, grunted a hello.

As the males parted, he found what he'd expected. A shifted Parker chasing the toddling Sophia while Mia kept an eye on them. The boy was the girl's protector and playmate in one. No one looked at Sophia cross-eyed or got near her if Parker had any say about it.

Isaac sidled up to his eldest brother, easing onto the bench beside him, watching the romping children.

"What's up?" Ty started the conversation, and a sudden bout of nerves assaulted him. This would hurt his family, upset the women—especially his mother—and anger the males.

Well, there was no nice way to lay things out. They'd be pissed, but he wasn't changing his mind. There was no other choice at this point. "I'm leaving Grayslake. Permanently. Alone."

Alone was the important part of his statement. He'd left the town briefly with Mia's father when the older male acted as Guardian of his hometown. Seven months later, he returned. It'd been a year since, and things hadn't changed. It was time.

Maybe after he accomplished his goals, he could return to Grayslake, but for now he needed to be gone.

Tension filled Ty, the man's muscles frozen and firm, hand stilling halfway to his mouth. Without lowering the glass, his brother turned his head and stared at him.

"I don't think I heard you right." The words weren't the deep rumble of his brother, but the chilling calm of Isaac's Itan.

He was damned if he'd call the words back. "No, your hearing is fine."

"No," the word was slow and consumed with deadly quiet. "I did not."

Deadly? Did it matter? No, Ty wouldn't hurt a hair on his head. Not after everything Isaac had "sacrificed" for the clan.

"Yes." Isaac nodded. "It's time. You know it. You don't have to like it, but you know it."

Part of Ty's change rippled over the man, skin swelling and relaxing in unhurried waves. Fur slid from his pores, peppering his arm, and Isaac fought to keep his own bear in check. Ty was angrier than he anticipated, but Isaac refused to back down. Not about this.

"I deny your petition." Of course Ty did.

After nearly losing Keen due to the family's stupidity, Ty had become very devoted to Van, Keen, and Isaac. The clan den rested atop a high hill and Van lived at its base. Ty was actively trying to get Keen to build a home beside Van's.

Isaac shrugged. "And Terrence already approved my application for relocation."

Terrence Jensen was the Southeast Itan, a scary as hell bear, but also Keen's uncle-in-law. The male was happy to help Isaac, which in turn helped his niece's family.

"He can't…" A shudder overtook Ty's body and his brother made a tight fist.

Unfortunately, it was the hand still clutching his cup. Berry infused tea splashed over Ty's pants, soaking him in the sweet mixture. The rush of liquid and ice had Ty freezing in place. The Itan tilted his head down and then refocused on Isaac. His brother's anger at his announcement was filled with frustration as well.

Rather than give his brother a chance to collect his thoughts, Isaac plowed on. "You know he's authorized to take petitions in the event a clan's Itan is prejudiced against—"

Ty snarled, "I'm not prejudiced—"

"You wouldn't let me leave if he hadn't already—"

"Damn right, you're not leaving," Ty snapped.

"Ty!" Mia's gasped yell didn't slow Isaac in the least.

"Yes, I am. There's nothing here for me, Ty. You know it. In your heart, you know if I stay I'll never have what you have with Mia, Parker, and Sophia." The words were hard to say, the naked truth always something he shied from, but there was no denying reality.

"Isaac—" Ty's voice was overridden by Sophia's high-pitched squeal. She wobbled toward them, apparently indifferent to the tension that lingered between Isaac and his brother. The moment she was within reaching distance, she raised her arms, calling for Isaac.

"A-a-a-a." Sophia still babbled, but she had specific sounds for most of the family members, the girl quickly taught *them* what *she* wanted.

Isaac was powerless beneath her bright-eyed gaze. "Hey, cub-cub."

He picked her up, settling her on his lap, tiny toes on his thighs as she clutched his hands. She loved bouncing, standing on his legs, and giving him toothy grins. "A-a-a-a."

Ty's voice was low, much calmer now that Sophia was present. "You'll miss this if you leave."

Isaac turned his attention back to Ty, careful of his precious cargo but also intent on his brother. "I'll never have this if I stay."

* * *

Kira rubbed her forehead, fighting the headache that threatened. She wasn't sure if it came from the stress of moving or the constant yammering of her best friend.

She clutched her cell phone, pushing back the tears that loomed, and tried explaining things to Zoey once again. "You know why I couldn't stay."

"I do, but I don't."

Another crash, the tinkling and crunching of glass had stinging moisture blurring her vision. Or rather, blurring it more than it was naturally blurred. Er. Right. The point was, no matter the destruction, she wasn't gonna let the tears trail down her cheeks. No crying, no whining, no sniffling, and no boo-hooing. Nope. None of it.

"Yes, you really do, Zoey. We've talked about this." And talked about it and talked about it and… Yeah.

"I don't understand, though. You're the Alpha's *daughter*. Why are you running away? If you'd just…"

The next sound was a heavy thud, and she wondered if that was her couch or her dining room table slamming onto the hundred-year-old wood floors.

Nope, no tears, but maybe a pity party was okay. A big one. Huge even. A ginormous of gigalactious proportions pity party of the millennium was totally called for.

Because, really, *saying* she wasn't going to take anyone's crap was not the same as actually *not* taking anyone's crap. Even though she left her old pack behind, the residual effects of their abuse still lingered. She was prey, she couldn't ever forget that.

"Being the Alpha's daughter doesn't make me dominant. Are you forgetting my other half?" The half that had her running and scurrying whenever a wolf trotted past or they pushed her around. "That's what I live with, Zoey. That's the reason I couldn't stay. I don't have fangs and claws like the rest of the pack." Okay, she sorta did, on a much smaller scale. They weren't enough to scare anyone, least of all a werewolf. "I couldn't fight back and I got tired of struggling to stay alive."

She was so very tired.

"Did you hafta go so far, though?" her friend whined, and Kira wondered if the woman was a werewolf or a big baby.

Another crash was followed by more shattering of glass except this time the sound wasn't muffled by a box. Dear God, what did they break now?

Zoey sniffled as if she was crying and Kira knew that was the furthest from the truth. The woman was trying to play on Kira's people-pleaser half. Not happening.

"Yes, I did," she snapped, hating that she'd turned into an über bitch. "We talked about this. You helped me do this."

Kira never would have gotten away without Zoey's help.

"I know, I just…"

God, she loved Zoey more than life itself, but she couldn't deal with this bout of "woe is me." Not when she had so much going on at that moment. Later, Zoey would apologize. Her friend would remember how many times she'd patched Kira up and how many times Kira had edged too close to death for anyone's comfort.

"Alpha was never any help. *Ever*. Which means if *he*," Kira hated, hated, hated that male. "If *he* got his hands on me, there's no telling how far he would go. You've seen the damage, Zoey." Her best friend had seen a little. Kira tried to shield the spunky she-wolf from the worst. "For once in my life, I'm thinking of me." Kira's heart thudded and pumped, threatening to burst from her chest. Anger coursed through her. Outright *anger*.

"Rawr, bitch—"

Kira tore the phone from her ear and pressed the button to end the call. Maybe tomorrow she could laugh and joke with Zoey.

She tucked the cell in her pocket and pushed away from the wall. The men were outside, grunting and groaning with a dash of grumbling as they grabbed more of her stuff. The half of her that was patient and kind warred with the ferocity of her inner-animal because that bit of her wanted to go rabid on their asshole asses.

Unfortunately, they were at least a foot taller and a good fifty pounds heavier than she was. Plus, well, they were werebears.

Short, fluffy Kira was no match for them. Hell, even in her shifted form, the most she could do was nibble on them and then dig and hide.

I am weremole, hear me run for my life.

Shaking her head, she made her way down the nearby hallway, running her fingers over the aged wallpaper and smiling at the thump of her shoes on the worn wood. History surrounded her, the past welcoming her in its embrace.

Her dog's repetitive barks drew her, the animal's attempts at protecting her easily heard. He was a wonderful, adorable, shitty guide dog. But he was hers. And he probably would be a great guide if she took the time to train with him. Except… she liked him the way he was. She didn't want him to become something he wasn't, didn't want to mold him into what she desired or what was expected.

She'd had enough of that in life. She wasn't about to inflict it on another being.

Ignoring yet another crashing thump, she tugged on the back door and the dog's barks immediately transformed from threatening woofs to happy cries. His approach was unmistakable, the scramble of clawed feet on grass and then weathered wood easily discernible from the rest of the world.

Kira crouched and held her arms wide as the blur of her pup ran to her. She supposed she had to be thankful for some things and the fact she was only partially blind was a blessing. Colorful blurs marked her world, allowing her to get around on her own. Mostly.

A wet tongue lapped at her, coating her face in dog saliva, and she nudged him away. "Hey, now, quit it."

He woofed and paused in his attentions, the animal's fun loving personality quickly shifting to enraged and protective in an instant.

A low growl came from her dog, rumbling and vibrating through her, and she took in a deep breath, sorting through the scents. The pup obviously objected to whoever was behind her and she needed to know who she faced.

The first inhale brought the stink of sweat and unwashed skin coupled with a good dose of anger that was quickly transforming into rage.

Could her day get any worse?

Kira pushed to her feet, intent on facing off with the male. God only knew what his problem was, but she wouldn't face it on her knees.

Spinning, she came face to chest with one of the males. "Can I help you?"

"Yeah," he sniffed, and she bit her tongue. Blatantly scenting someone was just *rude*. Sure, she did the same, but she was *half blind*. "Yeah, you can help me."

She couldn't see his expression, but his scent was unmistakable. *Lust.* She fought back the threatening panic. There was no reason to worry. She was in a crowded neighborhood and the

13

woman across the street was nosy as hell and had been spying on Kira's house. Well, she assumed it was spying. Otherwise, she merely liked to sit at her front window a lot. Like, all day.

He sniffed again. "You can help me real good."

He reached down and his gesture was unmistakable. The man rubbed his crotch, and she managed to keep her shudder of revulsion under wraps.

Yeah, she couldn't help him at all.

Her dog snarled, darting forward and snapping his teeth.

"What the fuck is wrong with your fuck—"

"Tommy Taylor, I know I didn't hear what I thought I heard." The feminine voice was quick and sharp, cutting through his words like a knife. "Because by my last count you already owe the swear jar over a thousand dollars."

The change in the male was instantaneous. All hints of lust and arousal disappeared in the wake of those words and fear moved into place.

Fear.

The man stepped back, putting several feet between their bodies while also allowing Kira to get a look at the newcomer. The woman was short, as short as she was and appeared to be as curvy, as well.

Kira glanced at the large male easing farther away and deeper into her kitchen as if to put even more distance between him and the newcomer.

Whoever put that bolt of terror zinging through the man before her was a woman Kira wanted to get to know. How did she do that and was it teachable?

Inquiring, pussyfooted, cowering minds wanted to know.

The woman focused on the mover for a moment longer before she turned that attention on Kira. She strode forward, arm outstretched. The aromas of happiness and welcome filled the air. "Hi, I'm Mia. Welcome to Grayslake."

For the first time since she'd begun this wild relocation across the country, Kira smiled. And meant it. Because in the wake of the woman's welcoming words, some of Kira's old self emerged, the part of her that smiled and laughed and loved life.

And when Mia hugged her hard, squeezing her until she thought her bones would break, Kira realized she would be okay. That everything would be okay.

chapter two

Isaac grimaced at the stacks of boxes littering the house. As a Healer who worked in a sterile environment more often than not… this was not okay.

He'd only been on his own a year, and still he'd managed to collect so much *stuff*. When he came back to town, the clan den hadn't been big enough for both him and Ty's little family. Moving into Mia's grandfather's home had been the answer. The place was old, but gorgeous with its hand-carved banister and doorframes. The worn spots on the floor at the bottom of the stairs represented years of running cubs while a large discoloration in the dining room spoke of messy kids eating breakfast.

It was a house built to be filled with a happy couple and children. Which was good since he'd soon be moving out and leaving it empty for a to-be-found happy couple and children.

With a shake of his head, he dispelled the pang of loss in his heart. He needed to think positively and not worry about everything he'd be leaving. He had another six weeks of packing and organizing to do before he moved. Between working at the local werebear clinic and volunteering his time at the human hospital, he didn't have much time to prepare. He needed to snatch every available moment.

Isaac snared another folded box and opened the stiff square. It took no time to make the appropriate folds and slap tape on the seams. With most of the living room done and the dining room empty, he headed to the kitchen. The worn wood floor was cool beneath his feet, smooth from decades of use.

History, the house had a truck full of history, and for a moment he wished he weren't leaving. There was so much to explore, so much to do to restore the old place until it looked almost new. It was always something he'd wanted to do—each time he found a new dent in the plaster or a jiggling step.

God, when did he become so attached to a house that didn't even belong to him?

Probably about the same time he realized he was ready to settle down and have a family. The same time he envisioned raising his family in this house.

On the heels of those dreams came yet another female's rejection. He had to accept that Grayslake wasn't home any longer.

Huffing, he went into the kitchen and placed the box on the table before moving toward the cabinets. He had so many different pots and pans—it was ridiculous. But he used each one. Maybe not every day, but who knew when he'd have a craving for fresh pasta or homemade marinara? Whenever that happened, he'd have the right tool.

It didn't take long for him to get lost in the monotony of packing, wrapping glass pans, and placing packing paper between metal ones. Of course, the whole process would go quicker if he had one of his brothers or their mates at his side. Hell, he'd even take his interfering mother and gruff father.

Too bad they were all "busy."

Busy showing their disapproval.

Dammit.

Isaac paused for a moment and breathed deeply, ignoring the small ache in his chest. His inner bear helped soothe the pain. It knew the truth just as his human mind did, and both parts of him were in agreement. They wanted a family, they wanted a mate and cubs and everything that came with being a good mate and father.

He delved deeper into one of the corner cabinets, cursing the person who'd designed them so deep. Isaac wasn't a small man and sure as hell wasn't designed for crawling that far into a wood framed hole. Of course, he was pretty damned sure his favorite cast-iron skillet had wiggled just out of reach.

Bastard piece of metal.

"Hello?" A sweet feminine voice drifted to him, sliding through the quiet of his house.

He jerked in surprise and banged his head on the underside of the drawer above him.

"Dammit." He eased back, rubbing his skull the moment he was clear. The bear was quick to heal him and brush away the ache, but it couldn't banish the owner of the voice.

"Heellloooo?" The word was drawn out into a faux howl. "I'm speaking, are you listening?"

He didn't recognize the voice's owner, but that didn't mean much. He kept to himself for the most part and Ty welcomed other bears to the clan here and there. Plus the hyena's poison hadn't stopped at his skin. No, it'd dug deeper, stroking his mind and his memory wasn't what it once was. A beast could only heal so much when faced with the devastating toxin, and he'd been too intent on healing—

A gasp came from the other room before a heavy thud accompanied by the tinkling of glass reached him. "Shit, that sounds expensive. You'd think you'd pay better attention, Kira."

The scrape of shuffling steps reached him and Isaac pushed to his feet, shoving the half-filled box out of his way. It was obvious the woman wasn't leaving, so he'd give her a reason to. One quick look at his face and then she would scamper back the way she came. He didn't have a humped back or scarring like the Phantom of the Opera, but it repulsed the women in his clan, so it would get this stranger to run, too.

He retraced his earlier path, passing the corner where the wallpaper peeled and the spot where it'd faded until pure white. He would have hunted new paper, one original to the age of the house, and redone the smooth surface. The old girl deserved a face-lift.

Instead…

Another tumbling crash reached him and he growled, the bear along with him. He didn't have a lot of expensive belongings, but—cheap or not—they were his, dammit. The least the stranger could do was keep her house-trashing hands to herself.

Isaac rounded the last corner, striding into the entryway. He passed the open front door and headed into the living room, more smashes reaching out to him.

"Dammit. Shit. Oh, that one was really expensive," she muttered. "I am the biggest ass known to ass-dom. Just stop moving and wait. Did you learn anything from your friggin' movers? Obviously not."

Isaac slid to a silent stop, freezing and simply staring at the muttering woman before him. She wasn't familiar, that much he knew. He would remember that ass, the trim waist that led to wide hips and the sleek line of her back. Deep brown curls nearly reached the top curve of her butt and... damn. Just... damn.

His bear had a similar reaction, perking up at the sight of this unknown female. His cock half hardened in his worn jeans, slowly easing to attention the longer he stared. She bent over, wiggling her ass as she lowered. Hand outstretched, she reached for one of the boxes that'd tumbled to the ground, only to bump her head on another. At least that one didn't fall.

"Ouch." She rose to her full, short, height. "Hello?" Her voice was raised once again. "It would be helpful if—"

"You stopped destroying my home."

She squeaked and spun to face him, hands pressed to her chest. Her ample, full chest. Her breasts strained against her top, seeming ready to burst past the thin fabric.

He wouldn't mind that. Not at all.

"Oh! There you are."

Isaac dragged his attention from her chest, traced the slim line of her neck and finally settled his gaze on her face. Her heart shaped face with her pert nose and full lips. They were spread in a wide smile, the expression pushing away some of his annoyance.

He only wished he could see her eyes, glimpse them before she focused on his scarring and turned away. Unfortunately, dark sunglasses covered them, keeping them hidden.

She eased closer, hand outstretched, smile still in place. A *sincere* smile—not forced and not filled with strain. Huh.

"Hi, I'm Kira Kolanowski." She took another two steps and promptly tripped. Her arms pin wheeled as she tipped forward. Isaac was quick to catch her and haul her close. He tried to ignore the feel of her curved body against his hard muscles. He was toned and firm, his bear keeping him fit, but she was a study in soft flesh and sweetness.

Sweetness. Yes. Blueberries and sweet cream wriggled in his arms, the scents embodied by Kira Kolanowski.

"Shit. You should really put all this stuff in order. I mean a half-blind someone could—"

Isaac growled. *He* should put *his* stuff in order? Gorgeous or not, she'd come into his home.

"Look, lady—"

"Kira. Or KK to some of my friends. Colon to the mean ones, but my best friend Zoey tends to straighten out those guys and now they only whisper real quiet," she whispered, apparently attempting to mimic the "mean ones" and then she huffed. "They seem to forget I have amazing hearing and can—"

22

Kira—or KK—jabbered against his chest, seeming not to care that he held her so close and that his body reacted to her nearness. His cock twitched, interested in the luscious female. It filled and hardened, aching to sink into her heat.

Did she pull away? Nope, she kept going.

Isaac tore himself from her and stepped back, pressing a finger to her lips as he did so. He still clung to his frustration at her destruction, but her frown, her bow-shaped mouth tipping down, had it vanishing.

"What are you doing in my house?" He winced that his voice was rough, but he had his bear to blame. The animal reveled in Kira's touch, in the way she didn't pull away and seemed to sink into him. Horny bastard.

"Well," she sniffed a quick breath of annoyance, but that turned into a deeper, slower inhale and her frown disappeared. "I came to introduce myself. I moved in next door." She waved her hand behind herself, actually gesturing toward the park across the street. "And thought I'd come by. Count your house so if I wanna come over I can—"

"Count my house?"

"Uh-huh." She nodded. "You see, my best friend and I—"

"The one who defends you from…"

"Oh, yeah." She flapped her hand as if it was inconsequential. He didn't think anything was trivial with Kira. "It's the whole Kolanowski thing. Kolanowski—colon." She shrugged. "Anyway, so what I do is—"

A series of rapid, deep barks echoed off the walls a split second before a massive golden retriever bounded into his house. Of course, *it* knocked over yet another box, sending it crashing to the ground.

Kira gasped and then yelled at the mangy animal. "Ebenezer Hufflesnuffle, stop that right now."

She even stomped, and Isaac wanted her to do it again. Her breasts bounced and stretched the material when she made the jerky motion. Yeah, he wouldn't mind the beast tearing up his place if it meant she stomped a time, or twenty.

The dog didn't listen to her, choosing to sniffle and snuffle Isaac's belongings. When it paused and slowly lifted its leg, Kira not moving to stop the damned animal, Isaac reacted.

He hissed and snapped his fingers as he whipped out the pup's name. "Ebenezer."

The dog slowly panned its attention to Isaac, and he could swear the thing glared at him. He opened his mouth to issue another reprimand but got distracted by Kira poking him.

"Hey, why are you yelling at my dog?" She prodded him again. "You shouldn't interfere between a guide dog and its owner."

"Your dog was about to piss on my stuff. You know, the boxes that managed to survive your entrance."

"Oh. Well, I wouldn't have tripped if you had the lights on in this place." She quieted and then focused on the dog. Well, in the general direction of the dog. "Ebenezer Snuffletruffle, you shouldn't pee on people's things."

He ignored her words and instead focused on what she'd said combined with her actions.

Guide dog.

Half-blind.

"You can't see?"

That had Kira snapping her hidden gaze to him. "Half-blind. A little bit blind, really." She raised a hand and brought her pointer finger and thumb near each other. "Just a tiny bit. And it's more fuzziness than anything."

"So tiny, you knocked over three boxes—"

"No, just two. And it's dark."

"And you need a guide dog?" He crossed his arms over his chest. The vision issues didn't bother him. She was gorgeous no matter what, and her scent did things to him *and* his bear. The pissing "guide" dog was an issue.

"More like a faux guide dog." She sighed and glanced toward the animal. The animal pissing on his fucking boxes. "Oh, Ebenezer Snoffleblossom, what am I gonna do with you?"

When the dog moved on to another box and lifted his leg, Isaac had a good idea what she could do with the beast. It involved his bear and a nice run through the forest.

Two may go in…

Then the animal flopped and hopped its way toward her, slobbering all over her fingers and bringing out her smile once again.

Isaac mentally grumbled. He couldn't eat the thing if it made her smile.

Dammit.

*

Kira *could not believe* that not only had she sent *two* boxes—not three—of the hottie's belongings to the ground, but then Ebenezer also tinkled on his things.

Could. Not. Believe.

He was never gonna let her count his house. Well, count her steps inside his house and jot things down so she could... She mentally sighed. Hell, he probably wouldn't let her near him ever, ever again. And he smelled *so* good. So, so, so, *so* good.

A million, gajillion, billion goods.

Her little twitching nose beastie wanted to snuffle and sniff him. In stereo. Her kind could do that. Her inner animal agreed. It rubbed and rolled, wriggling as if it chased the tastiest worm and this man held it between his fingers.

She took a deep breath, bringing in more of his scents, and released the air with a sigh. Deep, dark chocolate mixed with fresh turned earth. Utter. Perfection.

She also sensed a hint of anger coming from the male. Which, if she was honest, was to be expected when she was in the area. It was as if she were a life-size anger-mobile.

After twenty-nine-ish years, she expected it. Hated the reality, but accepted the truth. She always managed to piss off someone. But she didn't piss *on* them. That was Ebenezer's job.

Ebenezer slowly inched away from her.

"Ebenezer Hufflehaffle." She snapped her fingers. "Get back here, right now."

A low whine followed by a doggie huff preceded the clicking plod of the dog approaching. She always had to rely on her other senses, her inner animal's domination over her sight making it difficult to see. She recognized colors, but everything else existed as blurs and blobs. She'd probably hate the condition if she knew any better. But she didn't. So… she didn't.

"Look, lady. It's nice to mee—"

"Kira." She'd told him her name, hadn't she? She was pretty sure she had. Post-box tumbling, but pre-dog peeing. She did remember that she'd vomited way too much information about her name.

"Kira," he sighed except it wasn't a dreamy one. Nope, it was filled with frustration. Typical.

At least it wasn't tinged by impending violence. Grayslake had quite a few dominant and massive bears, but for the most part, they were nice and welcoming. And if they weren't, she had to tell Mia. Apparently, the woman was a disorganized unpacker and kind of a Big Deal in the tiny town.

She wished for once, she could make a good impression. The man she now dubbed "Mr. Unnamed" sounded so damned sexy. Just a big bowl of cookie dough and sin. But she'd already annoyed him. Her only option now was a not-so-graceful retreat.

"Look, Kira, it was wonderful—"

"What's your name?" She wasn't sure why she blurted out the question. It wasn't like she'd see him again. Well, she still hadn't seen him, but… whatever.

Another sigh. She wondered if he had a breathing problem. "Isaac Abrams."

"Oh." *Oh.* He was a bear. A big deal kind of bear, hence the scents of nature clinging to him. She should have guessed since she was now living in a bear town, but he'd seemed… different.

Her animal hadn't been afraid of him even a tiny bit. It was the reason she'd tromped up his front porch steps and wiggled her way into the house. The little beastie wanted to meet the man behind the scent and Kira went along with the critter.

It wasn't good to deny her animal side.

"So, you're related to the Itan then?" *Of course* her dog pissed on one of the Itan's relatives. *Of course.*

Maybe her best friend was right. Maybe she should have just stayed in her old home, managing to avoid her family and the rest of the pack. Avoidance meant a lot less pain.

Maybe she shouldn't have…

"Yes, he's my brother."

"Oh… that's… that's nice." Her little beastie whimpered and curled into a tiny ball inside her. Great. "So that makes you the clan's…"

Please don't say Enforcer. Please don't say Enforcer.

She'd heard bears could be big—duh—and mean and that Enforcers were the *worst*. Everyone in town was welcoming-ish

28

so far, but destroying the Enforcer's property was never a good thing.

"Healer." He snapped off the word, and she sensed a big old ball of persnickety rolling in.

She released a relieved sigh. "Oh, that really *is* nice."

He moved, easing his weight from foot to foot and his shoulders shifted as the rustle of cloth reached her sensitive ears. She imagined him crossing his arms, and she knew without touching his face that he had a frown in place.

Which meant it was time for her to skedaddle.

"So, uh, I guess I should go. Since you're not gonna let me count your house or anything and I bet Ebenezer needs to tinkle and—"

"He already 'tinkled.'"

"Oh. Well, I bet he's hungry, so—"

"He's currently eating a cardboard box. I doubt he's hungry."

She was gonna die. Or rather, wanted to die. Right then. After peeing on the man's boxes, Ebenezer was now eating one. The most delicious man she'd *ever* met, and she'd all around ruined everything. She didn't expect him to worship at her hooha altar, but she wouldn't mind spending more time with him. She could have invited him to dinner, or cooked for him, or made up any excuse she could to be in his presence a little longer, but no, Ebie had to ruin it.

"Right. So, I'll take him and go home and feed him real food and…" She let the words trail off, not really sure what she was saying. Zoey often told her she thought Kira talked to talk and didn't really have anything to say.

She wasn't sure Zoey was wrong.

"Ebie." She clapped her hands, and the munching ceased. "C'mere, boy."

Kira gazed around the room, hunting the shadows for her wayward dog. The sun waned while she'd spoken with Isaac and now most of the room was dark shadows. Shadows which made it difficult to see her dog. Great.

"Ebenezer Bafflepuffle, I mean it." She snapped her fingers again. Not that it'd do anything. Other than the confrontation with the mover, the pup had been enjoying Kira's new carefree attitude. Out from under the oppressive weight of the pack, she was now able to let her true personality free.

Ebenezer was letting something free.

She sought out the darkest corner, sure that she saw it move, and glared at the spot. "Get. Over. Here."

"Kira?" It almost sounded as if he were choking back laughter, the chuckles muffled, but still present.

She drew in a bit of air around her, scenting his emotions. He was laughing at her. Wonderful. Her embarrassment was complete. Tears pricked her eyes and she fought back the urge to let them fall. It was as if she were living at home again, listening to her pack snicker and giggle when they weren't trying to kill her. She always imagined them pointing and laughing as well, but at least she'd been too blind to see them.

Kira shoved her humiliation back and drew herself to her full height. It wasn't much, but she refused to let this *bear* belittle her or make her feel bad. She may not be the best shifter and she may be half-blind, but she was her deceased mother's weremole daughter and the youngest of Alpha Clarke's two children. Okay, she was his bastard daughter brought to the pack after his true mate died, and the Alpha part didn't matter since she hadn't inherited his strength. She'd endured a lifetime as prey in the middle of a wolf pack.

She would be *damned* if she cried in front of this big, dumb bear.

Kira pulled on every ounce of the haughty bitch demeanor she'd learned at Alpha Clarke's knee and blasted it at Isaac. "Obviously, Ebenezer is not nearby and while I'm sure you find my near blindness amusing, I would appreciate it if you could refrain from laughing until I've left. Can you please point me in the direction of my dog? I'd like to depart."

Silence greeted her statement, her words slamming to the ground between them like a leaden ball.

"Kira," remorse filled the word, but she didn't give a damn— even more, her give a damn was buried six feet under and she'd stomped on the ground to flatten the mound of dirt. She refused to dig it back up.

Ignoring his tone, she tugged on her purse and slid her hand into the well-organized bag. It took no time to find the specially printed business card she sought. While the pieces of cardstock weren't marked with braille, they were printed in a way that allowed her to easily discern what she touched. Tugging the card free, she held it in his general direction.

"Forward a bill for your broken belongings to my accountant. He will ensure you're paid for the damage Ebenezer and I caused." She kept that arrogant tone, speaking to him as if he were less than the dirt she enjoyed. She fought to keep up appearances, to not let him catch any hint of the tears lurking near her eyes. She hated the need to wear the dark glasses, but loved them at that moment.

"Kira—"

The rhythmic click clack of Ebie's claws on the wood reached her. She splayed her fingers and waited for the dog to near. The animal didn't behave half the time, but he always managed to sense her moods. When Kira needed him, Ebie was there and ready to work.

She glanced at the blob beside her, noting the animal's position and she knew he stared at her, waiting for direction. "Home, Ebenezer. Take us home."

The dog went to work, rising to all four feet and leading her forward. She knew Isaac stood to her left, his massive body easing aside as she approached, and she paused beside him, still holding the small piece of cardstock.

"We apologize for the intrusion and damage our presence caused. I will inform my accountant to expect your bill." Shaky words pushed past her lips, and she refocused on getting the hell out of Isaac Abrams's home and away from the too-tempting man.

Ebenezer eased her around the boxes she'd destroyed as well as the one that smelled of urine. As they passed a larger pile, she placed her card on the top. He hadn't taken it, but she was sure as hell gonna give it to him.

Instead of roughly bounding forward and dragging her along, the animal was gentle and slow. Ebie cared for her—it was obvious in his interactions with her—but he was also a puppy at heart. She was glad that he'd settled into work.

"Kira…" Isaac kept repeating her name, remorse filling the syllables as if it'd make a difference. "Wait."

She was an adult. She wasn't held captive by her father's decrees and sure as hell wasn't living on his land any longer. The bounds of the law aside, she didn't have to do a damned thing anyone demanded.

His heavy tread followed her and Ebenezer increased their pace, carefully leading her down the porch steps and along the walkway. They turned left when they reached the sidewalk, Isaac on their heels.

Kira ignored him. She'd ignored every other idiot who laughed at her expense, she could ignore this one. To think, she'd been thrilled to meet her bear neighbors. At least the couple to her left was nice and their little cub was adorable. Then there was Mia. She'd helped Kira unpack her kitchen and dig in her newly tilled garden. Heck, even the woman's little cub Parker enjoyed time digging in the dirt. Her young daughter liked eating the dirt, but Kira did as well when she was mole-shaped and didn't see anything wrong with that. It'd only been a few days, but she already felt a kinship with the female half-werebear and her small family.

Ebie paused, and she reached out, fingers colliding with the wooden gate. She stroked the wood and one nudge caused the attached bell to jiggle, telling her they'd arrived at the right house. She pushed the panel so it swung wide to grant them entrance. When it didn't immediately slam shut, she knew Isaac still followed.

She climbed the stairs with her dog's help. She'd counted out her steps in her new place, making sure she could navigate her property with ease. She was simply too upset to bother at the moment.

Digging out her keys as they neared the door, she ignored Isaac's heavy tread on the wood porch and the heat of his nearness. She ignored the way his scent called to her animal. She definitely ignored the way a sense of safety settled on her shoulders with him close by.

Kira easily unlocked her home, and nudged the door open, releasing Ebenezer as she did. The dog, normally thrilled at being released, remained nearby. He whined and danced on his paws, obviously uneasy, and she didn't have it in her to soothe the animal. Not when she was still dealing with Isaac.

"I appreciate your escort, Mr. Abrams." She kept her tone cool.

"I wasn't—" The words were a growl.

"Again, I apologize for my behavior and while I violated the boundaries of your home without permission, I do request that you respect my wishes." She kept the words smooth. "At this juncture, you are trespassing."

"I'm," he breathed deeply and held the air a moment before releasing it.

More of his scent slid over her skin, and Kira's inner mole both whined and growled at the man. The beast wanted and hated Isaac in equal measure.

"I'm sorry for laughing, Kira. You're just so cute and you don't seem to care that I have these—"

Cute. Right.

She shook her head. "Thank you for the apology. Please leave."

Before she broke down and cried like a baby.

"All right. I'll leave you alone. Maybe I can—"

"Good night, Mr. Abrams." Not sure she could utter another word without sobbing, she stepped back and pushed her front door closed.

Kira locked herself in her new sanctuary, away from the laughter that lurked on the other side.

Away from the pain.

Away from it all.

Maybe Grayslake wasn't so different after all. Then again, no one had tried to kill her. At least, not yet.

chapter three

Isaac sipped his coffee, the blueberry flavored bitter brew sweetened with a hint of sugar and cream. It calmed his bear's immediate desire for breakfast, which meant he could take some time to enjoy the sunrise. Shades of pink, blue, and orange colored the sky, painting the air in a glorious riot of hues.

The backyard was his small sanctuary away from it all.

A soft breeze blew across the yard, ruffling his hair and stroking his skin.

Quiet mornings like this he missed most. The neighborhood was always slow to wake on the weekends which meant he got a couple of early hours of quiet before everyone bustled on with their day.

He took advantage of this time as often as he could. Even more now that his impending move neared.

Five more weeks and then he'd be on the road. He hadn't spread the news of his destination to his family—mainly because they'd never asked—but he'd train with the Southeast Healer. He'd live in Terrence Jensen's compound while he learned all he could. From there, he'd become a sort of traveling Healer, going wherever he was needed at the drop of a hat. The Southeast Healer was getting up there in years and couldn't always handle some of the emergency cases or visit various clans in the territory.

That would be Isaac's job once he was deemed fit by the Southeast Healer.

He hated that he'd be gone, but traveling from place to place would enable him to meet hundreds—thousands—of other bears, other women. A desperate man had to find a mate *somewhere.*

A sharp bark was followed by a tinkling laugh and the slam of a door, breaking into Isaac's solitude. Another growl split the air, which was followed by a giggle. A giggle that had his bear pushing to its feet and lumbering closer with a deep snuffle. A wet, cold nose pressed against his mind, the animal nosing him and encouraging him to go toward the happy sounds.

More yips and chuckles, the thump of someone hopping down the steps reaching him with ease.

Kira. KK to her friends and Colon to the mean ones.

He hadn't spied her in days and he was embarrassed to admit he'd been looking. He kept his eye out for the bright, curvaceous woman each time he left the house for work and every time the process was reversed when he got home. His bear would allow no less.

For some reason, the animal attached itself to Kira, to her vulnerability and strength. Contradictions surrounded the woman and his inner beast wanted to discover each of her secrets.

He'd already uncovered one source of pain. Found it and stomped it into the ground with his callous amusement.

God, he was an ass. Then again, that wasn't news to anyone.

Another yipping bark and another full-bellied laugh. It had him half out of his chair before he even realized he'd moved. The bear snared control for a moment, urging him to go to the fence that separated their properties. The tall, wooden barrier crept to six feet high, but he could peek over the edge.

The problem was, he shouldn't.

He'd apologized for his behavior, yet she hadn't accepted, had she? Nope. She had remained frigid in her anger as she slammed the door in his face.

Rustling of grass told him she'd made it off the porch and onto the lawn. The rapid patter of Ebenezer returning to her filled him and eased the bear's tension. He hadn't even known he'd worried about her until that moment. He didn't realize his animal cared about her that way.

Fuck. He accepted his attraction to her. Even when she was all wrapped up in her snit, she was gorgeous. Hell, that haughty attitude made her more beautiful. He'd wanted to ruffle her feathers more. Well, after she was done being *really* mad at him.

After leaving her at the door, his bear tore through him and he'd bolted for clan lands, anxious to release his animal and let it run off some of its anger. Anger that'd been directed at his human half.

A pissed off bear was a dangerous bear.

As soon as it'd regained control of its rage, the damned beast set off to hunt Kira. From there, Isaac wrestled the four-legged asshole back into its mental cage and returned home.

It'd been seven days and now he found himself on edge once again. His skin rippled, the animal stretching against its bindings and hunting for a weakness. It ached to nuzzle and sniff Kira. Was desperate to rub against her until her scent covered him.

Isaac stretched his neck, rolling his head from side to side and fought to release the growing tension. She already hated him, he wasn't about to vault over her fence and tackle her to the ground just because his bear was a needy whore.

The animal growled at him, the sound echoing in his mind, and it assured him they'd be at her side eventually.

Shaking his head, he appeased the animal by padding toward the fence, his bare feet not making a sound on the soft earth. He sank his toes into the grass and enjoyed the coolness against his soles. Hopefully that bit of cold would calm the bear.

It actually snorted.

More laughs. More barks. Her joy wrapped around him like a light-hearted blanket, banishing some of the heartache he'd carried the last few weeks. Ever since he'd spoken to his family about leaving, he'd been buried beneath a cloud of unease. And now…

The heavy thud of a body colliding with the ground was followed by a low "oomph" from Kira.

Isaac covered the remaining distance in two rapid steps and peered over the fence without a hint of remorse. "Kira?"

She lay sprawled in the middle of her yard, legs and arms thrown wide as Ebenezer slobbered all over her, sending her dark glasses askew. The moment she heard him, she froze, tension filling every inch of her lush body.

Ignoring the wave of anger that overtook her features, he continued speaking. "You okay?"

"I'm fine." She adopted that haughty tone again. The one that made him think of ruffling her and peeling away every layer of clothing she wore.

"Uh-huh."

She rolled to her feet, movements graceful as she straightened her glasses and then brushed dirt from her clothing. The shirt she wore was worn thin in several places and torn in others. The shorts that exposed her plump, pale thighs were ragged at the hem. Hell, there were a half-dozen holes in them as well.

Did the woman not own—

The thought came to a halt when Ebenezer bounded toward her, hunk of metal and plastic in his mouth. He nudged Kira's hand, and she accepted the tool with a smile. She now clutched a small trowel, and then he noticed what she'd done to the backyard.

Small patches of turned dirt were peppered throughout the lawn, obviously areas she'd intended for planting.

The dog disappeared and returned with a floppy hat covered in obnoxious flowers. She was quick to snatch it and plop it on her head, presenting him with a rag-wearing, disgusting hat covered gardener.

He wanted to kiss her. Right on that pert nose that now sported a smudge of dirt.

"Do you need any help?"

Can I come over?

"No." She quickly returned, posture still stiff.

"I don't mind. It'll feel good to be outside for a bit."

I want to spend time with you.

"Mr. Abrams—"

"Isaac." He didn't want her thinking of him as a mister. He was Isaac to her.

He couldn't get the woman out of his head, and he was determined to explore his attraction. Kira was the first one who simply treated him like any other man. Oh, her demeanor changed when she'd realized he was related to Ty, but it wasn't because of his scars. And that intrigued the hell out of him and excited his bear to no end.

"*Isaac.* I have things under control. I've been gardening all my life. It's what moles do. I can handle this."

She was a weremole.

Well, that explained the scent of earth that accompanied her blueberry flavor.

Did he care—did the bear care—that she was a weremole?

That anger-filled glare remained focused on him, the wind blowing her curly hair across her heart-shaped face, catching on the glasses that shielded her eyes from him.

Did they care?

Not a bit.

He let his gaze sweep her yard, hunting for a reason to vault over the fence. And… found it. Large bags of fertilizer infused topsoil were propped against the shed, looking like they merely waited to be spread over her patches.

Well, he could do that.

"I know you can handle it." He gripped the top of the barrier and leapt, using his bear's strength to get him over the wood. He grunted as he landed and a new tension filled Kira. He imagined her glaring at him behind those midnight glasses, and he merely grinned in response. He gestured toward the shed. "But I see some topsoil over there. I figured I can work up a sweat and help you at the same time. As an apology. What do ya say?"

Kira crossed her arms over her chest. Or rather, under her breasts which had them straining against the tattered material of her top. "No."

"Uh-huh." He moved beyond the fence, striding past section after section of barren dirt. He wondered how much she'd done and what was left to accomplish. With luck, and a lot of charm, he could convince her to let him stick around. "C'mon. You know you don't wanna haul those bags around."

He shot her a wicked grin, even if she couldn't see his expression. Or could she? He knew she claimed to be half-blind, but he didn't really know what that meant. He'd learn soon enough.

"Isaac…" A warning lurked in her tone.

He ignored it.

"I'm just gonna grab one. Wanna tell me where you want it?"

"I don't need your help. Yours or anyone else's. I'm fine." He glanced at her, noting the tremble that wracked her. "I can do this myself. I'm not some…"

Isaac froze, heart clenching and gut tightening. "I know you can. I just wanna help." He changed direction, padding toward her. "I don't think you *can't* take care of your own garden, Kira." He stopped just shy of touching her and he knew if she weren't so upset, she'd probably bolt. "I was an ass for laughing. In my defense, you were adorable. I wasn't laughing because you couldn't find Ebenezer. I was chuckling because you're a little bit of a thing trying to call a dog that's almost as tall as you. You were angry, and it was adorable. That's all." He held his breath, waiting for her to respond. When it didn't look like she was getting angrier, he kept going. "This is my way of apologizing." Another strand caught on her glasses and he tucked his hands in his pockets to keep from reaching for her. "And it lets me spend time with you."

Kira shuffled back, quickly putting space between them, and he resisted the urge to follow her, to chase his prey and feel her beneath him. Her scent called to the bear, beckoned it forth, and he pushed it back with each exhale.

She was already skittish and hurt by his earlier actions. Nothing good could come of chasing her.

"Why?" Disbelief filled her tone.

"Why?" Isaac furrowed his brow. "What do you mean why? You're fun. Filled with life when you're not glaring at me." He cleared his throat. "There's no reason *not* to at least become your friend."

She deflated, some of her tension lessening. "Friends. Friends, I can do."

He didn't mention that the more time he spent in her presence, the more he wanted a lot *more* than friendship.

"All right then. Wanna show me what to do?"

The bear had plenty of ideas that involved Kira spread out on the ground, calling for him. For *him*. The Grayslake Healer, Itan's brother, and scarred as hell werebear.

*

Kira remained acutely aware of him all morning. *Him.*

When he shifted position and dropped another handful of soil, she knew exactly where he crouched. When he moved on, bare soles softly scuffling over the grass, she knew how many feet had passed. When he dropped *way too much* fertilizer on her tomato patch, she was right beside him and scooping up the excess.

The man was ready to drown her tomatoes!

It was risky to plant tomatoes. Period. She'd heard of a carnivorous wererabbit garden serial killer in Jamesburg and from all reports, the woman was rabid for tomatoes and *hated* carrots. Kira had both.

She turned her head to gaze toward the steel carrot cage she'd brought with her. Supposedly, it was bunny proof. She wasn't sure if that applied to rabid wererabbits though.

The risk to her garden was great, but she loved tomatoes and carrots. In salad, on a sandwich… Then there was homemade pasta sauce… Not that there were carrots in the sauce, obviously.

She used her trowel to dig a small hole and then dropped in a seed, carefully refilling the dip in the dirt before moving on. Her animal was snuffling and sniffling the air, happy they were digging through the earth while also remaining near Isaac. Her inner mole whined at her each day they were apart. Screeching at her to march their happy ass to his house right this worm-hunting second.

Heck no!

She'd left those laughs and chuckles back at home with her father's pack. She wasn't about to fall into the same trap. Giggles were the first step, breaking into her house and moving things around was the second. The third… potentially, hypothetically, involved dodging quiet electric cars or running from shifted animals.

The fourth at the hands of her brother… The burning, the scars, the blood…

The telltale brush of skin on skin, palms slapping together, alerted her to the completion of Isaac's task. She should have expected he'd finish before her. Spreading soil and fertilizer across her small patches was a lot easier than planting. And as precious as her new babies were, she couldn't trust him with creating new life.

Nothing for it. If she couldn't get rid of him, her day of gardening was over.

If she was honest, it was nice—maybe—to have a reason to quit. As much as she enjoyed digging in dirt, it also made her icky with sweat. Blech.

"Kira?" The uncertainty in the massive bear's voice had her smiling. To think, a big, bad werebear was timid around her.

She echoed his earlier move, brushing off her hands before gathering her tools and pushing to her feet. The moment she stood, Ebenezer was there, rubbing and pushing against her in his excitement. She stumbled a step, staggering from the dog's shoves.

Immediately, Isaac was there, arm around her waist as he steadied her. She breathed deeply, enjoying the scents of earth and man, allowing herself to appreciate his flavors for the few moments he was close.

Except... he didn't release her. Not at first. No, he inhaled as well, and she turned her gaze to him, focusing on his features as much as she could. For the first time in her life, she wished she could see. She wished the world wasn't fuzzy forms. Was he smiling? She saw-ish his teeth, so he could be smiling. Or silently snarling?

She had no idea.

He bent toward her, easing his face down until his lips pressed against her hairline and he nuzzled her strands. He repeated the breath, pulling her scent into his lungs and she wondered how he'd take it if she did the same to him. Would he allow her to rub his chest and take in his aroma?

She wasn't sure, so she remained still, stiffening when she sensed his lips almost kissing her rather than resting against her skin. Her muscles went tight and Isaac did the same, stilling before easing away from her.

"Sorry. I, uh, sorry." He seemed unsure as he put more space between them. "I shouldn't have… I really am an ass, huh?"

Kira furrowed her brow, trying to pick apart the reason for his unease and she couldn't find a thing. All righty then.

"Um. Okay. I'm about done here." She waved her hand, careful to avoid him as she gestured to the yard. "So…"

So, he could go home now.

"Oh." One disappointment-filled word, and it made her feel like a great big meanie.

How did she go from being totally and justifiably mad at him, to the bad guy? Where did that happen?

She didn't know, but she did feel like a heel, which meant the next words out of her mouth had her cringing, but a tiny bit hopeful. "Would you like to come inside? The place is a mess, but I do have…" She thought about what she had in her fridge and cabinets. She could figure out something. "I have food?"

"If I chuckle do you promise not to get angry? You're just so damn…" She heard the smile, but wondered if it really graced his features.

She wondered further if it was teasing or evil. Taking in another deep breath, she filtered through the scents surrounding her and found a hint of arousal, of attraction that were all him. For her?

She tilted her head, listening for anyone else nearby, anyone approaching or invading on their hint of privacy. And she found nothing.

For her, then.

"Adorable. Beautiful." He coughed and cleared his throat. "Um, but yeah, food sounds good. If you don't wanna cook, you can come over. I've got plenty..."

Kira shook her head. "No, you helped me out today. The least I can do is cook for you. If there's something specific you'd like and I don't have the ingredients but you do, then I'll let you snare them. Otherwise, lunch is on me." She wrinkled her nose. "Well, not *on* me, on me. Just... I'm..." She huffed. "Follow me inside, already."

She spun on her heel and started toward the house, prepared to count steps and navigate the large space. It wasn't that she couldn't see, she noted the bottom of the stairs and the large porch. But... counting meant she didn't have to rely on her spotty depth perception.

"Kira?" His heat warmed her back, his scent sinking into her pores as he looked over her shoulder.

"Sorry, uh, I'm trying to remember the count." She'd been doing this for years, she couldn't figure out why her memory hadn't gotten better at, er, remembering.

"The count? Like the number of steps? You wanted to count my house," he murmured, his heat still bathing her flesh.

"Yes. I thought maybe... I mean, we're neighbors and..." She shook her head. Even now, after he'd helped her, she didn't want to get her hopes up that they'd become friends. Based on

49

his arousal, and her own attraction, she almost wished for more.

"We *will* be spending more time together, Kira." His lips brushed her ear, and she suppressed the shudder working along her spine. "Take your time and after lunch, we can go to my house and you can explore there as well. I'll apologize again because I was an insensitive ass, but I *do* want you to come over. Stay awhile. Just… stay."

Kira wasn't going to read into his words, wasn't going to take the deepening of his scent combined with his rough words and imagine a message that didn't exist.

"Kira?" His baritone vibrated along her nerves.

"Ahem, right. So, I go from place to place, retracing my steps to make sure the count is correct and I'm oriented right. The first few times I had some help from a friend." She cleared her throat, his nearness wreaking havoc on her body. "But I've got it down, I think."

"What's wrong with your voice?" A hint of growl accompanied the words and her inner animal shuddered. Not in fear. Nope, the damned thing got excited by his show of annoyance.

Crazy, worm-eating thing.

"Nothing." His cheek brushed hers, telling her exactly how close he'd come.

Her normal instinctual flinch didn't have her tugging away from him. She remained in place, her mole actually urging her to get closer.

Super crazy, worm-eating thing.

Her inner mole did not dispute the claim.

"Kira?"

She paused in her travels. "Yeah?"

"Is there a reason I can't lead you inside? Or Ebenezer?"

She squeezed her eyes shut and took a deep breath. He wasn't trying to be mean, he was trying to understand. She had to remember that fact. He wasn't her old pack. He wasn't the wolves who... He wasn't *him*.

"I prefer to be as independent as possible." *I don't want anyone's help. I can live my life on my own. I don't need to lean on people for the rest of my life.* She didn't say the words aloud. "It's best if I learn the layout before accepting assistance. This is my home. I should know where everything is."

And I can't afford to depend on someone. What will happen to me when you leave?

Again, words she kept inside her heart. She knew he had boxes packed and stacked throughout his home and the gossipy tidbits she'd picked up from Mia told her a few things about him.

1) Isaac was leaving his clan.

2) He had scars marring his face, marking him as ugly as far as the women were concerned.

3) The man earned every one of those deep gouges in a battle for his family and his clan and the dumbass women failed to see how wonderful he was.

Something else she'd learned on her outings—there were plenty of people in Grayslake who thought her partial blindness also equated to deafness. Oh, not Mia, just others. Good thing it was a lesson she'd learned long ago.

He leaned toward her and his warm breath fanned her neck. He scraped his rough cheek along her throat and nuzzled the sweet spot below her ear. "Lead on, then."

Right. The leading. With the on. And then… Kira was sure a long fang scraped her skin, and she squeaked. Ignoring her animal's desire to remain in place, she quickly stepped out of his embrace and got back on track, ignoring his teasing laugh.

And it was teasing—not sarcastic or mean or any other type her pack mates taught her over the years. Not the evil cackle from…

Nope, with each moment spent in Isaac's company, she was quickly realizing he was nothing like the wolves she'd lived with.

This had her balancing her fear against her excitement, and she wasn't sure which would come out the winner. Hell, who was she kidding?

Excitement was totally in the lead.

What the hell was she supposed to do with that?

Her mole told her it had plenty of ideas.

Stupid, sex-starved, worm-eating mole.

It agreed.

chapter four

Isaac followed Kira, keeping an eye on her slow, even steps. Watching where she put her feet had his gaze tracing her curvy thighs and then moving to the roundness of her ass. His fingers tingled with the need to stroke and cup the globes. Then thinking about globes had him thinking about her breasts and how much he'd like to suck and nibble her nipples. A low, arousal-tinged growl escaped before he could suppress the sound, and Kira froze in place.

"Isaac?" She glanced over her shoulder at him, dark glasses shielding her eyes from his gaze. He'd love to stare into the orbs, read the expressions that flitted across her face as he kissed and caressed her.

Maybe later.

"Sorry." He cleared his throat and thumped his inner bear on the nose at the same time. "My bear's just a tad hungry."

"Uh-huh." She resumed her trek, not commenting further.

Her strides brought her to the edge of the steps, and it took everything in him not to reach out and carry her to the porch. But he didn't. Instead, he fisted his hands, his bear's claws making his fingertips ache. The beast wanted to keep her from harm at all costs. Period. End of story. Pick her gorgeous ass up already.

Isaac wouldn't do that, though. He recognized her need for independence. While he didn't like the fact she wouldn't lean on him, he could respect it. He was doing something similar by leaving Grayslake, wasn't he? Finding his path and hopefully happiness.

The animal snarled, letting him know that leaving was slowly shifting from a certainty to a maybe-probably-not. Especially if Kira planned to settle in Grayslake permanently.

If he had her at his side, he thought the town might be tolerable.

He banished the thoughts from his mind. He'd already pissed her off, invaded her privacy, and now weaseled his way into her making lunch. Bulldozing a woman wasn't a relationship no matter what the bear said.

She slowly made her way up the steps with a careful shuffle until she reached her back door. She jumped in place, punching the air with a wiggle of her ass and a sharp "yes!"

Her excitement was contagious, her happiness transferring to him as if it were his own. She was thrilled with her progress and he was thrilled… just to be near her.

"Ha! Take that, Alpha Asshole!" She did another wiggle and her words solidified in his mind. "Who's finding shit now?"

"Who's Alpha Asshole?" His animal was no longer intent on pouncing on Kira and was more concerned with why his little weremole was mentioning an alpha.

The adorable, tempting wiggles and jiggles ended in an abrupt jerk and she took a sharp breath. "Uh…" She gulped, her neck undulating with the swallow. "You see… He's… I bet you're hungry, right? I'm hungry, so you're hungry. Let's eat."

She scrambled for the knob, scratching at the aged wood and metal until she finally grasped the handle. A quick turn had her tumbling into the house. He grasped her, wrapping his arms around her waist to keep her from falling. She could yell at him about helping her later. For now, the bear wouldn't entertain the idea of Kira getting hurt.

He hauled her against him, fighting to ignore the pleasure that filled him at having her curves aligned with his hard body. He was a study in stark, muscled lines while she was sweet softness. He could sink into her over and over again and never tire of her touch.

The thought had his cock twitching, blood slowly filling his length, and he was quick to release Kira before she realized the level of his attraction. He'd been interested even after she destroyed his things, but seeing her care for her garden and her strength as she fought to do things on her own… Well, that just sealed the deal.

Isaac wanted her. Badly. And he wouldn't stop until he had her in his arms, in his bed.

Because something else hovered between them, something that bothered him more than he'd ever admit to his family. Something that tarnished his day-to-day life. His parents thought they knew. Even his brothers felt as if they understood his pain.

But they didn't. Not even a tiny bit.

Kira did, though. He had no doubt she understood what it was like to be thought of as less. As worthless. To be whispered about and shunned.

He sounded like a fucking girl, but he didn't give a damn. The hyenas hadn't just torn his flesh, they'd stolen a part of him that he'd never get back.

Kira made him wonder if he ever needed it in the first place.

The sudden jumble and clang of pots and pans had him striding through her home, following the continued sounds until he came to a jarring stop in her kitchen. A few cookie sheets peppered the ground as well as a skillet or two. Then there were the pots...

"Kira?" He stepped over a flat sheet that'd seen better days and steadied himself by grasping the kitchen table when he slid on another. "You okay?"

She stood stock still in the middle of the mess, hands fisted, and he imagined her digging nails into that unmarred skin. Her face flushed, red inching past her ratty top and slowly painting her neck until it filled her face as well.

"Honey?" He reached for her, ignoring the tension that still pummeled her body. She didn't resist when he grasped her wrist or uncurled her fist. Nor when he tugged her close and ran his hand down her back. "You all right?"

Kira sniffled and breathed deeply, releasing the air in a slow exhale. "I'm fine. A new friend came over yesterday to help me unpack and she… obviously didn't listen or understand or… It's fine. *Fine.*" Another breath. "It just means I can't exactly make you anything and I had this great soup in mind and—"

She was talking a mile a minute, and he didn't understand half of what she said. The only thing he did understand was that she was upset by the mess.

"Okay," he ignored all the warnings in his human mind and let the bear's instincts rule. He eased closer, tugging slightly until she was alongside him. "How about you tell me what ingredients you need and we'll go to my place. Even with all the boxes, I've got plenty of pots and pans and anything you'd need."

She shuddered, releasing a soft sigh. "I'm being stupid, aren't I?"

She rubbed her nose against his shirt, glasses going askew with the move. When they threatened to clatter to the ground, he snatched them.

"Do you need these?"

Kira huffed and pulled away, tilting her head back to peer up at him. His gaze met the most gorgeous pair of glacier blue eyes he'd ever seen. They were lighter than the clear water off the coast of Florida and sparkled just as bright.

"Huh?" She blinked, hiding behind her lids for a moment before focusing on him once again.

He brought his hand up, holding them within her line of sight. He wasn't sure how much she could see, but he did it anyway. "Your glasses. Do you need them?"

"Oh." A trembling hand rose, and he met her half way, placing them in her grip. "I… Most people…" She grimaced. "I stare through people sometimes, you know. I try to focus on the shape I *think* is speaking but I'm not always right and…" She sighed. "I prefer to wear the glasses rather than make others uncomfortable."

Her grimace, combined with the sticky flavors of her embarrassment, called to his bear's protective instincts. He didn't want her to ever feel bad about who she was, about her body, or the way she lived.

It was *their* problem. Not hers. They didn't like looking? Then they could turn their heads. Anger over his own issues of the past year and a half burned him, enraging his animal at the thought she'd endured the same her entire life.

She stirred in his embrace, gently withdrawing, but a soft squeeze had her remaining in place.

"When you're with me, unless you need them, you don't have to wear these things." He stroked her nose, fingertip sliding over skin. She twitched, probably surprised at the touch, but remained still. "I like seeing your eyes. They're gorgeous."

She was breathtaking, but the disbelief rolling off her in waves told him he shouldn't push. He'd already shoved his presence on her, taking advantage and wiggling into her day.

He could wait.

A careful step back had him releasing her and putting space between their bodies. The bear roared in protest, but they couldn't exactly feed her if they didn't let go.

It agreed with an annoyed grumble.

"C'mon. Let's go to my place."

"But—"

"Grab your stuff, Kira, and then we're going over."

"But—"

"Here, lemme get this sorted and stacked. We can wash everything and then we can put it all away—together—after lunch." There, he didn't think he said anything offensive and was even giving her a chance to order him around.

Kira slumped her shoulders. "You're not giving up, are you?"

"Nope."

"Fine," she mumbled.

"Perfect." Isaac smiled widely, truly grinning for the first time since the battle with the hyenas.

And… he wasn't self-conscious. Part of him knew she couldn't see the scars, there was no physical reason for her to reject him due to the damage. But he also felt it wouldn't matter to her even if she could spy the large swaths of twisted skin.

Maybe he had a chance with her.

The thought sobered him, had him backpedaling and reining in his emotions.

He was moving. Period. In five weeks, he was out of Grayslake. Yet some part of him said leaving wouldn't be easy.

Shoving it aside, he focused on getting them to his place. He spun from her and bent down, gathering the mess of pots and pans, carefully stacking them according to size on the counter.

"Isaac?"

He glanced over his shoulder, hating the indecision on her face. He wanted her to trust him *now*, but he had to be patient. "I'm good. Piling things according to type and size. We'll wash 'em after lunch. I promise."

Kira nibbled her lip, biting that piece of plump flesh, and he held the bear in place when it threatened to rush forward and force his hand. Because, really, the action brought his attention to her mouth, and he'd love to delve into her with a passionate kiss.

Not now. Not today. Maybe never.

It really wasn't smart to get involved with her only to leave her behind.

Then she presented him with her back, with her rounded ass that begged for his hands.

Yeah, bad idea. Really.

She glanced at him over her shoulder and he tore his gaze from her butt. The one he'd like to nibble and lick and taste and... "Isaac?"

He cleared his throat. "Yeah?"

"Can Ebie come?"

60

Swallowing his groan and figuring he'd just have to buy a lot of new things when he got to the Southeast Itan's compound, he answered her. "Of course."

Kira's blinding smile, the one that sank into his soul, was more than worth the money he'd have to spend.

*

Nerves assaulted Kira, butterflies and rhinoceros battering her stomach as she snared Ebenezer's leash and clipped it on her dog's collar. The clang and scrape of metal meeting metal sounded from her kitchen as Isaac did exactly as he described. She was giving him a bit of her trust. For now. At least until he betrayed it… Like everyone else in the world.

She shook her head. She really needed to stop being such a fucking pessimist. Not everyone was like Alpha Asshole and her brother.

Well, there were a few bears… Nah, Grayslake was better than her life with her family.

Isaac's feet thumped down the hallway, and she turned her head toward him, watching his blurred shape approach.

Yes, it was definitely better. *At least until he moves.*

Which reminded her that she shouldn't get attached. Then he placed his large, warm hand on her lower back, sending a shiver down her spine, and urged her toward the door. Maybe it was already too late.

"Ready?" His deep baritone thrummed through her, vibrating her from outside in.

"Sure."

"Okay, then." He reached past her, gifting her with more of his scent. She quietly drew it into her lungs.

She'd never get enough of him and yet… she'd have to, wouldn't she?

It took no time for him to open the door and escort her out. Without a word he tugged her keys from her hand and locked up her house before moving to the steps. That's where he paused, his indecision practically choking her.

"Uh, um, do you want to… Or should I…" He sighed. "Am I leading you to my house or am I leaving you alone?"

Kira paused and tilted her head to the side, considering him as she absorbed the surrounding scents. She didn't sense any pity, merely a desire to… what?

"Why?"

"Huh?" He sounded confused and she couldn't blame him. He didn't know what it was like to live with pity and scorn. "Why what?"

"Why do you want to lead me down the steps? To your house?" she explained.

"Would it scare you if I tell you I just wanna hold you for a minute? If it would, then I'm merely a concerned citizen."

She grinned and shook her head as she padded forward, Ebie at her side. "Bend your arm and hold out your elbow. Don't pull. Lemme follow your movements."

With a gentle hand, she reached for him, letting her fingers trail over his bicep, softly pressing to cop a feel. They were as big as tree trunks, solid and wide, tensing beneath her fingertips. Then she slid her palm to his elbow and forced herself to stop. More than anything, she wanted to keep going, to take a moment to "see" him with her hands.

Instead, she did as she'd indicated and gripped the bend at his elbow with a firm touch. "All ready."

She listened as they moved, slowly going down the set of stairs and then counting the steps to the front gate. The hinge squeaked as always and the little bell announced that it'd opened.

"Is that so you know you've got the right house?" he murmured, and the question brought a smile to her lips.

"Yes."

"Smart."

She almost told him it was necessary, and that she had a few dozen replacement bells in the house. They'd been stolen more than once. Not necessarily in Grayslake but there was always a chance she'd come across someone…

The rest of the short trip was made in silence, Isaac's worry easily reaching her. It seemed like their travels were over in moments. With him being next door, she imagined only a few dozen feet separated their yards.

The jiggle of his latch penetrated their quiet, and it was further destroyed by the roar of a vehicle coming near. And nearer and then even nearer.

Images of the past, a dark SUV rushing forward as she remained held fast by her pack mates. The vehicle bearing down on her while she could do nothing to stop the impending collision. The scrapes and bruises caused by being shoved before the massive machine and the cackling laughs that followed her fresh tears. The wounds that'd been healing were then torn open, spilling her blood on the concrete.

Panic assaulted her, filling her body until it overflowed and air rasped in and out of her tightened lungs.

"Kira?"

She recognized his worried voice, but the fear had her captive.

"Kira?"

It wouldn't let her speak, wouldn't let her do anything but remain motionless.

Firm hands grabbed her shoulders, gently shaking her. "Kira?"

The click and thump of vehicle doors opening and closing preceded the rapid argument of two people approaching. A man and woman sniping at each other over speed and driving and missing the turn at Main Street and...

"Kira?" Isaac's voice was a deep, annoyed growl.

The couple entered her line of sight, the woman short and a little rounded like herself while the man was large, larger than Isaac. A deep breath revealed these two scented like the man at her side. Not the earthy musk that intrigued her mole, but familiar just the same.

"Kira?" he snapped, giving her another rough shake.

Kira blinked her eyes, fluttering her lashes as the panic receded and embarrassment took its place. "I'm sorry. I—"

"Isaac Jericho Abrams." The woman's lyrical voice held a snap of anger mixed with annoyance and he stiffened before releasing Kira with a rough sigh.

"Lemme say I'm sorry in advance." Another sigh accompanied the withdrawal of his hands for a moment before he laid one arm across her shoulders. "Mom. Dad."

His parents. *Of course* she'd meet his parents at the tail end of a panic attack. Then again, why should she care? They were friends, new friends, but still friends and nothing more.

"We have been calling you all morning—" His mother halted in her tracks, cutting off her words. "Oh, hello, dear. Isaac, introduce me to your friend."

His rumbling growl vibrated her, but the sound didn't hit the air. "You've been calling me?"

"Yes, yes."

Kira imagined the woman flapping her arm, a bright bracelet or cuff swinging through the air clued Kira in to her actions.

"Later. Who's your friend? Oh, never mind." Isaac's mother approached, that cuffed arm stretched wide, and she realized the other swung wide as well. A hug. The woman opened her arms for a— Suddenly she was tugged from his hold and embraced, wrapped in the woman's softness and warmth. The scents of sweetness and pure happiness sank into her, and a soothing calm immediately followed. "Hello, dear, I'm Margaret. You can call me Meg or Mom. Whichever you like."

"Mom. Really?" Isaac huffed. "Dad?"

The other visitor, obviously Isaac's father, merely grunted. What kind of answer was that?

"Oh, hush," Meg admonished as she released Kira and held her at arm's length. "Aren't you just gorgeous? That hair, those eyes. Oh, Isaac, isn't she beautiful? George, isn't she?"

Another grunt from his father, obviously George.

"Yes, Mom, she is. She's also hungry. So if you could let her go and tell me why you called…"

"Oh," Meg's pure joy rushed Kira, bowling her over. "This is wonderful. I was calling because we're having a barbeque and your brothers want you to come. So you will and you'll bring your friend. What's your name, dear?"

Kira cleared her throat. "Kira Kolanowski. My friends call me KK and the mean—"

A quick tug had her back in Isaac's grip, the hand on her shoulder holding tight. "This is Kira, she just moved in, uh…"

"Two weeks ago." She filled in his silence.

"Two weeks?" She sensed his scrutiny and turned her gaze to his down-turned face. "We only met a week ago. How did I not notice you?"

Kira shrugged. "I dunno. You're oblivious to the world at large?"

"I'm a Healer. I can't be that oblivious," he grumbled, and she smiled.

66

"Apparently you can," she countered.

"Oh," the rapid clap of hands had them both refocusing on Meg. "Look at your two bickering like an old married couple. Do you see that, George? Just like us."

"Uh, Mrs. Abrams, we're not—"

"Oh, honey." Another wave of her hand. "I know how you kids are today. It's fine." A firm, cool hand snared Kira's and tugged. "Come along now, the party is about to start and we don't want to be too late."

Isaac snatched her once again, and she felt as if she were the rope in a game of tug-o-war. "Kira isn't going, Mom. I'll be along soon, but I'm not inflicting the family on her. No matter what you think, we're not—"

"Of course you are. You just don't want to tell anyone yet. I understand. I'm a very hip mother. Aren't I, George?"

George grunted. Kira wondered if he could speak.

Kira tried, "Mrs. Abrams—"

"Meg or Mom."

She was gonna get the words out. "We're not anything but friends. We just—"

"With benefits?" The woman sounded so disappointed. "That's fine, dear. I really do know how you kids are. Friends with benefits today, mated tomorrow. I'm a very cool mother. You didn't answer me before. Aren't I a cool mother, George?"

George grunted again.

"See, he agrees."

Kira's head spun, and there she was in Isaac's arms once again.

"Mom. We're friends. There are no benefits and Kira is not coming."

Kira thought getting to sniff his hotness was a benefit but kept her mouth shut.

"Oh." One single syllable and she was smacked with the woman's disappointment. She imagined Meg's expression echoed the feeling as well and Isaac's annoyed sigh soon reached her.

"Mom."

"No, no, it's fine." His mother was a subdued husk of her former self. Did Kira hear a sniffle? Yes. She heard a sniffle.

Immediately regret and sympathy filled her. She'd seemed so excited only moments ago. Kira reached up and patted Isaac's hand where he gripped her shoulder, drawing his attention.

When he looked to her, she spoke, "If you won't leave me…"

Parties were hard in general. Add in the fact she wouldn't know anyone or the area, it'd be doubly difficult.

"You sure?"

Kira nodded, and he huffed, "Fine, Mom, we'll come."

More excited clapping. "Perfect, let's get you two in the SUV and—"

"Kira and I will take my car."

"Oh." The disappointment was back, and this time Kira refused to give in. "Well, at least you're coming and I'll get to show Kira off to Nancy Brown. She thinks her son's mate is everything and sliced bread. Just wait until she sees yours. Ha!" Meg patted Kira's arm a couple of times. "We'll see you two soon, dear."

Then his parents were gone, bustling back to their vehicle, and suddenly they were alone once again.

Quiet reigned, and Isaac broke the silence. "Dear God. I'll straighten her out about the mate thing. She's… her. And I won't leave your side and I'll make sure they all know to give you space."

Kira shook her head. "No, it's fine. They'll figure it out soon enough and bringing it to everyone's attention makes it…"

Weird.

"Okay then, let's shower and then we can go. On the way, I'll apologize for my mother—a lot—and tell you about my family."

Oh. Goodie.

chapter five

Oh. Goodie.

When his mom said "family," she really meant the whole clan.

A mole amongst lions, er, bears.

Isaac popped his car into park, smiling when he caught Kira's wide grin and the halo of windswept hair captured by the breeze. He had a classic 70s Chevy Chevelle SS convertible that purred almost as often as it roared down the road. The ride got even better with the top down and wind whipping through his strands.

It seemed Kira felt the same.

"Hold tight, lemme get Ebenezer hooked up, and then I'll help you out."

"I know how to get out of a car, Isaac."

He flushed, face heating, and was thankful she couldn't see him. "And I know you know. Humor me."

71

She gave him a long-suffering sigh but stayed put as he rounded the car and hauled a squirming, barking dog from his back seat. The animal remained in place while he assisted Kira. The pup settled the moment she held his leash, plopping his furry ass on the driveway, seeming to wait for her orders.

At least Ebenezer occasionally behaved.

"Okay," she huffed and held out a hand for him. "Let's do this."

He was there without hesitation, elbow crooked and waiting for her touch.

Traversing the driveway seemed easy, the party truly happening behind the house, which left the front mostly abandoned. They did pass a few other bears, and he got head tips with low "hellos" from the men while the women pretended he didn't exist. Kira was a passing attraction though, feminine whispers following in their wake. The words that did reach him were filled with pity… for her.

When they entered the house, he tugged her into the vacant living room. "Kira… People are gonna…"

Bright blue eyes met his, her orbs exposed. At least for now. He'd brought along her glasses in case she became uncomfortable, but he hoped she'd keep them off. He couldn't help staring at her, at her beauty.

On second thought, that meant others would be staring too. Maybe she should put them back on.

"They're going to gossip," she finished for him. "About me. About you. About you and me being together." She shrugged. "I don't care. Who are they to judge? Perfect? Obviously not if

72

they think it's okay to spew that kind of talk." So, she eased closer, and he fought the urge to wrap his arms around her and lower his head to capture her mouth. "I don't care. I mean, I care because words can hurt. But if you don't mind leading me around, being seen with me, or if you're not bothered by their assumptions, then," another shrug, "they don't matter. You still need to straighten out your mother, though."

He winced at the reminder of his mom's massive, leaping thoughts that had them going from little more than acquaintances to friends with benefits and a planned mating.

But the rest… Not giving a damn about his clan's thoughts…

If he couldn't kiss her, he could at least touch her a tiny bit. He lowered his head, but instead of a kiss, he pressed his forehead to hers and allowed himself the luxury of taking in her scent. "You're amazing, you know that?" She was. So beyond amazing that he didn't have the words.

"Isaac?" The click clack of his mother's high heels on the tile reached him and he forced himself to pull away from Kira. "I know I saw that monstrosity of a car," Mom mumbled. "Isaac Jericho?"

Kira chuckled.

She knew he glared at her even if she couldn't quite make out his expression.

And his mother entered the room.

"There you are. C'mon, your father is about to ruin the cow with all his fiddling. You need to stop him before he destroys lunch all together."

Kira wrapped her arms around one of his, cuddling close. Her hold wasn't the gentle grip she adopted when they walked into the house, but one much more intimate.

He liked intimate. He wanted intimate. He craved intima—

"Isaac?" Mom snapped.

"Sure, we're coming. But why *I* have to handle Dad and barbequing is beyond me."

"You're a Healer, dear. If you can fix something, I'm sure you can take it apart again. It was breathing at one point, right?" His mother patted his shoulder as he passed, and he refused to address what she'd said.

It just… She… He didn't even know what…

"Now, I'll take Kira and introduce—"

"No."

"No," Isaac's snap overrode Kira's firm denial.

Mom sniffed. "Fine then, destroy a mother's deepest wish to introduce her son's future mate to the clan." With that, she spun on her very high heels and click clacked the way she'd come.

"I'm sorry." Isaac was pretty sure he'd be doing the same thing over and over again today. "She's…"

"Don't be. She's wonderful, but overwhelming. Today's gonna be hard enough. I'd prefer to stay with you."

"Then that's what will happen." Isaac went into action and one of those wide, joyful smiles graced his lips once again. He really needed to get his mother under control.

The bear told him to leave his mother alone. It liked the idea of mating Kira.

When he urged her to walk with him, she didn't release her firm hold on his arm, clutching him in an intimate grasp. He enjoyed it way too much and his cock twitched, reaffirming his pleasure at the touch.

Kira might not be able to see very well, but she could sure as hell smell and he needed to put a cap on his arousal. Now.

All too soon they emerged onto the back porch, the low rumble of the crowd filling the air. His bear both bristled and huffed in approval—enjoying that they were surrounded by other bears, yet hating that they were surrounded by other bears. Kira was theirs, even if she was unmated. So while the clan could protect her if needed, someone could also try to steal her.

The thoughts had his heart stuttering, faltering in its regular beat.

Unmated. And he was possessive and aggressive and…

And he wasn't thinking about mates and Kira. At all. He was leaving—*leaving*—soon.

The bear's snort said he was delusional.

Instead of fighting, he murmured the number of steps to Kira, outlining any uneven areas and glaring at anyone who didn't move aside fast enough.

75

Interested glances passed over her and he met each one with a glower. Men needed to stop checking her out. He knew she was curved and lush in all the right places, but they didn't have to drool over her.

Whispers followed in their wake, some about him. Okay, they were mostly about him. And he fought to ignore each one as he prayed Kira would do the same.

One particular, vicious whisper reached them. "*She has to be blind to be with him.*"

When she paused in the middle of their travels, he realized she wasn't going to let it go. Dammit. She was a little clumsy, a little absent minded, but those traits paled against her backbone of steel.

With unerring precision, she released him and spun to face the source of the words.

"Kira, wait." He reached for her again, hating that she was exposed to this acidic side of the clan, but he didn't want her fighting his battles. As cocky as he tried to act, there was no hiding the truth of his damaged features.

Of course, she didn't wait. No, she shrugged off his touch and padded toward the bitchy bear. Ebenezer stayed at her side, his nose touching her palm, seeming to communicate any difficulties in her path. She strode forward, strong and tall without hesitation.

"I would have to be blind to be with him? Isaac?" Kira snorted.

The woman, Vanessa, returned with a vicious laugh. "Of course. I mean, look at him."

The bitch waved toward him and he rolled his eyes.

"Uh-huh." Kira didn't drop Ebenezer's leash as she propped her hands on her hips.

Tension filled her, tightening her muscles, but not in fear. Nope, she was settling in, and as his mother often said, "getting ready to release a big old ball of hatefire."

"All right. I admit, I'm fairly blind. I'm a mole, it's just one of those things." Kira nodded.

Vanessa scoffed. "So I'm right. That *is* the only way he could get a woman."

Damn, that made Kira tense even more, and he sidled up to her, ready to step between Vanessa and Kira if needed. If it came to bear versus mole, he knew Vanessa would win.

"The thing about being a mole is that we live and die by our noses." Kira lifted a hand and tapped her nose. "If you can't see, you need some way to get around. That means I can scent a hell of a lot more than you. And I do it in stereo. No matter where you stand, no matter the sway of the wind. I can find you."

"Whatever." Vanessa crossed her arms over her chest. "You're just a blind chick feeling sorry for the clan's broken bear. Or he's feeling sorry for you. Either way, you deserve each other."

Rage suffused him, his bear rushing forward and ready to tear the woman apart for her hateful words. He didn't care about himself. No, his anger was due to what she flung at the woman he'd quickly come to care about. The only thing that stayed him was the small touch to his hand, her fingertips ghosting over his forearm. She granted the connection just as fast as she removed it, but it was enough to soothe the animal and hold it back. For now.

"Uh-huh. All right. How about I tell you something? Hmm…"

Oh shit. She'd adopted a tone he often had when arguing with his brothers. One that said "I'm about to teach you a lesson and make you feel dumb, shit for brains."

"Let's start with the man at your side." Kira gestured toward Hugh, one of the weaker bears in their clan. "He's been half hard since I came within ten feet of you. Fully hard just after I passed."

Isaac glared at the blushing man. There would be a reckoning there. He refused to have competition nearby.

"And I bet you know he's just shy of coming in his pants. All that arousal clouds the air. From him, it almost made me gag, but whatever."

Hugh was so dead. Ty would get over losing a bear.

But even when Vanessa gasped and turned her own glare on the man at her side, Kira continued. "As for you… you reacted the same way. You creamed your panties like you were watching God's gift to pornos with a rabbit vibe in your hoo-ha. Now, you could claim you're a lesbian and I'm your dream woman or that your arousal is due to the guy next to you, but I'm thinking it's for Isaac. You want him, except all these other women, their opinions, keep you from going after him. And now it's too late for two reasons: One, you're a bitch, and two, I don't share." With that parting shot, Kira spun on her heel, snared Isaac's arm and tugged, silently urging him to lead her away.

He couldn't withhold the wide smile that blossomed on his lips or the pride that filled his heart. She'd gone after the bitch and won, cutting the woman down with her quiet words. Kira hadn't said them very loudly, each one mostly whispered, but he knew the story would be spread through the gathering within the hour.

Vanessa's low growl had him freezing and spinning, but Ebenezer got there before Isaac. The happy, slobbering, goofy puppy transformed before his eyes, quickly becoming a vicious dog more than prepared to take on a werebear bitch. Saliva dripped from his jaws, teeth bared, and fur on end as he released a savage growl.

Vanessa slid to a stop, feet scraping on dirt and damp grass, and the move had her flailing her arms to stay upright. "What the fuck?"

Isaac's animal shoved against his skin and the slight sting of fur emerging from his pores was quickly followed by a deep ache in his bones. The bear was damn near ready to take over whether he liked it or not.

"Isaac?" Kira's voice was low, a slight tremble to his name, and the animal fought harder to come forth.

The woman would *dare* frighten Kira? She was his and Vanessa… He took a step forward, edging partially in front of Kira as he faced off with the bitchy female.

Ebenezer kept up his rolling growl, the threat more than evident in the animal's stance and each step he took toward the she-bitch.

"Itan!" Vanessa released a warbling scream. "Help!"

He suppressed his snort. Barely. Vanessa was pulling Ty in as the official leader of their clan, not as Isaac's brother. Over what? A dog scaring the shit outta her? Seriously?

Isaac sensed his brother's approach, Ty's dominance pushing forward like a bulldozer pounding down everything in his path. Kira leaned into him with a low whimper and the sound had Ebenezer snarling once again, the growl louder than before.

"Kira. Call off Ebenezer, for now. I'll take care of it." He turned his head and pressed a kiss to her crown. "I'll keep you safe."

"Ebie, come to me." Kira's whisper was low, but it had an immediate effect on the dog. His growling threats immediately ceased, and the animal slowly backed toward them, moving until the furry ass brushed Kira's leg.

Vanessa snorted. "Take care of it? Your brother is gonna kick—"

Isaac leveled a black gaze on the woman and allowed it to transform into an evil smile, one that made his scars stark white against his tanned skin. "The *Itan* is going to make a judgment on one of his bears. A bear who attempted to attack an invited guest."

He noted his father's strength and mother's calm easing close as well. He knew Ty would kick Vanessa out of the gathering, but it was his mother's opinion that would put the nail in the bitch's coffin. He reached behind him and eased Kira to his side, Ebenezer shifting his position to match her movement.

"Who invited her? You?" Another snort from Vanessa. "Who are *you*? You might have been somebody, but you're nothing now."

Thankfully, Mom burst onto the scene a bare moment before Ty and Dad, and she was sharp as a tack. In one glance and hearing those few words, his mother became the protective Momma Bear he'd grown up with. At six, it'd been stifling, at sixteen it was embarrassing, over thirty it was welcome.

"*I* invited her, you two-bit-hussy of a bear. You are looking at my newest daughter-in-law, and so help me, I will have George put you over his knee if you even *think* about being nasty to her. Your momma raised you better." Mom advanced on the woman and Isaac almost felt bad for her. Almost. "Just wait until I tell her how you're acting. You. Just. Wait. Now, get out of here." Mom waved her hands in a shooing motion. "*Get.*"

"Mom." Ty's long-suffering sigh overrode their father's grunt.

"Don't you 'Mom' me. Vanessa is leaving. I heard enough to know she went after Kira, *our* guest. Look at that poor pup. He's still got his fur on end." His mother bent down to Ebenezer. "You're a good dog, aren't you? Trying to protect Kira." Mom straightened. "Your father and I invited her and I *will not* have a guest treated that way. I'm sure as heck not having my daughter-in-law treated that way." Mom bustled forward, arms outstretched for Kira, and Isaac made sure his grip remained firm. His intention to keep her at his side was reaffirmed by her threading his fingers with hers and squeezing tight. Good, he didn't want to let her go.

Isaac met Ty's gaze over her head, his brother's eyebrow raised in question and Isaac shrugged. His mother had invited them, and well, he wouldn't be upset to have Kira at his side for the rest of his life.

In fact, his bear thought that was a very, very good idea.

Now he just had to figure out if Kira agreed. And if she didn't, how hard would he have to work to change her mind?

*

The whole barbeque-meeting-family thing had been a very, very bad idea. Huge. Because if she wasn't pissing off other bears—*good going Kira*—she was embarrassing herself in front of Isaac's family. Who, apparently, were her new in-laws-to-be. Which… she wasn't sure if she was excited, scared, or about to vomit all over Isaac.

Wait, she knew. Vomiting was coming out the winner at the moment.

She should have stayed home in her happy little house with its happy little yard and her happy little garden.

Lots of happy going on there.

Then Isaac squeezed her hand, tightening ever so slightly, and the tension of the confrontation drifted away. The person she identified as Were-bitch quickly vanished after Meg's tirade, and the male left as well.

Before long, the crowd disbursed, leaving Kira surrounded by a ton of people who smelled related in some way or another. Including Isaac's mother. She really needed to straighten that woman out. But how could it be clarified after she'd practically shouted it to the clan? Because, really, there was no way a man like Isaac Abrams would ever look at her twice and now the woman had… With the announcing and pronouncing…

She was ready to go home.

Instead of allowing her to escape, Isaac drew her toward the heavy scents of cooking meat and she realized he'd brought her to the grill area. In no time she was settled on a picnic table bench, Isaac at her side. Others lurked nearby but didn't encroach.

Well, almost. The delicate scent of blooming flowers reached her, and they reminded her of the first hints of spring. That was overlaid by the aromas of dirt and boy.

"Hi, Kira. Mim said I couldn't say it before, but she's not here and you smell like prey. Didja know you smell like prey? You do, but Mim said you're not for eating because you're *were*prey." The boy's voice was a tinkling alto, high-pitched and innocent despite his macabre words.

"Parker!" Mia's gasp told her the woman was nearby.

"What? That's what you said." The child harrumphed and fell silent for a moment. "Can I play with Ebenezer? I'm doing real good with playing and I haven't eaten Sophia, yet. Hey, how come he got away with going after Vanessa? He's not a were-anything, and he almost got to eat a werebear."

"*Parker Abrams*," Mia, aka the not-very-good organizer of kitchen pans, hissed at Parker. Abrams. As in Isaac Abrams and Ty Abrams and... *Those* Abrams.

Dear God, just days ago in her home, she whined and complained to an Abrams. Hell, she put the woman to work!

An *Abrams*.

The boy, obviously Parker, sighed. "Can I play with him? You can't see me because you're a little bit blind, but I'll be good."

The trembles of Isaac's body told her the man was shaking with laughter or anger. Considering the sweet-filled scent coming from him, he was amused by Parker's words and not the least bit worried.

Well, she was worried. Worried as hell. What had the woman shared with the family? Hell, what had Kira shared with *her*?

"Yes, you can play with Ebenezer PalffleSnowfle, but you have to give him back before we leave and you need to remember he's a real dog. Not a weredog." Kira smiled widely, the little boy's whoop of excitement was enough to banish any lingering distress from her confrontation with the woman.

Unfortunately, it wasn't enough to banish the renewed panic over the fact she was near Mia *Abrams*. The woman who'd helped her unpack became someone else with the knowledge she was an *Abrams*.

Isaac's warmth invaded her, his shoulder brushing hers as he leaned close. "I thought it was Hufflesnuffle."

She grinned and shrugged, ignoring the mounting worry. "When I rescued him they claimed he was a purebred, and he had a first, last, and middle name. I totally forgot the middle, and most of the last, but he doesn't seem to mind."

Listening to the pup's barks echoed by the tiny roars and squeaks told Kira the dog couldn't care less.

More warmth surrounded her, shadows blocking out the brightness of the sun and an inhale clued her in on the newcomers and their relation to the man at her side. As did Isaac's warning, rumbling growl.

"What do you want, Ty? Don't glare at Kira."

The tallest of the shadows shifted in place, weight moving from one foot to the other. She didn't feel any animosity or anger from the male. Which meant… she could be herself. At this point, there wasn't much more she could do to give them a bad opinion of her, so she didn't censor herself. Between the confrontation with the were-bitch and whatever she'd shared with Mia…

"Isaac," she released a faux whisper, lowering her voice a tiny bit and softening her words. "He can glare all he wants."

A sense of satisfaction from Ty hit her and she inwardly smiled.

"No—"

"Of course, he can. He's the Itan, right?" Another wave of cocky happiness. "Besides, it's not like I can see him. He's just wasting the effort." She turned her blurred gaze to the Itan. She'd have to find the brass balls she grew when living with Alpha Asshole and dust them off. Fake it 'til you make it. "You should really try and smell angry. Actually *being* angry would help. Do you want me to show you how? First you—"

A woman's tinkling laugh overlaid Kira's words, and the large men were pushed aside by a small, brightly dressed woman. Her joy was palpable and Kira found herself smiling in response.

"Take that, Ty Abrams. Your stares are as effective on her as they are on me." With that, the woman blew a raspberry. "Pft. Move along now. Women talk and all that."

The grumbling men backed away, mumbling about interfering women and ruining their fun. She wondered when it'd become fun to frighten females and the words sent a stuttering unease through her.

85

"Kira?" Isaac leaned toward her, keeping his voice to a murmur.

"Maybe this was a bad idea." She didn't give him a reason, didn't want to get into why his brother's words upset her.

He stroked her forearm, sliding his fingers over her skin until he twined their fingers together. "Wanna tell me why?"

"Not really."

At all. Ever. She'd left all that drama-llama crap behind with her old pack. Did she truly believe the men in Isaac's clan were that mean? No. Well, not really anyway. The ones she'd encountered so far had been nice. Well nice-ish. That one guy had been scary, but Mia took care of him. And now that she knew who Mia was, the guy's fear made sense.

"Kira."

She lifted her head and focused on him, wishing she could see his face and gauge the expression that passed over his features. Instead, she got a vague outline of brown eyes, sharp cheekbones, a strong jaw and lips that were definitely closed. In a frown?

"I'd like to go home, Isaac. Please." Knowing his brothers were kidding and trusting them were two very different things.

Silence enveloped them and she wondered if he'd agree or push her feelings aside. In less than a second, she had her answer. "Okay then, lemme get Ebenezer and say goodbye to my parents. Will you be okay for a minute?"

"I…"

The nearby woman suddenly drew her attention. She'd completely forgotten about the female who'd driven off the brothers. No hint of desire or arousal came from the female. No, Kira only found the essence of one of Isaac's brothers clinging to her. A mate? "Hey, Isaac. I was sent on reconnaissance since it's not like you'll talk to Ty, Van, and Keen. Plus, everyone assumes you'll walk on eggshells with me. 'Cause, you know, *me*." The unknown woman scented vaguely of bear and… hyena? Weird.

Isaac's huff of annoyance brought a small grin to her lips and earned her a teasing growl. "What's got you smiling?"

Kira shrugged. "Just the fact I'm not the only one who makes you snarl like that."

"I'll show you a snarl." He upped the volume, attempting to sound threatening when her nose told her the truth. Attraction eased from him and she knew, without a doubt, it was all for her.

She leaned close, ignoring the woman. When Isaac was nearby, she couldn't focus on anything but him. With his attention on her, she didn't think that was a bad thing.

"You should try to grab the emotions that go with the sound, otherwise I'm gonna think you're nothing but a big pussy cat."

"Pussy cat?" The intruding female snorted. "Pussy cat? Isaac? How about vicious? Or deadly. You should hear how he tore into—"

The lid on his playful happiness slammed shut and not a single emotion escaped him and drifted toward her. He was a blank slate and that, more than anything, worried her. "Trista, we're leaving. Can you let the family know?"

With that, Isaac hauled her from the bench and tugged her along.

Trista sputtered and called after them. "What about food? And Mia wanted to—"

"I'm perfectly capable of feeding Kira and we'll catch up with everyone else later." The words were tossed at Trista and his retreat didn't slow.

He pulled her back toward the house while he yelled for Ebenezer to come. She could have told him the dog wouldn't abandon his fun for anyone but her and even then, the animal's response was fifty-fifty.

Except Ebie listened to him since suddenly a warm, wet tongue lapped at her fingers.

All right, then.

Within moments they were back in his car, the engine rumbling once again as the vehicle tore down the clan house's driveway and onto the road. Wind whipped her hair, and the breeze brought a feeling of joyful freedom to her heart. It made her forget about the reason she'd wanted to leave the party as well as what pushed Isaac to suddenly change his mind about staying.

Something had them both… running. There was no other explanation for their reactions. She knew why she ran scared, but what about Isaac?

She hoped he'd trust her enough to tell her. Even more, she hoped she could trust him enough to tell him.

She also hoped they could get Ebie out of the car before he pissed all over Isaac's seats. The outlook was not good.

chapter six

It'd been a damned week since the thwarted barbeque from hell and Kira decided if Isaac could invade her space, she could invade his. Though, if she were honest, his invasion was probably in response to her first one, and now she was perpetuating the invasion circle of life…

It didn't matter. The man had burst into her backyard, *gardened* with her, and then allowed his mother to shout her wishes to the treetops as he dragged her through a family barbeque. Then he'd had the gall, *the gall*, to drop her at her front door with a fast goodbye.

Was there a mention of the mother-in-law stuff? Or mentions of how it'd be straightened out since they were not friends with benefits or mates? No.

No explanations for anything. Not even a handful of lame excuses. Yes, she'd been uncomfortable due to his brother's words and asked to leave, but she hadn't said, "Hey, abandon me."

It was time for a "come to Jesus" meeting. Past time. The man owed her, and she was collecting. Who did he think he was? Hugging her and offering to help her straighten out her kitchen situation.

Ha!

Another thing to add to her list of annoyances.

Kira counted her steps, Ebenezer at her side as she traversed her front porch and pathway. All she had to do was repeat Isaac's name to the dog and then they were off, Ebie pausing beside a nearby gate. She breathed deeply and smiled when she found the man's aroma surrounding the area.

She fumbled with the latch, tugging it until the metal granted her entrance to Isaac's yard. She wasn't quite sure what she was gonna do when she found him, but if he did nothing but make a phone call and got her what she needed, she'd consider them even.

No, he needed to get the mate-not-mate situation handled as well.

Ebenezer nudged her, announcing an impending obstacle, and she slowed her rapid pace. Stairs. The rough outline filled her vision, and she carefully stepped on them. She counted as she went, remembering the number from her last visit. It'd been two weeks since that fateful, box-breaking, pee-laden day. A week since she'd last spoken with him.

The rumble of his car told her he'd arrived home, and he wasn't about to hide from her now.

A few more steps brought her to his front door and before she could chicken out, she banged on the wood panel.

No answer.

Ha! He thought he could hide. She wasn't sure why he was hiding—what did she do to send the man scurrying away—but promises were promises.

Kira knocked again, hitting a smidge harder and ignoring the sting that came from her actions. That was his fault too.

When there was, yet again, no answer, Ebie got in on the action, scratching lightly at the panel.

"Isaac! I know you're in there!" She needed to get to him while righteous indignation filled her. Otherwise she'd apologize for bothering him and scurry away. Maybe shift and hide in her garden. She could stay there for days. Weeks even. She'd dropped a crap-ton of earthworms shortly after tilling her garden and her mole couldn't wait to feast on them.

No. Nope. Not happening. She had to be strong. And angry. The fury was slowly slipping away, and she clung to the emotion, determined to keep it hanging around.

The ground beneath her vibrated, the pounding of steps sounding from inside the home, and she realized she'd finally attracted his attention.

Was she still annoyed enough to give him a piece of her mind? Yes. She could do this.

Kira tasted the surrounding air, and the clean scents of Isaac had her mole dancing and squeaking for him. Oh yeah, the man had *also* denied her a single moment of peace with her inner animal.

Another strike against him. The beastie wouldn't let go of Isaac's promise to help her even after the kitchen was cleaned up.

Stupid stubborn mole.

The click and scrape of locks being twisted and turned reached her a bare moment before the squeaking grate of oil-craving hinges hit her. Then she was filled with Isaac, with his natural flavors and sweet musk. Even better, the aroma was crisp and clean, unhindered by any deodorant or cologne. A shower. He'd been in the shower which meant what surrounded her was all Isaac.

And he wasn't wearing a shirt. A glance below his waist and the swath of dark blue covering his hips and thighs had her imagining he'd only donned a towel before answering her knocks.

A whimper escaped her lips and she really, really hated that her vision was so screwed up. She'd love to trace the lines of his body with her gaze, focus on the ridges of muscle that she knew he possessed. Well, knew in an abstract sense, anyway.

The handful of times he'd held her, he felt firm. And she knew from her own experiences that shifters tended to be rock solid muscle and strength.

But she wasn't concerned about shifters in general. Nope, her focus was on the freshly showered, half-naked werebear before her.

"Kira?" His voice was deep and husky, and it went straight to the happy pink parts of her body. She'd had days upon days to gather a few naughty fantasies and they seemed to rush forward with the throaty word. "Is something wrong?"

The concern was readily evident, but she was still having trouble with the thinking part of her brain. She was too preoccupied with wondering if Isaac had man-noms.

Kira had laughed at Zoey when she'd first heard the term. The woman went into detail about a man's hips and the sexy line that seemed carved into his body. When the she-wolf saw that sensual spot, she'd wanted to nibble and lick there. Basically, she wanted to "nom" on that part of her man. Man-noms.

Did he have them?

She stared at the edge of his towel, at his hips, fighting to see anything that'd confirm her hopes. Unfortunately, she was still a little of a lot blind.

Dammit, man.

"Kira?" His repeat of her name had more concern attached, and she forced herself to meet his gaze. Any longer and she would have drooled all over herself. "Did you need something?"

Did she need something… Did she…

"Oh!" She glared and pointed at him. "Yes. You."

Isaac took a step back, and she had no doubt he was surprised at her tone. "Me? What'd I do?"

She ceased pointing at him and instead used her fingers to count off the reasons she was annoyed. "You broke into my backyard."

"After you invaded my house," he countered.

Yeah, she knew that first point wasn't very sound. "You weaseled into my garden."

"I helped, though."

Kira kept her glare in place. Yeah, that point was good, too. "You followed me into the house and when I ended up with pans everywhere, you *promised* to help me wash them and put them away. Do you know how many of them ended up *back* on the floor, collapsing from the stacks you created? Lots."

His flinch told her he felt bad about that one. Good.

"And *then*." She was on a roll now. She had this rant going, and the rage-train wasn't stopping until she was done. "Then your mother is all about pretty eyes and gorgeousness and family gatherings *and* mother-in-law. And Parker eating the dog. And what the hell did Mia tell you all about me? And…" she kept ticking off her issues, finally losing count and huffing in frustration. "You left me and never came back."

Well, there was the crux of the matter and the source of her… hurt. Not frustration, not annoyance, not even anger. Hurt. He'd… and the brief holds… and the family…

The rush of spending time with him let her hopes rise a tiny bit and then they'd crashed into a pile of broken almost-dreams. She admitted she'd pulled away due to her own insecurities and his brother's words. But why had he?

"Kira…"

"No, I'm not done." Well, she was done, but she had a feeling he'd kick her out since his tone didn't leave her with a very optimistic feeling in her gut. "The point I'm getting around to is that you," she wracked her brain for something that didn't sound *too* insane, "you didn't feed me."

Way to call attention to food, and thus, the size of your ass, Kira.

Too late to pull the words back now.

His body shook, frame kinda trembling, and she wrinkled her nose. "Are you laughing or cold?"

"Damn, Kira. You don't make it easy, do you?"

"I'm very easy," she snapped and winced. "Okay, not that kind of easy. Dammit."

Now his laughs burst from his chest and he reached for her, fingers encircling her wrist and tugging her forward. She allowed him to pull her, then her shoe had to get caught on the doorsill, which sent her tumbling… right into the half-dressed Isaac. Isaac without a shirt, water still clinging to his chest. She splayed her hands on his abs, catching herself, but she also let her touch wander a tiny bit south and…

Boom. Man-noms.

She wanted to trace them with her fingers, her tongue. Instead, she fumbled and pushed and managed to stagger herself upright.

"Oh, God, I'm so sorry."

His hands were busy tugging at his towel, securing it around his waist and she whimpered when he pulled it higher.

Buh-bye, man-noms.

Still chuckling, Isaac took two steps and then he was before her, his heat enveloping her in a warm, moist embrace. She was tempted to lean into him, to pretend to fall again and cop a feel. Instead, she remained in place and enjoyed his nearness.

"You're sorry?" he whispered. "Why? It got your hands on me. I'm not sorry at all."

Kira huffed and glared at him. "Nice of you to act that way, to say that now. They could have been all over you this whole time had you *not abandoned me*."

She should shut the hell up. Now even.

Ebie barked his agreement, so she didn't feel *too* stupid.

"Yeah?" One word and it was filled to the brim with sexiness.

She needed to get a handle on these emotions flip-flopping through her. Angry, happy, annoyed, aroused. God, why couldn't she settle on one? It was his fault.

She rolled the options through her head and realized exactly *why* she couldn't. Because she'd pick aroused and their relationship would go from being a hint more than acquaintances and right on to Bang Town.

"No. No 'yeah.' That's not what I meant. I didn't mean your hands would have been on me and, um…"

"Uh-huh." He agreed with her, but it didn't sound like he *agreed* with her.

Sexy bastard.

"Look," she needed to stay on task. "You made me believe you were gonna help me clean up and feed me. Two things that did

98

not happen. I cleaned up, and no food entered this mouth." She pointed at said mouth to reiterate her statement.

Another bark from Ebenezer. Her dog was so smart. Plus, he knew which side of the bowl his dog chow came from.

Er, right.

Happiness tinged with cocky bravado blew toward her, the emotions rich and full with his closeness. She could swear he was smiling. A swath of white appeared above his chin. Yeah, he was grinning wide.

But she wanted to see just *how* wide. Not asking permission like she normally would, Kira reached for his face, fingers tingling in anticipation. She didn't care about "seeing" random strangers, but her few encounters with Isaac had her wanting to memorize the rise and fall of his features. The way he smiled and the different expressions that accompanied each tone of voice.

Basically, she wanted to know him.

Except the cold, hard grip on her wrists kept her from her destination. The twitch and tug of his upper-body told her that he'd flinched from her touch, pushed her away as he jerked back.

She tried not to let his rejection of her touch pierce her heart.

Tried and failed.

Then she reminded herself that for all her dreaming and wishing, they didn't know each other well. She swallowed her sigh and resolved to change that.

"I'll feed you." His voice was gruff and brisk. "I was going to cook for you, right? That's fine, but I don't have much of anything in the house. Do you want to go grocery shopping or do you have something at your place I can whip up for us?"

Kira grimaced. "Well, I ordered groceries, but they haven't exactly shown up yet. It's another reason I came over. You know people and I was wondering if you could maybe... I don't know... Just..."

Hemming and hawing wasn't solving her problem. She was hungry and her order hadn't appeared yet.

Isaac released her wrist, but didn't lower it, popping into a pose she associated with someone checking the time. "It's after six. Did you order from Miller's?" At her nod, he continued. "They're usually done with deliveries by now."

"Well," she winced more. "You see... They..." She sighed. She hated saying anything negative about the bears in her new home, but it wasn't exactly gossiping if he was asking, was it? "I ordered groceries the day before yesterday, but they're really busy and they said—"

"Really?" Isaac's tone told her a massive throw down was imminent.

Dammit.

"I spoke with Vaness—"

"Uh-huh." He grabbed her hand once again, this time twining their fingers, as he led her deeper into the house.

They passed stacks of boxes, a reminder that he'd be leaving Grayslake soon, but she didn't have much time to be sad about

100

that fact. She found herself nudged toward a small table with a few chairs surrounding the piece of furniture.

"Have a seat."

He didn't leave her much choice since he practically shoved her onto the chair.

The moment he left her, he had a phone in his hand, the telltale beeps as he dialed reaching her. Apparently it didn't take them long to answer because he spoke almost immediately.

"Emily? It's Isaac. I need your father."

Emily, Emily, Emily... Kira remembered the woman was part of the Miller Grocery family. The youngest or eldest of Mr. Miller's cubs? She wasn't sure. She didn't get *that* much gossip passing by her house. She did, however, get enough to know that Vanessa at Miller Grocery was the same Vanessa that Kira embarrassed at the barbeque. Which was probably why she still hadn't received her food. Great.

"Miller, hey, it's Isaac. How's the ticker?" Isaac sounded jovial, but tension in his body was unmistakable. "Good, good. Come by the office if you have any issues. Listen, I'm calling for a personal reason. Your youngest, Vanessa, is causing problems and I don't appreciate it. I sure as hell don't appreciate her delaying an order to Kira Kolanowski. You know about Kira. My mom's talking about her all over town."

Kira groaned and laid her head on the kitchen table. She didn't even want to know what Meg Abrams was spreading. After a five minute meeting, she'd gone from friends with benefits to soon-to-be-mated. Was she somehow, miraculously mated and pregnant now?

"She's special to me, Miller." That had her whipping her head up and focusing on Isaac. While his expression was unreadable, his scent and position of his body were not. There was no hint of a lie. He spoke the truth. She was… "Yeah, she's real special. Which is why I don't like hearing that an order she made days ago still hasn't shown up at her door. You can understand my feelings here, Miller. She's—"

She what? She was the ugliest woman on Earth? She was annoying? She was a walking goddess and he should kiss the ground she floated upon?

Coincidentally, she voted for the last one.

"Right. Exactly. I'll see Rick in the next twenty minutes."

A beep announced the end of the call and then it was just the two of them. Well, the two of them and a dog padding toward her that smelled suspiciously like urine. Dammit, she'd forgotten about Ebie.

Ebenezer nudged her palm and she turned her attention to the whining pup, taking another whiff. Yup, he'd done his business somewhere in the house *and* stepped in it which meant he'd tracked it through the place.

"Ebie, what am I gonna do with you?"

*

Isaac had a few ideas but not one of them revolved around what she could do about Ebenezer and centered entirely on what *he* could do with Kira. His cock had a handful of requests of its own and if he didn't get some jeans on, she'd realize it as well.

102

Then again, he didn't have to worry about her seeing his towel tented by his stiff dick. She'd be able to figure out his feelings if she breathed in his scent.

The dog came to his rescue. The damned dog who protected its owner with fierce snarls but also pissed in his house. Fucker. With a sigh, he dropped the phone to the counter and padded toward the duo, one he'd like to kill and one he'd like to fu-make love to. He couldn't think of Kira as a hard and fast fuck. Ever.

Crossing his arms over his chest, he glared at the pup, baring a fang when the animal merely gave him a lolling dog smile. "Taking him to the animal shelter seems like a good idea." The dog whined, Kira gasped, and he released another sigh. "But that's not gonna happen."

"He doesn't mean to—"

"Oh, he does." Isaac lowered to a crouch until he was eye level with the mutt. "You're just trying to keep your mom from getting hurt, but lemme tell ya, I'm not gonna do that."

Kira barked out a laugh. "Not hurt me? Ignoring me isn't supposed to hurt?"

He pulled his attention from the dog and focused on her, on her flowing brown hair and those pale blue eyes that seemed to see into his soul. He hated himself for the hurt in her gaze and he knew he had a new fight ahead of him. She was one hundred percent right. After their afternoon together, he shouldn't have abandoned her and then avoided her at all costs. He shouldn't have let his sister-in-law's comments about his ferocity and the battle with the hyenas upset him so badly that he stayed away. Then after one day of hiding, he'd been a girl and continued avoiding her, which compounded the problem.

He opened his mouth to tell her that, to assure her that wasn't going to happen again, but her giggles had his teeth clacking together. She tried to suppress them, but the chuckles and snorts won that battle.

Isaac raised his eyebrows. "What's so funny?"

She drew in a calming breath, blowing it out slowly though half of the time she giggled again before she could speak. "Calm," she pressed a hand to her stomach as she tipped her head back and focused on the ceiling. She spoke to herself again. "Calm."

Kira brought her attention back to him and then it drifted lower and lower…

Isaac followed her line of sight and pushed to his feet with a rumbling growl. She couldn't see his glare, but that didn't mean he'd stop.

"I'm sorry! I'm sorry!" The laughs were back. "It's just hard to yell at you and stay mad when you're sitting there with your junk flapping around."

Flapping? *Flapping?*

"I was not flapping. I'm hard as a goddamned rock around you." His bear was annoyed and forced another rumbling sound from him. He'd tipped his hand and pushed when he should have made a graceful retreat.

The chuckles silenced as quickly as they'd begun. "Oh. I… *oh.*"

Her gaze remained focused below his hips and he turned his back to her, cursing himself for revealing so much and then beating himself up because his damned cock was still standing tall. Fucking wayward body.

He tried to calm his need, and then the stench of Ebenezer's most recent "accident" reached him, reminding him of what had to be done. He kept his back to her as he moved to the kitchen entry, careful of the dog's wet footprints.

"I'll get dressed and then clean this up." He paused in the archway and glanced over his shoulder. "Why don't you go back to your place with Ebenezer? As soon as I'm done, I'll come over. We can wash him real quick and then see about dinner. Miller's grandson, Rick, should be there by the time I'm done."

"But—"

"I shouldn't be too long." He didn't want to hear "buts" or "maybes" or, "I'm just not that into you."

At least, not right then. Not when his bear raged at him over his carelessly spilled words.

Without waiting for her reply, he carefully made his way to the stairs. He didn't see any damp paw prints and was grateful the damned dog stayed on the first floor.

A few thumps to his dick to reduce his erection later, and he was dressed and back downstairs.

Thankful he hadn't packed away his cleaning supplies—hell, he hadn't packed anything after meeting Kira—he got to work cleaning up the house. Most of the mess was kept to the main hallway and... another one of Isaac's boxes.

Man, he *loved* that dog.

His bear grunted. The animal obviously didn't understand sarcasm.

His twenty minutes were spent unpacking the soaked box, cleaning the contents and then packing everything into a *new* box. The drenched cardboard went into a plastic bag and straight to the trashcan situated at the side of the house.

When he and Kira finally got together that dog would need...

Isaac pummeled and kicked that idea away.

He was leaving—going somewhere new and away from everyone who knew he wasn't good enough for any woman.

Slamming the lid down with a resounding thump, he padded toward the front door. He just needed to grab his cell phone and keys and then he could head to Kira's.

Back in his kitchen, he ignored the lingering scents of her presence, the sweetness and earth that clung to her. Her flavors rose above the stinging air filled with evidence of his recent cleaning. They called to the bear, luring it forward with the promise of more, and he shoved it back.

They were leaving town. *Leaving.*

Besides, even if he were staying, she deserved better than him.

Shaking his head, he snared what he needed and turned toward the front of the house. Even if she was too good for him, he was anxious to be with her again.

Yeah, he was a glutton for punishment and a mind-fuck combined.

A high-pitched screech broke the quiet of the neighborhood, zinging through him and shaking him from inside out. What the… Another came, panic in the scraping sound. Then a third followed by the unmistakable snarl of a bear.

The fourth had his heart stopping as the source finally registered. Kira. It had to be her. She was one of the few non-bear residents in Grayslake and she was the only one close enough to be heard.

Isaac didn't know what the fuck was going on, but he knew she was in trouble. His woman was in trouble.

He burst through his back door, vaulting over the porch railing and not hesitating to do the same to the six-foot fence separating their yards.

The scene before him froze his heart, the muscle unmoving as he stared. Kira's entire garden was destroyed; the carefully tended beds that'd sprouted new life were now nothing more than scattered dirt.

He ached for the loss, knowing it would hurt her.

It'd hurt her, but not as much as the massive bear intent on chasing her around the fenced-in area. Her little feet scrambled over the pitted ground, the small brown body fighting to dig into the earth.

Without hesitation, uncaring of the identity of the bear going after Kira, Isaac tore his clothing from his body as the beast rushed forward. It recognized a threat to the woman they thought of as theirs and was more than ready to battle for her.

Fur sprouted, bones snapping and reforming in rapid succession. One step had him coated in the deep brown of his animal, two had feet and hands turned into claws, and three and four had his inner animal stealing control. His pace didn't slow. No, it increased and had him racing to the she-bear attempting to kill Kira.

Yes. She-bear. *Vanessa.*

And killing was definitely on the woman's mind. Her rage was palpable and easily rising above the stench of Kira's fear.

Vanessa lifted her paw, claws flexed and extended as she aimed for the quivering, small ball of fur huddling in the back corner of the yard.

Isaac didn't hesitate. He tore across the expanse that separated him and Vanessa. He didn't slow. No, if anything, he went faster, pushed his bear harder in an effort to save Kira.

He released a bellowing, ground-shaking roar that drew Vanessa's attention away from the small animal at her feet. The woman swung her head toward him, her eyes widening when she spotted him. She immediately eased away from Kira, lowering her arm and backing down from the impending fight.

Fuck that.

He barreled into the she-bear, tackling her with his massive weight and sending them straight through the wooden barrier that encompassed Kira's lawn. They rolled, the much smaller bear crumbling beneath his weight and size.

She snarled and snapped at him while he did the same, sinking his teeth into her forearm when she batted at him and digging into her snout when she attempted to bite his.

Vanessa growled, pushing and scraping in an attempt to dislodge him, but he refused to relent, refused to allow this female to get away with attempting to kill Kira.

It would have meant his little mole's death. She'd been shifted, probably in an attempt to dig her way to safety. Based on the condition of the yard, she'd tried hard to run and Vanessa was relentless in her pursuit.

A scrape of claws down his side, her back nails digging into his flesh, had him releasing a bellowing roar. The following burn, the one that seared his veins and sent throbbing pain into his bones, was both familiar and hated.

She deserved to die now. His bear would have been content with Ty punishing her after Isaac got in a strike or two to avenge Kira's pain and fear. Now he knew the truth of the woman's intent.

If Vanessa's physical attack hadn't killed Kira, the poison coating her claws would have done the job.

It was a burning, deadly toxin that left hideous scars in its wake. One Isaac once felt pulsing through his veins while he healed and patched up other bears and wolves suffering the same fate as him.

The red haze of fury and rage blanketed his vision, dropping like a blood-lusting cascade of silken fabric across his eyes. The agony assaulting him was what his Kira would have endured, the pain unending until it was neutralized and purged from the body.

Isaac had a specific purging in mind. One that didn't involve Kira and was meant for Vanessa.

He bellowed again, announcing his plans to the world. It would take one more swipe, on more bite to her throat, and the threat to his little mole would be at an end.

Yes. The bear urged him. *Now.*

It craved the she-bear's blood and he couldn't blame the animal.

"Isaac!" The female's voice was known to him, but he needed to keep his attention on Vanessa.

"Dammit, Isaac!" That male was familiar as well. Mated, but still a threat to his connection to Kira.

The bear's possessiveness flooded him, battling with the desire to kill the bitch beneath him. Vanessa still struggled, scraping and cutting, and filling him with more of the deadly poison. He'd taken more into his body before. More and he'd survived.

"Isaac, stop!" The woman again.

Movement to his left had him tearing his attention from his prey with a snarl as he bared his teeth at the interloper. Only the sound died and delved back into his chest. She stood there, his Kira, naked and shaking. Dirt clung to her pale skin and those haunting blue eyes shined with tears.

"Please, stop."

Another movement. The male. He stood too close to his Kira.

The she-bear beneath him moved, raising her head toward him, fangs dripping with blood and saliva and aimed for his neck.

A roar, filled with every emotion living inside his heart, pierced the bright sky, echoing and vibrating the air surrounding them.

"*Isaac!*" The female again. Intruding. Interrupting.

He didn't want any distractions. He needed to end the threat to Kira and then hide her pale body from view. Another struggling squirm came from the she-bear and he raised his paw, claws ready to dig into flesh a final time. He had a plan now. Kill. Protect. Care.

Kill Vanessa.

Protect Kira from view.

Care for Kira.

"Isaac!" The bellow was deep and powerful and stronger than his own.

He brushed it aside. Despite the power, he was owed reparation and he would have his hundred pounds of flesh. The woman tried to hurt Kira. Why did no one understand that?

"Dammit, boy!" That strength he recognized. It rang through his mind, his bear immediately reacting to the words. They were ones he'd grown up with, ones that had both parts of him cringing the instant the tone met his ears.

Father Bear.

Males entered his vision. Large and intimidating. But not to him. No, the she-bear recoiled from the dominance that now enveloped them.

"Let her go." Ty. Brother Bear.

"Now, Isaac Jericho." Papa Bear. It was his turn to flinch.

Ty crouched beside him. "Let Vanessa go. I have her."

Isaac growled, curling his lip. He didn't want to release the bitch. No, he wanted to finish what he'd started.

"Dammit, boy. Kira needs you now. Ty and I have this one. You go care for her."

He released a rumbling growl. No. They were taking his retribution from him.

"Your woman is naked and Keen is standing not ten feet from her." Ty thumped him and he snapped at the retreating fist. "You want him to go after your girl?"

Narrowing his eyes, he sought out Kira with his gaze and found his brother spoke the truth. Keen was easing closer to his woman. His nude woman. The male was mated to Trista, but... Kira was beautiful. Definitely more so than Trista.

He snarled at his brother and father before pushing Vanessa aside, vengeance forgotten in the face of Kira being lured away from him. He closed the distance with rapid ease, nudging Kira back while putting his massive bulk between her and Keen.

No one should see her nude. No one. Hell, not even him until he had her permission to look, kiss, and touch.

The crack and snap of bone had him looking toward his father and brother, the two men keeping an eye on Vanessa as she shifted. By the time the final muscles settled into place, the woman was a dirt-covered, blood-strewn, sobbing mess. She babbled and cried, pointing at him as she accused him of attacking her and trying to kill her for no reason.

The trio all stared at him, his brother with speculation, his father with exasperation and annoyance from the female's words.

A glance at Keen showed he didn't believe Vanessa's lies.

Maybe Brother Bear Keen wasn't all bad. But his Kira was still nude.

"Isaac, shift back." His father gave no room for argument.

Which was fine. Isaac wasn't arguing, he simply wasn't going to listen. Not when the only thing keeping them from seeing Kira's nude form was his bulk.

Ty growled at him, but the human sounds were far from threatening. "Shift. Back."

Screw their orders, and fuck the pain assaulting him from Vanessa's poison-laced attack, he was not exposing his woman.

His father sighed and shook his head before reaching for the buttons of his shirt. "He's not gonna do anything while she's nude. You know better than that, Ty."

In no time, Dad was bare chested and slowly padding forward, his steps quiet. Isaac fought back the urge to release a warning growl to the older man. Dad was mated to Mom and wasn't one to stare at other women. They'd been together for years. He was a safe male. The thoughts spun through his head as the feet separating them lessened and he stopped with a handful of feet separating them.

"I'm going to lean over you and hand her my shirt." Dad was smart, approaching with caution but without fear.

Isaac nodded and kept an eye on the male's movements. Kira pressed into his side, gasping when she encountered one of his seeping wounds. He swallowed the snarl that filled his chest.

More pain assaulted him, emanating from the wound and beating at all the others. No, he kept the sounds of pain at bay.

The soft rustling of cloth had him focusing on her, watching her slow and careful movements as she donned Dad's shirt. He hated another male's scent on her, but it couldn't be helped.

The moment the final button was fastened, he let his shift wash over him, the bear readily sliding to the back while his human half pushed forward. They knew that healing couldn't happen on four legs. No, he needed his hands to wash the wounds and thread the needles that would put him together again. The pain was reminiscent of the agony he'd experienced over a year ago, his blood on fire and killing him slowly. At least this time he only had to worry about healing himself. There was no concern for others while he was eaten alive by poison and pain.

The torturous sensations of his bear's recession pulsed through his body, beating in time with the pounding of his heart.

The only thing that kept him sane was the feeling of Kira's palm on his flesh, the warmth of her fingers stroking his skin until he knelt on the disturbed dirt of her lawn. He panted and heaved, fighting for breath, battling to move past the stench of blood and toxins until he found the sweetness of her. He focused on that aroma, on the calm it brought forward. He was not fully soothed, not in the least, but he was no longer craving Vanessa's death with every ounce of blood in his veins.

He could wait an hour or two for that. First, he needed to care for his woman.

Isaac pushed to his knees and turned his attention to her, noting the dirt marring her nose and the scratches that decorated her face. New rage assaulted him, but he tamped it down. He had to take the time to count the number of injuries

Vanessa still deserved. Arms covered by his father's shirt, he continued his inspection at her knees, seeing past the mud and earth and on to the bruises and scratches that lingered.

She reached for him, hand trembling, and he noted the blood and the way her nails were ragged and torn.

She'd fought. Run. Tried to dig and hide.

A whimper from his left reminded him of Vanessa's presence, of the woman who'd caused Kira pain. The she-bear was dead. She just didn't know it yet.

chapter seven

Kira trembled, shaking from fear and anger in equal measure. If she were stronger, larger, and fiercer, she'd kill the were-bitch. But she wasn't.

So instead, she followed a limping Isaac into her home, swallowing the sobs that threatened to burst free from her chest. Not in pain, the wounds Vanessa caused were nothing compared to what she'd endured through the years in her father's pack. No, the desperate need to cry was on Isaac's behalf. She wasn't able to inspect the deep gouges in his skin and flesh, but the large swaths of red told her enough.

The tumble and roll of two brown-furred bodies shocked her, the ground shaking and trembling beneath the onslaught of Isaac and Vanessa's battle. Then the scent of blood and… something deeper had filled her nose.

A scent she knew well.

Isaac slowly shuffled toward her back porch and she remained close in his wake, unwilling to let him out of her sight. When they passed by the first male who'd joined them, Isaac snarled.

The stranger backed away, arms raised. The man reminded her of Isaac, the scent close, but not quite a perfect match for the man she followed.

A brother? A brother, yet Isaac voiced a warning.

He had three and she already recognized Ty, the Itan, nearby. George was there as well. So, Keen or Van.

The other aroma that clung to the mystery male was of one of the women she met at the barbeque. He was mated. Trista? Was that her name? So, Keen which meant that Van was dealing with the were-bitch.

He gripped the stair railing, the wood creaking beneath his hold, and she was quick to step around him and race for the door. She was thankful she'd spent the week acclimating herself to her new home. She knew her house now, knew where to find the things she'd need. She couldn't stitch him up, not with her blurred sight, but she could end the pain that wracked his body.

The heavy tread of the other males followed their progress, but she didn't have time to worry about strangers in her house moving things around and turning her space into a minefield of accidents and pain.

Isaac came first.

"George, are you in here?" she called back to Isaac's father, knowing the man would help. More than anything, she knew of his tolerance and patience when it came to women. Meg was a formidable force.

A grunt was her answer.

"Take him to the top of the stairs, last door on the left. Get the water running. Cold. Not even a hint of heat." She strode into her kitchen, confident in her movements.

She bent over and snared her two largest pitchers from one of the lower cabinets. When she straightened, she noticed no one had moved. No one followed her directions.

Oh, screw that. She might not know a lot about a lot of things, but this… She knew more about this than she ever cared to.

"Is there a problem?" she snapped, uncaring that she spoke to the Itan and his father. Not to mention Keen, the clan's Keeper. He didn't make the laws, but he sure as hell knew each one.

The red-covered male swayed and she spouted orders again. "Get him upstairs. Start the shower. Cold. Don't put him in it yet. I'm following you."

"Kira?" Isaac's voice was thread and hoarse.

"We don't have time for this." She glared in George's general direction. She understood their worry for Isaac, and she accepted that he was the clan's Healer. If anyone should give orders about medical care, it'd be him. Except she knew they were working on borrowed time. "Do you want him to live? Do you want him to thrive? Because right now, you're killing him."

She ignored the anger and worry assaulting her and simply returned to her task. If they wouldn't help her, she'd drag Isaac's ass to the shower herself. She was small, but she had pure rage and adrenaline on her side.

She flung open one of the upper cabinets and spied the orange-yellow boxes she needed. It wasn't just tinkling bells that she stockpiled. It'd only taken one experience for her to learn that baking soda needed to be a well-stocked staple in the Kolanowski household.

Without missing a beat, she snared one of her kitchen chairs, placed it near the counter and crawled atop it. She grabbed two boxes and then glanced at Isaac before snaring a third.

Kira hopped down and tossed the boxes inside one of the empty pitchers. She strode forward, hand outstretched for Isaac.

"What are you doing?" Ty took a step toward her, his massive bulk overshadowing her. His concern and anger hit her hard, but she didn't give a damn.

She took a deep breath and fought for calm. It didn't work. Her mole was freaking the fuck out because Isaac was not only hurt, but was injured while defending them. He was theirs now and these males were keeping her from caring for him.

Fuck that noise.

"Do you wanna know what's happening to him right now because you won't help me? The woman had poison on her claws—"

"Wha—"

Kira spoke over him. "But it's not poison. It's an acid that attacks organic material. Cells. Half the drug slows you down, puts you to sleep so the acid can eat through your flesh. So right now," her voice rose with every syllable, becoming shrill as she screamed at them. "Right now, your brother is being eaten alive because *you won't fucking help me!*"

The words echoed off her aged wooden walls, bouncing off every hard surface, but Isaac's voice rose from beneath the sounds. "Yes."

A flurry of movement surrounded her, George's mass brushing past her as he moved to Isaac while Ty came closer, hands outstretched.

"Oh, fuck that. This is my house. That's my ma—I'm helping him. You go deal with the were-bitch outside. I don't need your kind of help," she sneered and then turned to follow the slowly shuffling men.

She didn't give a damn what Keen and Ty did as long as it didn't hinder her as she cared for Isaac.

Kira caught up to them on the stairs, George supporting Isaac and slowly bringing them toward the second floor. More of Isaac's strength drained with each step and fear attacked her, pummeling as her heart threatened to freeze in place.

It seemed to take forever, but they finally entered her room and she raced past them, flinging her shower door open and quickly climbing into the tiled space. A yank on the knob had ice-cold water raining down on her and goose bumps covered her skin. George's shirt retained the cold liquid, making her shudder, but it didn't matter when faced with Isaac's injuries.

She grabbed one of the pitchers and set it beneath the spray before reaching for a box of baking soda. She ripped at the cardboard packaging and dumped a handful into the slowly filling jug.

121

George dragged Isaac into the shower, soaking himself when he entered. "What do you need?"

Kira didn't stop in her preparations. "Lower him to the ground in the corner. Lean him against the wall and then get out."

"You don't—"

"George, I'm on the clock here. Set him down. If you want to be helpful," she snatched up the other pitcher and shoved it at him. "Fill this from the sink. Cold. You can also yell for another couple boxes of baking soda. I think I brought enough, but I'd rather be safe."

When the empty jug was grabbed from her hands, she assumed he was following her instructions. That left her to deal with the male before her.

Never in her life had she hated her handicap. She kidded with herself and whined about not seeing his body or someone's smile, but… But right now, when healing Isaac depended on being able to see his wounds, she wished she'd inherited her father's strengths instead of her mother's weaknesses.

Kira reached up and redirected the spray, grimacing at Isaac's shout when the water struck his body. Yeah, it hurt. She, more than anyone, knew that.

She dipped her hand into the pitcher sitting on the floor, measuring the volume of water. Finding it held enough to do the job for the initial dousing, she hefted it and approached the moaning and whimpering male.

Wincing, she did what had to be done. It'd hurt, sometimes more than the burn of the acid, but it was necessary.

The first rush of liquid drew a snarl and the second had fur rippling over his cheeks, darkening it from tan to deep brown. Dammit. He needed to stay human. Shifting to a bear wouldn't help him with this.

Hating herself, she reached out slapped his face, forcing him to focus on her and not the pain. She barely yanked her hand away in enough time to avoid being bitten, the clack of his teeth snapping together telling her just how near the edge he lingered.

"Isaac, you need to stay human." She dumped more of the liquid on him, washing away the streaks of blood, and filling the open wounds. If any of them healed over, covering the damage beneath, they'd have to dig into them again.

It couldn't linger—eating and eating and eating until there wasn't much left to discover.

He snarled again, baring a nearly-bear fang and she bracketed his head with her hands. She let a hint of her shift wash through her fingers. As a mole, she was tiny, but the animal did let her have some of the perks of moledom when still human. Such as sharp nails and teeth. She only needed the nails.

Kira dug them into his skin, tips rested above the arteries in his neck. "Stay. Human." She released her own version of a growl. "I will kill you before I let you continue suffering. Do you understand me? You promise to stay human or I'll save us both the trouble."

She was bluffing. She'd sooner kill herself than do more harm to Isaac, but with the pain riding him and the water and baking soda filling the air, he couldn't smell the lie.

He responded with a grunt that sounded very similar to his father's, but she took it as agreement.

She got back to work. More of the baking soda filled water drenched him, sliding over his skin to be washed away by the shower. The rain would keep him cool as she fought to cease the poison's progress. Time ticked past, everything outside her care for Isaac disappearing from her thoughts.

Slowly he regained his strength, the suppressant aspect of the poison working its way through his increased metabolism. The bear part of him burned it off, leaving behind the pain and debilitating wounds.

His skin sliding beneath her fingers was ragged, some injuries deeper than others, but slowly healing. She memorized each one, the heat of the cuts telling her of the healing while the coolness of others informed her the toxin still lingered.

While he lay injured before her, his movements sluggish when she urged him to twist and turn so she could reach all parts of him, she took advantage. She took advantage of an injured male and memorized the planes of his body, the strength of his muscles and the old wounds that had scarred and left permanent marks on him.

The one that laid open his chest stretched from shoulder to ribs on the opposite side. Another encased his shoulder. There were even more on his back that stretched to his legs.

Then… dear God, the one that destroyed his face. The *pain* he'd endured. The agony. It was astounding to her. A thick line of scar tissue went from hairline to chin, amazingly missing his eye. She had no idea if it was usable, but it remained in place. Shapeshifters couldn't tolerate foreign material within their bodies. Especially during the change. So he definitely didn't have a glass eye.

But the suffering.

"K'ra?" Isaac's voice was a slur, but it was enough to snare her attention.

She placed the half-empty jug on the ground and crouched before him. She cupped his cheeks, helping him raise his head as she stared into his eyes. Claws weren't involved this time. Now she needed to care for him, give him a reason to fight and lure him to the land of the living. "You with me?"

"Wh' h'ppned? Wh're we?"

"Kira?" George's low, rumbling voice bounced off the tiled walls. Even after she'd exhausted all three boxes of baking soda, he'd stuck around. His words were quiet, almost a whisper, but she heard. As did Isaac.

The man before her snarled and the sound transformed into a rolling growl, overriding all others. "Mine."

"Easy," she was quick to soothe him. "Be easy. It's your father. You worried us and he is helping me."

Isaac grumbled and snatched one of her hands, fingers wrapping around her wrist. He tugged her, forcing her to fall against him. He didn't even wince, not when her weight landed on him nor when her fingers dug into still-pink flesh. "Mine."

"For the love of…" she mumbled. "Isaac, you're injured. Do you remember?"

She'd experienced this often enough that she knew what recovery was like. Reinforce recent events, remind the person, reinforce them again, touch them, anchor them to reality. Repeat until their eyes were no longer filled with the blackness of their pupils and they met your gaze.

"Huh?" He shook his head and she knew he focused on her.

"Vanessa came to my house. She attacked me and you saved me. You fought her. Her claws were tipped with poison. Your father and I healed you."

"Wha—?" He shook his head, but the anger was gone, memories slowly resurfacing.

"You fought Vanessa, she poisoned you, we healed you."

"We?"

Kira reached for the wound on his bicep, testing the temperature of his skin. It was the worst and one that'd needed several washings. Now only a ridge of swollen skin remained. He was nearly back to her.

"Your father and me. Do you remember?"

"Dad?" He was hoarse from the constant growls and yells as she'd treated him, but after that first slap, he'd stayed human.

The shower door slowly swung open, George's familiar form coming into view. The more time she spent with the male, the more she'd be able to recognize him with or without his scent.

"Isaac?" Hope filled the single word.

"Vanessa?"

"I've been up here with you and Kira. Your brothers are dealing with her. At least until your mother gets her hands on her." George's voice was grim, but she didn't hear a hint of remorse.

"So, she's dead then. Mom won't stand for anything less," Isaac rumbled, and his skin darkened with his bear's fur.

Hell no. Not after all she'd done. She gripped his cheeks once again and forced him to turn to her. "You need to calm down. I did not put you back together just so you can ruin it. The more you're exposed to this, the worse it gets, every single time." Didn't she know the truth of that statement? She reached up and traced the scar that ran the length of his face. "And I think you know that already."

Isaac's gaze was already on her, but it became heavy and charged, weighing her down. "I do. But the question is: how do you?"

Dammit.

*

Dammit, Isaac hurt all over. His bear gradually healed his wounds, but it couldn't return his strength. He needed time and food.

And Kira. He definitely needed her. Unfortunately, he couldn't find her even in her own home.

The moment she decreed he couldn't be moved from her care, his family descended. His father, Keen, and Ty were already present, but then *everyone else* came over.

127

His father helped him onto Kira's bed and that's where he'd remained. On one hand, he wanted to stay with her. On the other, he wanted all the fucking males out of her fucking bedroom.

Instead, what he got was his father and brothers surrounding him in bed and she was nowhere in sight.

Dammit. Again.

He still hadn't gotten an explanation as to how she knew of the poison, what it did, and how to treat it.

But he would.

Just as soon as he got rid of everyone.

The four men of the family stood before him, encircling him in their massive presence. Well, they could fuck off. He didn't have the energy to deal with the bullshit with Vanessa. He had more important things on his mind.

Kira-shaped things.

"You need to explain what happened." Ty's voice was harsh, but Isaac ignored him.

"Where's Kira?" He looked to his father. Ty may be his Itan, but his father was his father. When Dad showed up, they were all back on an even playing field. "Is she okay?"

Dad grunted and rolled his eyes.

Raised voices of a handful of women reached him, his mother's, Mia's, Lauren's, and Trista's overlapping. Right. The women had descended.

"Isaac," Ty snapped.

He glared at his brother. "What?"

"I need you to tell me why I have a half-dead she-bear on her way to the hospital and how you got poisoned and beat to hell."

Isaac's bear snarled. He wasn't beat to hell. Yes, he'd been poisoned, but adrenaline would have carried him through ending the threat to Kira. Just a few more moments…

"It was necessary." He looked past the men, staring at the doorway. "I want Kira."

He needed her beside him, needed to know she was healing after her confrontation with Vanessa and that coming in contact with the toxins hadn't harmed her. It ate through flesh and bone, but it could be just as dangerous to skin. And then… one nick, one cut, and it'd burn through her blood.

Ty shifted his position, blocking Isaac's view. "I want to know what the fuck happened to one of my bears."

Dad grunted and shot Ty a glare. Good. Let the man get slapped down by their father.

Isaac snarled at his Itan. "You mean me? Or your precious Vanessa? Good to know you're worried about me."

"Dammit, Isaac. That's not what I meant."

He sighed. "Yeah, you did. One of your bears, Ty. Not me, just 'one of' them."

Another reason he needed to get the fuck out.

Isaac was breathing. Isaac was healing. Isaac was doing this or that for the good of the clan, so let's forget that Isaac could feel pain like any other man. Let's forget that he's not a robot.

He mentally shook his head and took a deep breath. He wasn't going to turn into a wailing baby. He didn't have the right to whine like a bitch. Not when Ty's attitude wasn't anywhere near what they'd all done to Keen long ago. The pain and agony his youngest brother endured over the years, his struggle for control… It was nothing compared to a little thoughtlessness.

"Dammit, Isaac."

"Fuck you, Ty," he volleyed back.

His anger brought forward a rush of adrenaline, heart-pumping blood through his veins, and the transition shoved more of his pain forward. A wound or two split open beneath the new onslaught. He hadn't had a real chance to heal and it showed. The sting on his side was the worst, but the other on his thigh pulsed with an ache as well.

Their father grunted. One that told them to shut the fuck up already. "What happened?"

Isaac sighed. He could fight with his brothers, but he couldn't ignore Dad. So, he repeated the events. Skipping over Kira's visit, and rushing forward to him hearing her screeches and her animal's calls for help. Even now, after all this time had passed, the sounds haunted him. Her pleas and wails bouncing through his head and enraging the bear once again.

His skin rippled, fur sliding through his pores and then retracting when he urged the animal to calm. Kira was safe. She was downstairs with his mother and his brothers' mates. Just because the mates couldn't shift didn't mean she was unprotected. Mom clearly claimed her, which meant she was now a deadly Momma Bear who'd defend her family to the bitter end.

"I remember making it to the house. It gets a little hazy for a bit and then my memories pick up in the shower with Kira dumping a baking soda mix over me." He shrugged, the action pulling at his skin.

"How'd she know? Is the poison so common that she knew how to treat it?" Keen, the analytical one, the one who used his mind to do battle rather than his fangs and claws. Mainly because if his youngest brother actually brought out the bear... *everyone* better run.

"No, it's not. Obviously the hyenas knew of it." That was how Isaac received his scars during the battle with the bastards. Of course, he'd have a few extras to decorate his body now. "But other than that, it's not common. The Southeast Healer knows, of course. Your average clan or other shifters..." He shook his head. "No, it's not something they'd be familiar with. Hell, the only way to get it is home brewing or through a chemist willing to risk his life for it. Manufacturing the good stuff is a very delicate process."

"I doubt Vanessa is smart enough to do it on her own," Ty mumbled and none of them disputed his words. The woman wasn't the brightest crayon in the box. "And Grayslake isn't exactly a hotbed of illegal activity or brilliant chemists."

True again.

"So where'd she get it?" Van voiced the question in everyone's minds.

"I have no idea. Why don't you guys go investigate? Send Kira up on your way out." That earned him four equally threatening glares.

"Seriously, Ty. Vanessa went after Kira. She's my ma—" He wasn't going there. Not with his brothers and father hanging around and definitely not before he spent more time with her. He loved—liked—everything he knew about her, but it was still so little. A man couldn't claim a mate on next to no time spent together. Then again… Ty had. And Van. And Keen.

Maybe…

"Vanessa had poison on her claws. I admit, I might have gone a little overboard." Though his bear didn't agree with his statement. If they'd had their way, Vanessa never would have gotten off the ground. "But that doesn't change the fact she tried to kill someone. Not in a challenge. Not because she was threatened. She was pissed at Kira and decided a mole didn't need to live in a bear town. Period."

Two of the four glares disappeared, Keen and Van no longer as angry and his father was slowly easing toward annoyed. Ty though, he still appeared ready to do battle.

Well, the male could wait until Isaac healed. It was a rule in the family. No hitting a cub when he's down. They were far from cubs, but he figured his father would make them stick to the spirit of the words.

"That's not the story Vanessa told."

Isaac snorted. "Of course not. She probably said I attacked for no reason. That I'd gone crazy." Ty's slow nod confirmed his statement. "Yeah, well, did anyone get a good look at Kira before she saved me? Because that's what she did, by the way.

132

She saved my life. Each time a person is exposed to this shit, it gets worse. After last year," he huffed. "Without her, you'd have one less brother right now. Did you see the blood and scratches on her? The raw, broken fingernails? The way one…" Her condition came back to him in a rush, reminding him that more than one finger looked and felt crooked as she'd touched and stroked him. "She broke at least two fingers trying to get away, Ty. And even with that damage, she made sure I lived."

He leveled a steady glower at his eldest brother, at his Itan. "So before you discount my story—before you brush aside the words that come from the woman I saved—you should think about how we got this way." He tore his gaze from Ty and focused on his dad. "Can you send her up?"

A nod and grunt came from Dad, the sound followed by a tip of his head. The universal sign for "get the fuck out" and his brothers listened. No one gainsaid Dad.

Ty, Van, and Keen filed out and his father was the last. The old man paused by the door, turning back to him. "You did this before. People tell me you cared for them before yourself after that fight."

That fight. Nice way to put the battle that existed in Isaac's hazy, agony-laden memories. He didn't want to go back to that time. Didn't want to think about every seeping wound…

"Yeah," he pushed the word past the emotions clouding his throat.

Dad held up a hand, the palm red and rough indicating a recent wound. "Cut m'self getting you in the shower. Got some of that acid on me." He shook his head. "Don't know how you survived that. All them bears and wolves, and you not treating yourself for hours." His dad looked away and a small shudder wracked the old man's body.

Isaac pretended not to see the slight sheen to his dad's eyes and waited for him to speak. "I saw her, Isaac. I couldn't help but see her legs and her back through my shirt." Another shaking breath. "I don't know how either of you survived that. The pain…" Dad cleared his throat. "I'm just glad you're good. Don't stay in bed too long. Can't be lazy."

With that, his father was gone, striding through the doorway. The heavy thump of his retreat slowly lessened until he really was alone on the second floor of Kira's home.

Alone and hurting, he wondered who the hell exposed her to the shit that damned near killed him. Then, he could kill them for hurting her.

chapter eight

The glares of the Grayslake inner circle were no less fierce when they tromped down her stairs. The women had been welcoming enough. They'd thanked her for saving Isaac and patched up the raw spots on her arms, hands, feet, and shins with baking soda solution. She hadn't even realized the toxin assaulted her, not with adrenaline filling her veins, allowing her to feel no pain.

When she'd instructed Mia on how to prepare the neutralizing treatment she'd used on Isaac, the Itana tugged open the appropriate cabinet and stared at row after row of Kira's baking soda boxes. She'd turned to Kira, the woman's emotional pain and pity swarming her like a blanket, and whispered, "Do I want to know why you have so much of this?"

"No." A simple word that brooked no further discussion. She didn't want to talk about it and she sure as hell wasn't going to take a trip down memory lane while Isaac lay in her bed and faced off against his brothers.

The sound of the men thumping down her stairs had all conversation halting, and the men's flaring rage whipped her before they entered the kitchen. At her? At Isaac? It sure as hell better have been because of Vanessa.

"Mia, I have to interview Vanessa. I want you to ride back to the house with Van and Lauren." Ty's voice was flat and unbending leaving no room for denial. The anger flowing off him smacked her. Had it been a physical part of him, solid and firm, she would have crumbled beneath the strength.

"Excuse me?" Mia's voice was soft but just as firm as Ty's.

Lauren snorted. "Who said *I* was leaving?"

"Lauren," Van warned.

"Keen, you better not try to send me home, too." Trista gave her mate a warning.

Kira was able to discern the family's scents now, so she knew it was Keen who approached and tugged Trista to him. "I wouldn't dream of it. If Kira's okay with it and you wanna stay, you stay."

"How can you—"

"One second, sweetheart." The familiar meeting of lips preceded the rest of Keen's statement, the words directed at Ty. "How can I be okay with Trista staying here? I can because unlike you assholes—"

"Language." After that first day Mia assisted Kira in unpacking, she'd learned that cursing did *not* happen in her presence.

Keen tried again. "Unlike you *jerks*, I know Isaac took Vanessa down for Kira, which means she's part of the family."

Ty sighed. "I have to look out for the clan, Keen."

136

"And Kira is as good as part of this clan, Ty. Remember when you decided to mate Mia? And everyone told you not to mate a half-shifter because you may not have fully shifting cubs? You put family above clan.

"Do that now and quit being an idiot. Heck, how many times do you two have to screw up before you realize family is more important than anything? You almost lost me. You're about to lose Isaac. It's about time you think of something other than yourselves and the clan." Another kiss from Keen to Trista. "Give me a call when you're ready to come home and I'll come get you."

The weight of Keen's words told Kira something deeper hovered between the family members.

"We… We didn't…" Ty sputtered.

"Ask everyone in the room if they knew of my struggles, Ty. Ask them and see who raises their hand… and who doesn't." The shift of Keen's shoulders projected his shrug. "Then you'll know exactly who is oblivious and who isn't." A murmured *love you* came before the youngest Abrams left.

With that, the eldest family member entered, the massive form of George Abrams seeming to take up every available space in the small kitchen. "What're you all fighting about?"

"Dad—"

"He—"

"They're idiots." Meg's voice rolled over Ty's and Van's. "Which is nothing new." She tsk'ed. "You'd think after all that mess with your brother, you'd learn to pay attention." She sighed. "Are we ready, George? Does Isaac need anything?"

137

"Nope, we're good." The massive male's attention shifted to Kira. "You let us know if you need anything. Isaac will, but I'm talking about you, too. We'll be at the clan house, but it won't take much time to get here."

"Is no one listening to me?" Ty raised his voice to be heard over his father's.

"No." Everyone in the kitchen voiced the word. Including Van.

Whatever Ty's problem with her, he'd been overruled.

With a good bit of grumbling and growling, everyone left. Including the women.

Well, they mostly left. They'd really gone over to Isaac's to see about his packing and visit with each other though they assured Kira they were available if she needed them. They just didn't want to be "under foot" while they chit-chatted since she'd need to check on Isaac soon.

That was followed by a pat on the arm and wink from Meg.

Kira was not going there and she sure as hell wasn't asking Isaac's *mother* what she meant by that.

Alone, she padded through the house, noting the waning light, but unworried about her path to the stairs. She should flick on a light but bright or dark, she still wouldn't see well. Besides, she knew how to get where she was go—

Whatever was in her path sent her sprawling, arms waving and pin wheeling as she fell forward. She reached for the wall, fingers scraping against the flat surface, sending a new wave of agony down her spine. She'd straightened her digits while caring for Isaac, taking a moment to pop the bones into place

138

and begging her mole for help in quickly healing the injuries. They'd come to a sort of agreement through the years. Kira would ask for assistance to heal the part of her body which needed it most and it would comply, accepting that human-Kira knew what would help them survive.

The fingers were first, convincing the small beast that they were safe despite the pain elsewhere and that she needed them to help Isaac.

It listened, but it'd only been hours. The bones weren't quite solid enough to take her weight, and her ring finger ached and cracked beneath the sudden pressure. The snap buzzed through her, sending a bolt of pain along her nerves, and she swallowed the whimper threatening to escape. She'd feel better if she voiced the pain, but long-taught lessons were hard to override.

Despite her attempt to halt her fall, she continued tumbling toward the ground, her other hand outstretched and prepared to catch her weight. It'd still hurt, the burns on her arms not quite closed, but it couldn't be helped.

The ground grew closer, or rather she continued to race toward the ground, until finally she collided with the worn wood. Her head bounced against the hard surface, sending yet more agony flaring through her.

God, today was a day of pain. Both emotional and physical agony battered her, memories brought forth by the aches assaulted her with every beat of her heart.

Thump. Thump. Thump.

Her pulse mimicked each strike of her half-brother's fists on flesh, each tear of his teeth through skin.

Thump. Thump. Thump.

She gasped and fought for air, refusing to allow injuries to steal her control. She'd been through this and survived. Hell, she'd endured worse. She could take this beating. The past overlaid the present, pulling her toward the last time he'd attacked. When he'd jumped her in the parking lot, ready to teach her how real wolves treated prey.

Thump. Thump. Thump.

He broke the wooden bat that day. The one that'd turned brown with her dried blood.

No one knew that though, did they?

No. Never. Only the weakest pack members whined to the alpha and Kira was not weak.

Thump. Thump. Thump.

The pool of blood surrounding her spread with every squeeze of her heart and tightening of muscles. She stopped feeling at one point, no longer sensing the pain he caused. Except… except she recognized his last actions, the spilling of liquid over her exposed flesh, the fiery burn that raced over her nerves.

"Here's a new present…"

The mole had trouble healing the damage, but it had. Slowly. Carefully. Painfully.

Thump. Thump. Thump.

Except it was more like *creak, thud, squeak, thump, gasp.*

The changing sounds were enough to pull her to the present, to force herself to think of her surroundings.

"Kira?" The deep baritone confirmed her brother wasn't lurking around the corner or pummeling her damaged body. "Kira?" Panic filled his voice. "*Kira!*"

Panic. She recognized panic. He should suppress that emotion. It only encouraged the rabid animals. The scent sent them into a frenzy that almost killed her. She couldn't be afraid, never afraid…

Warm hands touched her, squeezed her, pulled at her skin and she reacted without thought. She'd always fight. He knew that and she waited for his gleeful cackles to fill the air. He enjoyed it, claws digging into her as she battled him.

Wolf versus mole. Wolf would always win, but mole would go down fighting.

Always fighting. Always, always, always—

"Fuck, Kira. Dammit, stop." The snarl was… familiar? Yes, wasn't it always the same? Of course those who tried to kill her were familiar. It was the same group each and every time.

Her brother needed new friends. At least a few that'd put her out of her misery and do the job right already.

A heavy weight pressed against her, covering her from head to toe. Something new. They always reached for her arms and legs, leaving her stomach vulnerable.

"Fuck it. Stop, dammit."

He cursed. She should tell Mia so he could put ten bucks in the… swear…

Swear jar?

Mia?

Kira breathed deeply, pushing past her pain to taste the surrounding flavors. Sweet, heat, musk, man. Those aromas blanketed her, covering her in them. Not just in the air, but physically as well.

She blinked, finally seeing the blurry male above her, remembering the scent and man that held her captive.

"Isaac?"

"There you are," he murmured. "You scared the hell out of me."

Him? She scared herself. Or rather, the past assaulted her and captured her, refusing to be dislodged.

"What happened?"

No, she wasn't going to talk about it. About anything. She was Kira Kolanowski, woman without a past.

"Nothing. I tripped and my hand and…"

In one swift move, Isaac was on his knees beside her, hands moving over her body, pressing and sliding over her skin. She recognized his examination, knew it was a Healer taking stock of his patient. She'd lived through enough of them, after all. He was gentle, fingers carefully prodding and stroking. His hands stuttered when he got to hers, gliding over the bent digit.

"I need to splint this," his words were hoarse. "I'll call—"

"I have several under the bathroom sink upstairs."

He shot her a surprised look, eyes wide and eyebrows raised. "We're going to talk about why you have splints inside your house and why you fought me as if your life depended on it."

Kira grimaced and the words burst free before she could hold them back. "More often than not, it did."

The sudden stillness of his body wasn't a continued burst of surprise. No, it was a predator's quiet as it prepared to pounce. "I see."

He didn't, but she let him believe his own words. Zoey, her very best friend in the whole world, didn't even know the truth.

"Let's get you up." Those warm palms skated over her, his grip firm but gentle as he slowly helped her stand.

Wetness coated her right leg and a glance revealed she carried a new wound in the middle of her shin. She looked around and found the culprit. At some point, someone used her small stepstool. Instead of placing it back in the crawlspace beneath the stairs, they'd left it leaning against the wall. Had the sun been shining, she would have seen the bright colors that covered the handle. Had she bothered paying attention instead of depending on her memory to get her to the top of the steps, she would have walked around it. Instead, she stumbled and hurt herself further.

Oh, joy.

"C'mon. I have you." He kept his tone soothing and calm as he led her up the stairs.

143

The deep vibrations eased her continued anxiety and she followed him, allowing him to safeguard her.

Their trip took longer than normal, but not as long as expected, and suddenly she was in her bathroom, sitting on her counter as Isaac dug through the cabinets. It gave her a chance to look at him, to see the new red lines that were too bright to be healing skin.

"You shouldn't have gotten out of bed. You're not fully healed." She reached for a line on his bicep, fingers coming away sticky and stained. "You hurt yourself again."

She felt his glare but didn't care. Heh. She rhymed.

"And you re-broke your finger and sliced up your shin."

She didn't have to tell him he was right. It was a bit obvious.

Unhurried hands got to work, Isaac apologizing as he mended her. She remained quiet—another thing she'd learned over the years in her father's home. She could endure anything and not make a sound. A gift in some ways.

The snap of her finger popping into place didn't cause a flinch. Neither did the rush of agony on its heels. The shin was a simple gash that her mole would heal in no time, and she allowed the animal to focus on that wound. She was with Isaac and from what she'd heard, Vanessa was at the hospital. She wouldn't need to be in fighting shape right away. The beastie could do as it wished.

He secured the splint in place, additional twinges of pain hitting her nerves, but nothing alarming.

144

"How did you know I re-broke it?" She knew he'd been out of it. First when he was shifted and then ever more so in the shower.

One last piece of tape was pressed into place and then he traced her palm, finger sliding over the new scarring she'd acquired while caring for him. Even though they marred her skin, she couldn't regret them. The world was a better place with him in it.

"Because even through the haze of pain, I watched you. Because I know you." He raised his gaze to hers, his bear's black orbs peering from behind his normal chocolate irises. "Because you're mine."

"You're also naked." Not that she was ogling or anything. Okay, she ogled. Maybe not when he was hauled into her bed by his father, but definitely now.

Ogle, ogle, ogle—with another ogle for good measure.

Surreptitiously, of course. It was probably the only time she'd see him naked and even if she couldn't see him well… It was still a naked Isaac.

Naked, naked, naked—with another naked for good measure.

Thinking about his nakedness kept her from thinking about his words, how final they seemed, and how much she wanted them to be true.

*

Isaac tightened his muscles, tensing and curling his hands into fists so he wouldn't snatch Kira to him. So he wouldn't pull her close, rub his body against hers as he buried his face in her hair

145

and nuzzled her neck. He'd scrape his fangs along the column of her throat and then...

His cock twitched and his body's reaction was immediately followed by a twitch of her nose. His dick filled further, and she flared her nostrils, drawing in more air.

Dammit, he didn't want her scenting his arousal. Not when he was naked before her, bare to her blurry gaze as he patched her up. He focused on those facts, reminding his human body, and his eager bear, that she'd been injured. Her finger was broken, her skin was raw, and she had a seeping gash on her shin.

None of it was healing as fast as it should, but she was a weremole, not a bear. He didn't know how quickly they recovered from injuries, and it wasn't like there was a handbook he could consult.

"Yeah, well, I heard you fall and didn't want to stop and put on pants." He reached out, unable to keep his hands to himself, and stroked her cheek. "Especially when the scent of your blood called to me."

Kira wrinkled her little nose and he knew he was a goner when that little movement aroused him. "Is it a carnivore thing? Because moles aren't on the menu."

Oh, they were, just not the way she meant.

"No, it's a you thing." He didn't want to give her any more time to think about what he'd said.

His bear demanded they care for her, which included putting her into bed with them so she could heal and be under his protection as well. Vanessa's actions proved his Kira needed someone to look out for her, and he refused to allow that job to fall to anyone else. Not when she belonged to him.

"C'mon. Let's get you in bed." He nudged her, intent on getting her down from the counter and shuffling toward her welcoming pillow.

"Wait." She nudged him back. "Did you put everything away?"

He glanced at the scattered supplies. "No, but I'll do it when we get up."

She glared at him. "One, there is no 'we' getting up. You need to lie down, but I gotta—"

"Go to bed with me."

"Put things away and clean up downstairs. Everything has a place. If they're not put away, I trip, break a finger and slice up my shin." She pushed the words through gritted teeth and he paused, letting her words envelope him.

The bear snarled and demanded they do exactly as she asked. They couldn't risk their Kira. "You're right. I'll put you in bed and I promise I'll put the supplies back exactly where I found them." Her expression said she was skeptical, not quite believing him. "I promise."

"Not like Mia?"

Isaac frowned. "What about Mia?"

"*She* was the one who 'helped' put the pots and pans in the kitchen just before I met you."

"Ah." He understood now; both her frustration then and her worry now. Mia, while a wonderful Itana, wasn't exactly the

147

best at organization. Cleaning wasn't an issue, but tidy was still an abstract concept to the woman. Unable to keep his hands to himself, he reached for her unharmed hand and gave it a gentle squeeze. "I'll place it exactly as I found it, Kira. You can trust in this. I will never do anything that would cause you harm." He tightened his hold once again. "Now, let me take care of you."

"I don't need taking care of," she sniped, but there wasn't much heat in the words.

"Uh-huh." He didn't believe her. She was a woman he wanted to wrap in cotton and protect with every ounce of his strength. Which, at the moment, wasn't much. "Bed."

Isaac nudged her again, holding tight as he lowered her feet to the ground and not releasing her when he led her toward the bed in the middle of the room. When they reached the soft mattress, he tugged aside the blankets and helped her slide beneath the sheets and comforter. He hadn't walked her around to the clean side, to the spot unblemished by the remnants of his shower. No, he wanted her surrounded by his scent, wanted her mole to accept him.

When she let her eyes drift close with a soft sigh and wiggled into a more comfortable position, he figured the animal was well on its way to welcoming him.

Good. He didn't want to have to press too hard. He would have, of course. He wasn't letting her go. He didn't know what the fuck to do about the Southeast Itan or Healer. He didn't know what the hell he'd tell his family or moving or… anything.

Because no matter his choices, as long as any plan included Kira, he didn't give a damn about anyone else's opinions. Only hers.

The click-clack of nails on wood reached him a moment before Ebenezer peered around the corner, tongue hanging from his mouth.

Okay, he cared about hers and Ebenezer's.

But if the dog kept peeing on his fucking things… His bear recommended eating the animal, but Isaac knew the truth and sighed.

If the dog kept peeing on his stuff, he'd just buy more stuff.

He was such a pussy.

With a shake of his head, he padded his naked ass around the bed and crawled in beside Kira. He didn't touch her, didn't dare place a hand on her skin. If he did, he'd have her, coax her toward accepting him and that wasn't acceptable. Especially in her condition. Not because he couldn't be careful of her injuries, but because he wanted her to welcome him with open arms and knew if he held her, kissed and caressed her, he'd make love to her.

He'd claim her as his own.

They didn't know each other well enough for that.

Neither had Ty. Or Van. Or Keen…

He brushed aside the animal's thoughts. He wasn't his brothers.

So, instead of giving in to the desire to touch her, he simply stared. He allowed his gaze to trace the gentle curves of her

149

face, watching as her animal healed the bruises marring her cheek. The purple slowly faded to pale blue, then the disgusting yellow-green until pale, clear skin was left. Some of the scratches disappeared further, pink flesh left in their place.

He watched it all.

And it wasn't creepy. He reminded himself of that fact. He was ensuring his Kira was becoming whole once again, that's all.

Right. He might believe that someday.

Exhaustion pulled at him, and as much as he ached and his human body tugged him toward sleep, the bear gave him the strength to remain awake. They had to so they could watch over Kira.

Their Kira.

Minutes ticked past, Kira healing beneath his gaze while his body did the same. New scars formed, ruining his already damaged skin, but he didn't give a damn. He was alive, heart still beating, blood still pumping through his veins so he could lay here beside Kira and watch her sleep.

At least, until she spoke.

"You're watching me sleep," she huffed. "Is there a reason? Did I grow another head? Or are you lulling me into a sense of security before you wake me up with a knife against my throat. Or your claws. Teeth would have woken me before you got a good grip, though. Just as an F.Y.I."

Flat. Without hesitation. As if they were thoughts that regularly spun through her mind.

The bear rose up, enraged that her thoughts had *ever* gone in that direction. His skin stretched, poking and prodding his still-healing wounds, while his bones ached with the need to snap and reshape.

"Why," he paused and shoved his goddamned animal back in its cage. The bear wouldn't help them right now. Not when he scented the first flickering of fear from her. "Would you ever have to consider those options?"

She didn't say a word, simply kept her eyes closed and breathing even. Hell, Ebenezer's huffing breaths and pants silenced.

She still didn't speak.

"Kira?"

"I heard you."

"Are you going to answer?" *Before I tear this place apart.*

A knife… claws… teeth.

"Are you going to come after me if I fall asleep? Are you going to shift your hand and press your claw to my skin so if I jerk away it'll dig into my throat and kill me?"

Isaac forced himself to breathe. This was the anger-filled, politely raging Kira he'd met that first day. Not Kira, some of my friends call me KK and Colon to… the…

"No. I would never. You're mine. I said that and I sure as fuck meant it." He couldn't push the growl from his voice. Then again, he didn't try very hard either.

151

"We're gonna talk about that whole 'mine' thing. But I'll focus on your no first. If you're not going to attack me in my sleep, then the why and who don't matter." She wiggled and tugged the blanket tighter around herself.

Oh, it mattered.

He relaxed against the pillow, rolling to his side so he could continue staring at her, memorizing her profile. "Kira?"

"Hmm?"

"You're gonna tell me when you wake up."

She reached over and patted him, the fabric of the comforter not allowing her heat to sink into him. "You keep thinking that."

Oh, he would. And he wouldn't allow her to duck his question.

Her hand remained atop him, her warmth eventually reaching him and he refused to move. He didn't want to lose that hint of a touch.

"Isaac?" Kira's breathing remained normal and had she not spoken, he would have sworn she slept.

"Yeah?"

"Your scars don't bother me."

He halted, whole body locking into place. His heart stopped, lungs no longer drew air, and the blood in his veins froze. He couldn't have said a word had he tried. Not a single one.

He made a sound, a half-aborted "I" that came out as a wheeze.

I don't know what you're talking about.

"I know they make you uncomfortable. I figure that's why you wouldn't let me touch your face at your house." She shrugged, the sheet rustling with the movement. "But I have now and they don't bother me." She turned her head, opening her lids to reveal the glacial blue eyes that peered into his soul. The bear pushed through him, aching for a look himself. "We all have scars. Some on the outside and some on the inside." Another shrug. "But we have them."

"Where are yours?"

Kira gave him a rueful smile. "Both."

That was not the answer he wanted. Though it was one he should have expected.

His father told him about her scars, ones like his, and her own words told him about being afraid to even sleep.

His Kira had a past that had beaten her to hell. Fuck, even her present was painful. She'd already been attacked by a werebear, burned by poison, broken a finger, and ended up with a large gash in her shin. He refused to accept that all of it was due to him. Re. Fused.

No amount of refusal erased the truth.

No amount of truth could make him walk away.

Isaac cupped her cheek, enjoying the feel of her silken skin beneath his palm. This, through it all, remained unblemished. Her hands were raw and the flesh on her legs was blistered from the toxins, but the pale pink of thriving life still filled her face.

Kira stroked his skin, fingertips gliding along his forearm and tracing the lines of scarring. Some new, some old, all of them disgusting to see. He figured they were just as disgusting to touch.

Except she didn't seem to mind.

That tender stroke continued as she crept higher, petting his biceps and lingering over the curve of his shoulder. His neck was next, the one part that didn't have a single scar marring his flesh. No, the hyenas—and Vanessa—managed to miss slicing his head off.

Not that they hadn't tried.

She traced his jaw and he gritted his teeth, forcing himself to remain still. She inched even closer to the skin that no one had touched, not even another Healer, since that day.

His bear snarled and roared, urging him to fling her away. They'd rather have a pissed off mate than none at all. And it was sure she'd walk away the moment she traced the wicked line bisecting his face.

But she said she had already. So what did that mean?

"Do you know that I can tell more about a person by touching them than I can by scenting or hearing them speak? I obviously can't see you." Another rueful grin and he wanted to tell her to get rid of the self-deprecating talk. "A scent doesn't lie, does it? And you could lie, but your scent wouldn't. Expressions mean nothing. But feeling your skin, tracing the lines of your face, it tells me so much more."

His cock throbbed with the feel of her hand on him, desire burning hot and fast through his blood, and he cursed himself for being an insensitive asshole.

Didn't mean his cock softened. Nope, his dick remained hard while he focused on Kira, on the magic of her fingers.

"What does it tell you?"

Would it tell her that he refused to let her go? That he didn't give a flying fuck what anyone in the goddamned clan said? That even the Southeast Itan himself could throw a bitch-fit the size of Texas and Isaac would tell the man to go fuck himself?

Kira traced his jaw, from a spot beneath his ear on to his chin. Her finger scraped over his rough skin and he knew he needed a shave. When *she* shivered, and the light delicate scent of *her* arousal reached him, he figured he'd hold off on the shave for a little bit.

"Your jaw is square. Strong." She retraced her path. "You're stubborn as hell."

Isaac chuckled. She wasn't lying.

Her touch continued, outlining his lips from corner to corner. "You smile a lot. You're happy."

He wanted to tell her that used to be the truth but didn't. Not when she seemed to glow brighter and brighter each moment he let her continue feeling him.

Isaac barely felt the next stroke and the smile bled from his face. The skin was damaged and rough, the nerves severed and destroyed over the hours on that day.

"You still smile. Maybe not as much because of this, but you do." Her finger glided along the harsh line. It was about the width of his pinky, her first finger. "You should smile more, you know."

It was Isaac's turn to grimace. "Sometimes, after all the pain, there's not much to smile about."

God, she looked at him with those eyes, those bright blue eyes he wanted to stare into for the rest of his life, and said a few words that gutted him. They tore him apart for what they meant to him today and what they must have meant to her over the years.

"Sometimes the pain is the only thing that reminds you you're alive, and so you smile."

chapter nine

Isaac quietly crept down Kira's stairs, one of her towels snug around his waist. The third stair from the top creaked and he froze, listening for any sounds that told him she'd woken. He sighed when she didn't even mumble or shift in her sleep. She needed the time to heal, and he needed time to clean the floor and put things away. Particularly the stool she'd tripped over.

Then he'd hunt for the inconspicuous bits of tape she'd said decorated the floor. They were dark brown to blend with the wood, but they outlined exactly where her furniture was meant to be. He didn't want a repeat of earlier, so he'd be damned if an errant chair sent her sprawling again.

He also wanted clothes.

He reached the bottom of the steps and began his hunt, moving through room after room, nudging her coffee table back into place and then came her couch. Hell, even the TV table was askew. What the hell had his family done? Decide it was okay to destroy a person's home? Even an inch could mean Kira would tumble and hurt herself and—

His bear scraped its nails along his spine, adding to Isaac's frustration. Damned protective animal.

Well, that settled it. No one would ever come inside again. He couldn't risk her that way.

Ebenezer's click-clacking approach had him turning toward the entryway. The pup sat near the front door, whining when Isaac gave him his attention. He walked two steps toward the back of the house and then looked at him again with another whine.

"Got to go out, boy?"

Another whine.

"All right, let's go." He followed the dog, Ebie—God, *Ebie*—to the back door. One twist of the knob had it open and the dog raced into the yard, sniffing damn near everything before finally finding a place to do his business.

Of course, standing outside in nothing but a towel was the perfect time for Mia to come strolling out as well. The Itana spied the dog first, her face lighting up with happiness when she caught sight of him.

Then came the high-pitched squeal he knew belonged to little Sophia. Great. He figured Parker wasn't far away and when a small bundle of fur raced through the massive hole in the fence, his suspicions were confirmed.

"Kira? Is that you?" Damn Mia was loud and Kira was sleeping and he didn't give a flying fuck about his scars and the fact he was half-dressed.

Ignoring the mess of Kira's yard, he stomped to the hole. He couldn't even call it a hole, could he? A good fifteen feet of fence was completely missing, the large hunk of nailed together wood now lying on the ground.

"Kira?"

Isaac hissed, and Mia jolted, freezing in place. "She's sleeping."

"And you're…" The words began, but ended with a quick intake of breath. "Oh, Isaac."

Shit. He hadn't put on a… shit. If he'd had clothes, he should have put them on. But he hadn't and letting Ebenezer out was a necessity and he forgot about the women at his house and… Fuck.

She padded closer and he took a step back, unwilling to let anyone touch him but Kira. Yes, he had scars. He had wounds that were still healing and he had pain thrumming through him like a goddamned drum, but the only one who could touch him slept in the house at his back.

"You… Are they all from… then?"

Sophia kept him from answering, her giggles and yells drawing their attention. She held out her chubby little arms with her chubby little hands, and called to him. "A-a-a…"

Isaac reached toward the toddler, holding her for a moment, smiling where her small palms patted his face. She was adorable and would be a gorgeous woman when she grew up. Which annoyed the bear because her being pretty meant boys would sniff after her.

Another gasp from Mia, but he didn't spare her a glance. Yeah, he was smiling. Smiling because the pain told him he was alive, right?

The thud of a vehicle door slamming shut reached them, the heavy cadence of his brothers and father easily heard in his backyard.

Isaac brushed a kiss across Sophia's forehead and handed her back to Mia. "Uncle Isaac has a few things to take care of, little Ia." He finally looked to the Itana and pretended not to see her pity and tears. "Can you send one of them over with some clothes?"

"You could come over and—"

He shook his head. He wasn't about to leave Kira. "If they won't bring them, then I need Dad to stay with her while I'm gone."

"I'm sure they'll want to talk to you."

"Which they can do at Kira's," he countered. She looked as if she'd argue again, but he cut her off. "If it were you and Ty, no one would ask him to leave your side. Well, it's me and Kira, do you understand? Someone didn't put a stool back where they found it and she tripped over it after you guys left. She re-broke one of her fingers and I found her silently bleeding in the hallway. So no, I'm not leaving her alone."

"A stool…" Mia's face was white. "I didn't even realize she'd…"

"There's a lot of things no one knows. I don't even know. But she's mine now and I'm going to take care of her. So that means someone brings me clothes or Dad stays in the house while I get what I need. No matter what, she won't be alone again." He refused to budge on this and his bear was in full agreement. Him or Dad. Period. Ty was strong, Van was wicked fast, and Keen was deadly when the bear took over, but

Dad was fiercer than them all. The man was old, getting up there in years, but he knew more than he could teach any of them.

"I'll send one of them over." She paused. "Is she all right? Does she need anything? I— She told me once that things had to be organized a specific way. When I helped her unpack, she said where things had to go and just how and… I thought she was just a little OCD. I knew she couldn't see well, but she could *see*. I didn't think it mattered."

His animal swiftly rose to its back legs, snarling and roaring to be released. Of course it mattered. How could someone think— He took a deep breath and fought to calm his beast. Mia didn't know. She wasn't trying to be vicious. She just didn't understand.

"It was you?" Isaac remembered the scattered pans and finding a shaking Kira standing in the middle of them all.

"Well, I—"

He couldn't stand there, not when he'd already witnessed what happened when people were thoughtless and how it affected the woman he'd claimed. "Send someone over. I need to get back inside with Ebenezer."

Isaac spun on his heel, leaving Mia standing at the property line. A quick snap of his fingers had the dog racing toward him while a call from Mia had Parker trotting back into Isaac's yard.

He hated being short with Mia, hated being so gruff with the woman, but his emotions roiled. They alternated between happiness that he'd found Kira, anger that thoughtless actions harmed her, and enraged that Vanessa dared go near her.

He should calm and listen to what his brothers and father discovered after speaking with the she-bear, but that could wait. Clothes from his father and then he'd return to Kira's side. There. He had a plan.

A plan that was shot to shit shortly after he and the dog entered the house. He'd just refilled Ebenezer's water bowl when someone pounded on the front door. They didn't knock gently. No, they pounded.

If it was his brothers, he'd kill them all. Slowly.

He didn't even look through the peephole. No, he simply wrenched the door open and snarled at the men standing there. His brothers took a step back while his father merely tilted his head back and stared at the roof.

"What did I tell you boys when we walked over here?" Dad leveled a glare on Ty, Van, and Keen. "I told you to be quiet. Hell, I *told* you to stay at Isaac's while I took care of this. But what'd you do? I should let him kick your asses and send you limping home."

Damn Dad had to be really pissed. The man hardly ever did anything more than grunt. He even threw in a snarl or two to switch things up.

Ty snorted. "He could try."

Dad snorted back. "Your brother was half through his shift when he opened this door. Only thing that kept him back was me." His father looked at him. "Am I right?"

Isaac shrugged. It was true. Though he knew killing his brothers would upset his mom. Maybe even more than Dad.

"Ha, right." Ty kept on going. At least Van and Keen had the good sense to step back.

Isaac took a deep breath and slowly released it. "I'm gonna say this once and I want you to think about it. Take a minute and really think about it." He let his gaze travel from Ty to Van and back again. This was a lesson Keen already knew and it was one Isaac learned.

A year and a half of pain wasn't much compared to the years Keen struggled, but it was a fuck-ton more than his eldest brothers. "Sometimes the world doesn't revolve around you. Sometimes you don't know shit from sunshine. Sometimes you don't realize that you need to think about who the hell you're talking to and that your damned title doesn't mean shit when you're standing in front of a male who'll do anything—*anything*—to ensure his mate's happiness. That means if you pound on this door again, I'm gonna take your fucking hand."

With that, he took the clothes his father held and stepped back.

Unfortunately, his dad had to speak. "We need to talk to you."

Isaac huffed. How did he know his father would say that? Dammit. "Fine. Walk through to the kitchen. Don't move furniture, don't dick with things on a shelf, and" —he thought about what else could disrupt Kira's comfort in her own home— "don't move things around in the fridge." He turned toward the nearby stairs and threw his last words over his shoulder. "I'm gonna get dressed and I'll be back."

"What is he, a woman?" Van mumbled and the words were quickly followed by the sound of an all-too-familiar smack. "Dad, what was that for?"

163

"'Cause apparently I raised an idiot with a death wish. Get your ass to the kitchen."

The shuffling steps of their group reached him and he continued climbing the steps. Of course, that didn't mean he couldn't hear the whisper that followed him.

"What the fuck is up with those scars?"

Another slap. At least his dad was on his side.

Isaac ducked into the first room he found and tugged on the worn jeans and equally worn shirt his dad nabbed. A few holes decorated both pieces, but his father knew comfort when he saw it and brought Isaac exactly what he needed.

Outside the guest room, he tilted his head and listened for Kira, tried to discern if she was awake, and was glad to hear she was still sleeping. He wanted her with him, there was no doubt about that, but she needed a nice, healing rest.

It took him no time to get downstairs and to Kira's kitchen. Thankfully his brothers sat in the kitchen chairs and it didn't look like they'd messed with anything in the room. Though, the glare his father leveled at each of them told Isaac they'd tried.

"So." With his brothers and dad sitting around the table, Isaac pushed himself up and sat on the counter, feet dangling above the tiled floor—above tile that'd seen better days but was probably original. He'd see about fixing that for Kira after… He tore his thoughts from that direction. Telling her she belonged to him wasn't like her accepting him. And he needed to not go there right this second.

He cleared his throat. "What's going on?"

"We talked to Vanessa and she said…" Ty began and everyone stared at the man. Isaac tried to keep his face blank. It wasn't his brother's fault he was a bit of an ass.

Although it didn't look like anyone else had a problem revealing their emotions because three glares settle on Ty.

"What? I didn't do anything that time!" Ty raised his voice, now Isaac glared and Ebenezer released a low growl.

It seemed everyone had a problem with Ty, and his eldest brother sighed and slumped in his chair. "Fine," he grumbled. "You're gonna make me apologize for being an ass, aren't you?"

"Pretty much." Dad shrugged. "An ass. Oblivious. Uncaring."

"I care!" Ty shot up straight and then flinched when Ebie released another growl. "Can you shut that dog up?"

Isaac looked down at the pup, the animal had gone after Vanessa to protect Kira at the barbeque, stood by her bed when she was hurt, and played with Parker which made the boy happy. He figured Ebenezer earned his bit of retribution.

"Nope."

Ty moved to stand, but his father forestalled the movement by placing his hand on Ty's forearm. "Sit your ass down. Your mother is making me do this or I don't get laid ever again."

Moans and groans filled the room.

"Dad…"

"Gross…"

165

"Really?"

"C'mon…"

Dad grunted. "If y'all would get your shit together and quit fucking around, you wouldn't have to hear about your mother and me doing it." The old man leveled a flat expression on them all. "It's not like y'all sprouted from the ground like trees. Little annoying, dirty, smelly trees."

"I'm telling Mom you said 'fuck.'" Keen was such a tattletale. He was also grinning widely.

He hadn't really seen his brother smile before Trista.

Hell, Isaac hadn't really smiled before Kira.

It made sense that it took a mate to make a male realize nothing else mattered if you had your female. Nothing.

"And she doesn't give a damn as long as we have this come to Jesus meeting." Dad curled his lip, exposing a long fang.

Keen, being the ass he was, did it back except his was longer than their father's.

"Can we not do this in my mate's kitchen?"

That had the four of them focusing on Isaac. Dad didn't seem to care. No, he thought the old man might have even smiled. Keen looked happy, Van just shrugged like it didn't matter and Ty… looked like he swallowed a rotten fish.

"Oh, fuck you, Ty." He snarled the words.

"I didn't…" Ty shook his head and finally just leaned over and pressed his forehead to the table.

His dad released a snarl that had them all paying attention to him. "You four are acting like you aren't brothers. Van gave Ty shit for Mia. You gave Van shit because of Lauren and then all three of you gave Keen shit—"

"Not three," Isaac raised his hand. "I wasn't here to care about Trista being half-hyena. Not that I would." He shrugged. "It's not like she was, you know, *there*."

Dad shook his head while his brothers glared at him. Well, glared at him and then focused on his scars. "We'll talk about that in a minute." Dad got back to yelling at them. Only thing was he didn't yell. No, when he was real quiet, saying the words low, they knew they'd *really* pissed the man off. "And now you are all being dicks about this Kira-Vanessa bullshit when you *know* Vanessa is a two-bit bitch who can't take anyone getting the better of her."

"Well, she—"

"Get your head outta your ass," Dad snapped at Ty and Ty glared at Isaac like it was his damned fault his brother was a dick.

"The fact is, you're brothers. I don't give a flying fuck why one of you did anything. You stand behind the others. They start a fight, you finish it. They put their trust in someone, they claim a mate, and you better protect that person with your lives. You four are the heart of this clan and if you don't beat together, you're not beating at all." His dad harrumphed. "Now, your girl got any beer in there?" Dad grew serious. "We're gonna need a drink while we sort out how the she-bitch got her hands on that poison."

*

Kira stood in the hallway, leaning against the wall, using it to keep her upright. The words were harsh, but she heard the love in each syllable. There were problems between the brothers, obviously, but their father *cared*. Or rather, their mother cared and made their father deal with it, but he wasn't doing it with claws or fangs.

He shot out a few words that were followed by grumbles and then she heard Isaac pad across the kitchen, his stride unmistakable to her.

Making noise, not wanting them to continue digging into manly relationship stuff and embarrass themselves in front of a woman, she strode into the kitchen.

Anger, sorrow and regret hit her in the nose, but regret rose above everything.

And then… crisp, clean, and sweet, a man reached her. With unerring precision, she found Isaac, the man just reaching for the handle on her fridge. Then his happiness struck her and he smiled, exposing his teeth as his lips separated. She wanted to feel that smile. Without hesitation, she moved to him, depending on him to stop her if she came to an obstacle. But she didn't and managed to get to him unhindered. He didn't move, merely opened his arms and she walked into them, sighing when he held her close.

She raised a hand, stroking the side of his face, following the scar on his cheek and on to his mouth. His lips were spread wide, turned up at the corners. The left was slightly lower than the right, his wound tugging at his flesh, but… he smiled.

A gasp that turned into a manly cough came from her left, but she ignored the sound, too focused on Isaac to be distracted. "What's this smile for?"

He eased closer, his face almost coming into focus the nearer he got. Not entirely, never entirely, but she could see the warmth in his eyes. This man… With his man-noms and good heart and scars and… He was just… Hers. And she needed to accept that.

"You." She nuzzled his cheek when he got close enough, showing him she didn't care about his scars. "Just you."

Then a gag came from one of the brothers trying to be funny, but it was followed by a smack, then a disgruntled "hey" and finally a grunt.

She really liked Isaac's father.

With a shake of her head, she stepped from Isaac's arms and tugged on the refrigerator door. "I've got beer, but it's light."

She ignored the groans and smiled at Isaac's low growl. Smiling wider when Ebenezer joined in.

Isaac sidled closer, his heat consuming her. "It's perfect." He reached past her and snatched a couple of bottles as well as the one from her hand. "If I tell you you're perfect will you believe me?"

With a shake of her head—and ignoring another gag from the peanut gallery—she turned to face him, eyebrows raised. "Laying it on a little thick, aren't we?"

She liked that he was. Liked that he followed up his words upstairs with action in front of his family. He… wanted her.

"Maybe. It depends."

"On?"

"What'll get me back in your bed." He dropped his head, voice low. "Naked."

Warmth suffused her face and she didn't need to look in a mirror to know she was bright red.

"Quit." She nudged him. "I'm sure your dad wants to hear about Vanessa."

Isaac stepped away to give her room and she stood beside the fridge as she waited for everyone to take their drinks and settle down.

Except George nudged Ty before the Itan sat down. "Go sit on the counter."

"Why am I sitting on the counter?"

"Because your brother's mate isn't gonna sit on the counter. She's gonna sit in your chair. Did I raise you to be an asshole? I swear, I don't know why your mother thought I could come in here and deal with this shit. I *told* her I should just kick your ass and be done with it, but *no*," he huffed. "That woman thinks I should *talk* to you four." He took a swig of his beer. "Putting a few new holes in your head is talking as far as I'm concerned."

Kira grinned and leaned against Isaac.

"Move your ass." George nudged Ty's chair once again and the large male vacated the seat. "Kira, come sit already."

"I'm—"

George grunted and she let Isaac lead her across the space. She could have made it on her own, but with five large males occupying the small space, it was best to let him lead. Except, when they got there, Isaac sat first and tugged her onto his lap.

"Hey, how come—"

"Because you're an asshole." George didn't let Ty finish the words.

"Is this pick on Ty day?" A growl filled the Itan's words, but she didn't sense he was truly on edge. Just annoyed.

"Yes." George didn't miss a beat. "It is. Because we don't have better things to talk about than how big of a dick you are."

Isaac's arms around her felt too right to ignore and rather than pull away, she settled against him, enjoying the rightness of his embrace. She'd stand on her own two feet tomorrow. For now, she'd enjoy leaning on someone. Just for a little bit.

Rather than Ty, George began their discussion, his words unhurried and calm while tension thrummed through the rest of the men. Isaac included.

"Now, why don't you tell me what happened."

So, she did. From the moment Vanessa knocked on her front door, to the second the woman threw the heavy box of groceries at her and followed that with a rough shove.

Then came the mad race to the back yard, the rush to get away from the female whose body was rapidly transforming from lithe woman to fierce bear.

And the stench…

"Her hands were coated in Carvrix. Also known as Carve." She turned her attention to Van, the clan's Enforcer. "She has blisters, right? Maybe around her nails? Casual touch with the drug might sting a little. Like a lemon hitting a paper cut. But she had to have applied it between here and Miller's, which means she had it on her human skin for a good five to ten minutes. It doesn't need a lot of time to go to work on flesh. It works best with blood. Practically feeds on it. Skin isn't as vulnerable." She took a deep breath, prepared to tell them about the drug that'd haunted her for the last ten years of her life. "It's usually applied right before a shift or even after if there's someone around to brush it on. It doesn't attack nails the same way it does a body. Nails are dead, so it just," she shrugged. "I don't know the chemical properties. I just know how it works. I can't tell you the why."

"Okay," George drew her attention again. "Carvrix?" She nodded. "How did you know what it was? How did you know how to treat it? Do you know how she may have come across it?"

Memories rushed forward, burning her from inside out. One fucking drop of the stuff kicked her ass. Two had her screaming. Three had her almost passing out. Four... four took her too close to death. Of course, had they treated her before then, they could have played with her longer. Injure, neutralize, injure, neutralize.

She didn't say he was the smartest man alive, just the most evil, and she never told them how she managed to live through it all.

Zoey. Zoey was the how. It paid to be smart and have a friend willing to listen to Kira and ask few questions.

"We'll start at the end. You know it's an acid laced with a suppressant. It makes you tired so the acid can do its work. There are two ways to get your hands on it. Buy it or make it."

Isaac's heavy gaze landed on her, weighing her down with the question on his lips. "You can make it? I thought... It's a complex process."

"If you're looking for high grade, it is. You need a clean lab and advanced chemists. If you don't give a damn and want to hurt someone or if you're on a time crunch, you can whip up a batch in the kitchen." Their shock struck her, anger fast on its heels. Before they could push further, she explained. "It's like... human Meth. You can buy the better stuff on the streets, right? Dealers tend to have better stuff. But if you don't care about its strength and just need some, you can make your own. There's always danger, but if you're at that level of desperation," she shrugged. "It's worth the risk."

"Do you know the difference?" George sounded calm despite the anger and worry clouding him.

"Yes. I..." she fought past the growing ball of emotion in her throat. Past pain collided with today's stinging reminders. The skin along her arms was still hot and red. She'd need to treat herself again soon. She must not have washed it all away. Kira rubbed her arms, skin flaking off with each pass. "I do know. I've scented both, felt both. Both have torn flesh from my bones, nearly killing me."

She stared at the twists and turns of her old injuries, now as pale as her skin, lessened with age. That was the first test. It remained as evidence, the first batch's success all those years ago.

Kira shook her head. She'd come so damned far and still she couldn't escape the males.

Taking a deep breath, she let the air whoosh from her lungs in a slow glide. She turned to Isaac and cupped his cheeks, thumb

173

sliding over his long scar. His eyes remained on hers while she focused on the ribbon of stark white against tan.

"This one was weapon grade. That's the original design and application. It's expensive and designed to go down, not out. It digs deep and keeps digging until it's fallen through the body." She reached for his arm, the pink still contrasting with the warmth of his skin. "This is from today. It's the same. Down, not out. It's biological warfare at its finest. You don't have to encompass a body, to kill it. The drug just has to go deep enough."

"How do you know?" The words were hoarse, but the voice was unmistakable.

She turned toward Ty. "Who do you think was the guinea pig? Though, I doubt the company president knew it. Then again, he might have." She shrugged. "It doesn't matter now."

"Yeah, but…"

Kira ignored Ty and refocused on Isaac. She pulled him closer to nuzzle him. "You need to stay calm."

Already tension buzzed through him, his skin stretching and pressing where her palms rested. She pushed to her feet and tugged on her shirt, slowly lifting the billowing fabric. After all these years, several spots on her body were still sensitive. Regardless, she tugged it high while she nudged her shorts a hint lower on her hips. She knew what they saw, the gasps alone told her what she needed to know.

"This one on my hip stretches down to about mid-thigh. Home brewed. This single line," she traced the scar along her ribs. "That one's medical grade. That time it nicked my lung." She remembered the panic in Zoey's voice when it collapsed. She never told her best friend what happened. "The one on my back," she turned to show the combination of home brew and claws, but gentle hands eased her shirt from her grasp before turning her to face Isaac.

She didn't have to see his agony to feel it. The emotions burst through the air and drenched her in misery.

"Who did this, Kira?" The words weren't those of Isaac's human half but from the man's bear.

Kira flashed him a rueful smile. "Alpha Asshole. It's his company. He hired the chemists to create it and he sells it."

"And he did this to you?" Isaac's brown eyes bled black.

"No," she shook her head and let her eyes close, shutting out the world. "Those are all from his son. My…" She could push the words out. She could. And she would pretend it didn't matter. Pretend they wouldn't blame her for Isaac's injuries today and all those months ago. Because the reality was, his wounds were caused by a drug the Alpha created and sold to the clan's enemies. Somehow Vanessa got access to it. She pulled her hands from Isaac's face, removing her touch completely as she stepped back. As long as none of the men moved or tried to stop her, she could get away before anyone said a word. Before they registered her connection to Isaac's scarring and the death of their clan members. That it was all because her…

She kept her eyes closed when she finished her sentence. "They're from my brother."

Kira managed to get away, to race from the kitchen and make it to the back door and then the porch and then… then he caught

her and held her and told her it would be okay because he had
her and wasn't letting go.

chapter **ten**

Isaac held her, refusing to release her and let her run from him again. She hadn't made it far, but even if she had, he would have hunted her and brought her back.

He didn't care if that made him sound like a stalker or a psychopath.

She was his. Period. Full stop.

He heard his brothers and father talking quietly in the house and instead of returning there, he kept her close and sat on the back porch steps. He held her in his lap, snuggled against him, and ignored her tears. If he acknowledged them, his bear would tear free and hunt her family.

He was pretty sure she'd be on board with that plan, but if there were a chance she'd get pissed when he killed her brother… He'd wait. He could gut them tomorrow.

So, he held her, stroked her back and then her thigh. As much as he loved holding her, his cock didn't react to her presence. It seemed even his dick knew now was not the time.

Every once in a while she twitched, jerking in his embrace, but he didn't think she was fighting to get away. No, he knew they'd dredged up the past and when the mind remembered, sometimes the body did too.

He should know.

"I'm sorry," she whispered and it broke his heart.

"Why?" He remained just as quiet. His family could hear if they wanted, but he wanted to maintain the peace as long as he could.

Kira released a hoarse, mirthless laugh. "Why?" she shook her head. "My *family*," she spat the word as if it were poison, "developed the drug. They distribute it to whoever is willing to buy it. Your body is…" she sighed and leaned against him and he buried his face in her hair.

"My body is this way because a dozen or so hyenas decided to make me a pincushion and when they were done, instead of healing myself, I cared for the rest of my clan. My body is this way out of pure stubbornness and pride." He cupped her cheek, encouraging her to look at him, to accept the truth and conviction in his words. "And I wouldn't want to look any different. If I wasn't covered in scars and rejected by the women in my clan, I wouldn't have found you. And that is unacceptable to me."

A single tear slid from her eye, down her cheek followed by another.

"Don't cry."

"Can't help it." She sniffled.

"You're breakin' my heart."

Kira shook her head and he nodded. When she shook her head again, he stopped her the only way he knew how.

He kissed her. He closed the distance between them and brushed his lips across hers, nearly moaning as the blueberry sweetness filled him. With the next pass, he lapped at the seam of her mouth, gathering the alluring tastes. He did moan when she opened to him, allowing him entrance.

Tongues tangled as he lapped at her, drawing in more of her and simply breathing her in. The bear practically purred and rubbed against his mind, nudging its way forward. It accepted that they wouldn't claim her now, but it refused to be denied being present. So he let the bear see her, scent her, feel her beneath his palms.

The kiss continued, growing passionate and then cooling before flaring hot once again.

And it was just kissing. He stroked her hip and outer thigh, but didn't press further. He had his entire life to explore every inch of her. Now was simply a physical statement of intentions.

He continued stating, she continued listening, and his body responded to her touch, her taste, and her nearness. His cock throbbed, twitching and thickening with every whimper that escaped her. He fought to suppress his need, but it was futile.

Especially when her small hands inched to his shoulders and clutched him as she turned more fully toward him.

The shared warmth grew hotter, practically burning him with their passion, and he knew he needed to stop before it was too late. Halt before he ripped every piece of clothing from her body and made love to her on the back porch mere feet from the men of his family.

His bear snarled at the idea his brothers or father would get a look at his naked mate.

Which was why he slowly eased their kiss, lowering the heat and desire to a low simmer and finally pulling his mouth from hers.

He pressed his forehead to hers, sharing her breath and drawing her scent into his lungs. The bear savored her, overjoyed at the kiss they'd shared and knowing it was only a matter of time before they fully mated.

"You're mine, Kira Kolanowski, KK to your friends and Colon to anyone who's ready to die." He tightened his hold. "*Mine.*"

A rough throat cleared, jerking Kira in his embrace and Isaac tossed a snarl over his shoulder at whoever was dumb enough to interrupt them.

"Sorry. But I wanted to tell you that we're heading out. Our mates included." A silent, heavy pause and then Ty went on. "We're keeping Vanessa in custody until we find out how she got a hold of Carve and Keen is contacting Terrence to update him with this information." Another stretch of quiet. "Can I say something? Ask a question?"

Isaac wanted to tell his brother to go fuck himself, but Kira ended his dream of kicking his brother's ass.

"Yes." She moved and Isaac helped her stand.

He kept one arm around her waist and glared at Ty. If the man even *thought* of upsetting Kira, he'd be eating his teeth for dinner.

"Well," Ty rubbed the back of his neck. "It's more for both of you. I," he huffed. "I'm the Itan of my clan, but I'm also their older brother. So I have a responsibility to them as their leader and as family and sometimes I take that too far." Ty released a sad laugh. "I always take it too far. But I'm learning. And I want to welcome you to the family, and to the clan. I know I don't show it very well, but I'm glad you're here for him."

Ty met Isaac's gaze and he saw nothing but sincerity in the man's eyes. He was happy that Kira was in Grayslake. He was embarrassed as hell that he had to talk, but that didn't diminish his brother's feelings.

"I'm glad you're making Isaac happy. He deserves it, you know. After…" Ty shook his head. "We didn't know. We didn't even ask and Isaac kept working and… fuck me." The Itan looked torn to shreds, emotions bubbling at the surface, regret rising high. "We didn't know and being sorry about it isn't enough. I don't think anything can ever express…" Ty swallowed hard and focused on Kira, and Isaac pretended not to see the wetness in Ty's eyes. "He deserves to be happy and I can never thank you enough for coming into his life." Ty coughed. "Now, before I leave, I just need the name of your pack and, er, species group. They may not be doing anything illegal—"

Kira snorted. "They probably are."

"But I have to give Terrence all the facts and pass along how to combat it so the Healers can be notified."

Kira rubbed her forehead and he leaned toward her, pressing a soft kiss to the top of her head. He hated that she hurt, that the worry gave her headaches. He'd take care of her from now on. He wouldn't let her have a thing to be concerned about.

"Naper, Arizona and…" she buried her face against his chest with a rough shudder. "And wolves." She chuckled, but he didn't hear any joy in the sound. She turned her gaze to him, tilting her head back to meet his. "A mole among wolves. Funny, huh?"

Ty's voice drew their attention once again. "Well, now you're a mole among bears, among the Abrams, and we take care of our own. I may have forgotten that for a little while but," the power of the clan's Itan filled his brother's voice, "if they come here, if they even think of touching a hair on your head, they'll die for it."

With that, Ty left, his words hanging heavy in the air, and it was Kira's soft voice that broke the quiet. "Did he mean it?"

"Yes."

A small shudder had her trembling. "C'mon. Let's get you inside and feed you. Then I can tuck you back in bed."

Kira chuckled. "What about you? I got a little bump, you…"

Isaac stared down at her, wondering how the hell a broken finger and four-inch gash equaled a bump.

She rolled her eyes, seeming to read his question in his gaze. "Relatively speaking, it's nothing. I mean, you saw some of it. And maybe," she licked her lips and he ached to taste them again. "Maybe someday you'll see it all. But it's pretty obvious that today was nothing compared to the past."

"I hate that you endured that," he murmured. Hell, he more than hated it. The bear was perfectly prepared to take on a whole damned pack that turned a blind eye to what happened to Kira.

Every. Damn. One.

He wasn't sure how the regional or national alphas would take losing a whole pack.

Then he caught sight of a scar peering over the edge of her collar.

Fuck it. He didn't care.

*

Well, Kira hated that she'd endured all that pain and agony over the years, too. But just as Isaac said, if she'd changed anything about the past, she might not be here with him.

So she didn't care about the past. It could go fuck itself. She had now, and that's what mattered.

The wind picked up, making her hair flutter in the wind, and the porch creaked, announcing its objection to the shift in the breeze.

"It's fine." She stroked his chest, savoring the warmth that reached her. "I'm fine."

Today. Now. Maybe not then, but she had Isaac at her side. While she loved Zoey to pieces, her friendship was nothing compared to having this strong male.

Isaac leaned down and she tipped her head back, rising to her tiptoes to meet his mouth. This kiss was soft and sweet, but no

183

less arousing. Her mole wiggled and squirmed, urging her to go further, to take another step toward taking him as their own.

She wanted that, deep in her very soul she wanted Isaac to be theirs.

Maybe soon. Maybe after she knew there wasn't an ax hanging over her head.

Was it a coincidence that Vanessa's claws were tipped with Carvrix?

She didn't think so. Not even a little bit.

She wouldn't put spying outside of Alpha Asshole's list of happy-fun-times. Her only question was why Vanessa waited so long to attack. Which was something she'd bring to Isaac's attention. Just as soon as she was done with this kiss.

Kira's stomach grumbled, reminding her that she still hadn't eaten since Isaac had yet to feed her. Apparently he heard the sound as well because the sensuous kiss ended before it really began. It took everything in her to hold back the whimper that jumped to her lips when his mouth left hers.

"We can do more of this after I feed you." He whispered the word against her lips and she leaned into him, pushing higher on her toes in an attempt to recapture what he'd stolen.

Instead of humoring her, he chuckled and eased back. But not before dropping one last, hard kiss on her. She moaned then, taking in more of his scent and flavors.

He snared her hand, drawing her into the house, and she took a moment to admire the way his jeans barely clung to his hips and the wonderful way they cupped his ass. She wondered if he'd let her nibble. Just a little. Or at least rub him all over. Twice.

Because if she got her teeth rubbing on his skin… It'd be done. He'd be hers and there was no getting out of it.

When he glanced at her over his shoulder and a rush of need smacked her in the face, she didn't think he'd mind too much. Or at all.

He drew her inside, shuffling into the kitchen and then settled her in a chair. She watched him move around her kitchen, opening and closing cupboards while also peeking in the fridge.

She coughed, snagging his attention. "I'm pretty sure it was all destroyed during, you know. It's probably gone."

"Huh." Her stomach grumbled again and she scented his frustration. "I wanted to cook for you."

Kira grinned. "With my own food?"

He harrumphed. "Yeah, but it would have been a great meal."

"Uh-huh. With my food."

"You're awfully protective of your food now. Earlier you practically dragged me over here, demanding I submit to your overwhelming desires and—"

Laughing—*laughing*—she closed the distance between them and attacked, cutting off his laughs with a kiss. A carefree kiss that brewed a new heat, one of happiness and fun and everything she'd never had in her life. But right there, that second, she had it all.

185

Isaac eased her away with one last warm press of their lips and then stepped out of reach. "Nope. Food."

"Spoilsport." She pretended to be angry, tossing him a frown, but it was ruined when a giggle escaped.

A giggle!

"Yup." He didn't deny it. "Now, restaurant, drive-thru, or delivery?"

Kira froze, options rolling through her mind. She wouldn't mind going out with him, being seen on Isaac's arm and politely telling everyone he was hers. And yet…

"I'm not sure about going to a restaurant…"

They were dark, making her already iffy eyesight even worse, and she already had a hard enough time being tidy when eating. She'd learned how to handle things over the years, but she still had trouble now and again.

For Kira, soup was the devil. Its cousin was spaghetti.

"How about delivery then?" He stroked her back, soothing her even though she hadn't said a word. Then again, she noticed the small trembles attacking her and she realized words weren't necessary. "Telli's makes a great pizza or we can have Chinese delivered from the little place down the street. Carly's doesn't typically deliver, but if you're craving a burger, they'll come by too."

She quirked a brow. "Healer's privileges?"

"Uh…" His unease filled his voice and scent. "Well…"

"Or ex-girlfriend privileges?" She couldn't imagine Isaac never dating a woman. That didn't mean her mole liked the idea. Her teeth ached with the need to sink them into his shoulder and claim the man before anyone else darkened her doorstep.

She'd cut the next female who showed up and then she really would gnaw on the man.

"You see…" He drew one arm away and rubbed the back of his neck, his worry increasing.

Kira pressed her forehead to his chest, breathing in his scent and pushing past the emotions clouding the air. She dug down to the very base of his essence and let it sink into her.

"Here's the deal." She poked him. "You don't talk about exes and I won't ask. I won't talk about exes and *you* won't ask. Agreed?"

"Exes?" Isaac's rumble shook her, the sound vibrating the air.

She snorted. "Really?" She propped her chin on his chest. "Like you haven't boinked half of Grayslake?"

His turn to snort. "Hardly."

"A third then. The point is, there were lovers," —he snarled— "before we found each other. There's no growling allowed."

He paused a moment, head tilted to the side. "Is killing on the table?"

Kira sighed. "Only if they show up and give me a hard time. No hunting them down."

"You steal all the fun."

187

"It's my purpose in life." She rolled her eyes.

Of course her stomach complained of the lack of food, which put Isaac back on the food path. "Pick a place."

She sure as hell wasn't picking burgers. Fuck that noise. "If you don't mind watching me get a little pasta sauce kinda everywhere, then Telli's."

Isaac dropped a kiss to her lips and she pushed into the kiss only to have him pull away just when it was getting good.

"Telli's it is." He nudged her, encouraging her to turn around, and she went along with it. The moment her back was turned, he patted her ass. "Go have a seat. You need to heal."

"I'm fine, Isaac. You're injured too."

"I didn't break my finger a few hours ago."

"And mine isn't damaged any longer," she countered.

"Who's the Healer here?"

"But—"

"Go."

Kira froze and slowly turned on her heel, spinning until she faced Isaac once again. "You're sounding suspiciously like a parent speaking to a child. Which I know isn't the case because I'm a grown woman."

"Who is healing?"

"Who has healed from worse in her twenty-nine-ish years? Who also knows her own body," she countered.

"Yes, but I'm here now and I'm going to take care of you and your body." He sounded so patient. So caring and considerate.

If only she hadn't heard the same story from a half dozen other males through her life. "And I can take care of myself."

"Kira, you're…" He ran a hand through his hair. "I just wanna…"

She paused and pressed a hand to her stomach, fighting back nerves and urging her mole to calm. He could just be trying to help. He could simply be concerned. He might not be trying to wrap her in bubble wrap.

"One question and I need you to be honest." At his nod, she continued. "Do you want to take care of me because you want to claim me? Or because I'm nearly blind?"

She wished she could see his expression, but she'd rely on her nose and ears.

"Well, it's a bit of both. You see…"

"I think it's time you—"

Isaac rushed her, pressing a finger to her lips. "Don't get your back up and fluff your feathers. Just wait a second, okay?"

She glared. It wasn't like she could do much else.

"So, yeah, you have difficulty seeing and I wanna protect you. The bear is livid that you got hurt over something like a stepstool."

She wasn't all that happy about it either.

"The animal wants to feed you, but it also wants to keep you safe. If he had his way, you wouldn't ever leave the house and I'd feed you every bite by hand to make sure you get what you need."

Oh, *hell* no.

"Quit bristling. I said that's what he wants to do, dammit." He removed his finger and tugged her forward, into his arms. She wasn't going to speak just yet. He seemed like he might be on the road to redemption. "But *I* know that'd be a mistake. We're walking a fine line right now and I wanna try and balance my urge to protect my mate with the urge to protect someone who has difficulty seeing in a seeing world."

He cupped her cheeks and his sincerity wrapped around her like a soothing blanket, extinguishing some of her anger. "I need to care for you. No matter what, I want to do everything I can to protect you. I can try to not be an ass about it, but it'll never completely go away." He paused a moment before speaking again. "Lemme feed you, lemme fuss over you, and then lemme tuck you into bed," he murmured and her heart melted, just a little bit.

A lot. It melted a lot. He pricked her pride and annoyed her, but he did it in such a sweet way.

"Fine," she grumbled. "But when you tuck me in, will I be alone?"

chapter **eleven**

Isaac left Kira with a soft kiss and a smile. He planned on returning to her home as soon as he managed a shower and a change of clothes. Tugging on his own stuff after his injuries was fine, but he needed to be clean. If he got wet and naked at Kira's then she'd end up wet and naked and he was pretty sure they weren't ready for that step.

The bear disagreed.

He ignored the animal. They needed to be thankful she hadn't kicked them out and even more thankful that they'd be sleeping beside her.

Naked could come later. Like, tomorrow. Tomorrow was a good day for naked.

Shaking his head, he slid his key into the lock and a quick turn gave him entrance to his house. He stepped into the entryway, flicking on the light as he toed off his shoes and then froze.

He let his gaze slowly pan over the living and dining rooms. Noting one particular theme that pervaded his place.

There were no boxes. None. Not a single one in sight.

Not only were they gone, all of his belongings were back in place. The knick-knacks—ones his mother *insisted* he have—lined the shelves. Parker's drawings he'd framed graced his walls once again. His furniture was arranged exactly as it was before he began the ordeal of packing.

It was as if he'd never pressed tape to a single box.

What the fucking fuck?

He took a step into the living room and a small slip of paper on the coffee table caught his eye. He padded over and snared the note.

You're welcome.

Love,

Mia

You're welcome?

She was welcome?

What the…

He took a deep breath and pushed back his irritation. He knew his family didn't want him to leave, but she undid everything he'd accomplished. Everything.

Without hesitation, he stomped toward the kitchen and snatched the phone from its cradle. Seven button presses later and the damned thing was ringing. With each trilling sound, his anger and frustration grew. How dare she come into *his* house…

"'Lo?"

Isaac launched at Ty the moment he answered. "Your mate," he snapped.

Ty just sighed. "What'd she do and is it just an annoyance or did she break a clan law?"

"She…" Annoyed the hell out of him, but she hadn't *actually* broken a law. He'd asked her to go to his home which meant she, as well as Lauren and Trista, were left to their own devices. And none of them wanted Isaac to leave. "She unpacked my house, Ty. Everything."

He heard rather than saw his brother's shrug. "And? The family doesn't want you leaving the clan. You know that."

"I didn't expect her to tear my place apart."

"You know she didn't do that."

Isaac narrowed his eyes even though his brother couldn't see the glare. "And how do you know?"

"Hypothetically?"

He groaned. "God, you suck."

Hypothetically was a game they'd played with their parents.

Who brought a dead rabbit into this house?

Hypothetically, it may or may not have been…

"You've got Kira now, Isaac. Did you just assume she'd pick up her new life and follow you around?"

Yes, he had. "Mia still shouldn't have—"

"She wanted me to tell you that your porn collection is outdated and lame. You should get a subscription to—"

"Seriously? The woman who doesn't allow cursing is commenting on *my* porn collection? Really, Ty?"

Ty snorted. "You'd be surprised. Beneath that sweet exterior—"

"These are thoughts I don't need. Tell your mate to leave my crap alone and the decision to move, or not, is up to Kira and me." Dammit.

"She's it for you though, right?" His brother grew serious. "I mean… *it*."

Isaac thought of her smile, the radiant joy that lived inside her when he wasn't being an ass and she wasn't being attacked. Hell, even when she was healing, she still smiled wide and got her dander up at the drop of a hat.

"Yeah, yeah she is."

Silence stretched between them, but it wasn't uncomfortable.

"I'm sorry, you know. For being such a dick."

"I know." He nodded and fought the tightness in his throat. This wasn't a tossed aside apology. He sensed the truth and conviction in Ty's words.

"I gotta talk to Van and Keen. Fuck, we fucked over Keen. *I* fucked over Keen."

Isaac hadn't been around then, still with Mia's dad taking care of Cutler, but he'd only had to hear the story once. He wished he'd been there for his youngest brother. Maybe he could have talked some sense into Ty and Van. Maybe he could have…

Ty sighed. "How drunk do you gotta be to talk about the fight?"

The fight. It'd felt like World War Five Hundred at the time. Wolf after bear after wolf after bear… all struggling for breath and dying before his eyes. No one really knew how hard he'd fought for them. Every single male that walked away was because of him. Wolves, bears, he didn't give a damn when he patched them up.

"A fuck-ton drunker than I am now." Drunker than he could ever be.

"How'd I become a self-absorbed asshole?"

Isaac chuckled. "Practice."

"Dick."

"Bigger than yours. Don't be jealous."

"Don't make me kick your ass."

"You and what army?" It was familiar ground, a bickering that they'd shared for years.

"Was it bad, Isaac?" Ty was subdued, the chuckles no longer filling his voice.

He ran a hand through his hair and slumped onto his couch. "It was…"

The soft click of his front door, the squeak of the hinge, told him someone entered his space. The click-clack of nails on wood clued him into his visitor, and Kira eased into the living room behind Ebenezer.

Without a word, she padded toward him and he held out his arm, welcoming her onto his lap. With her there, cuddled against him, he could push through the story. Get it out once and for all and never talk about it again.

Kira drew her knees up and pressed her head to his shoulder, giving him the strength to talk.

"You remember the burn, huh?" he murmured, not waiting for an answer from Ty. The hyena alpha got his eldest brother first. The two leaders facing off before all hell broke loose. "The burn and the way your blood flowed like it wouldn't stop."

How many pints had he replaced in body after body by the time all was said and done? At some point, sterilization became secondary to saving lives. He could heal an infection. He couldn't bring someone back from the dead.

"Trent went down first. He fought at my side and some fucking hyena got him in the goddamned throat." He closed his eyes, recalling the flash of claws, the shine that coated them before they were embedded in Trent's neck.

Surprise flitted across his friend's face a split-second before pain suffused his features. Then... then death. The fucking hyena looked at him, eyes crazed, irises golden in the dim light, and Isaac lost it.

He went after the male, meeting strike after strike, taking a few and giving a few of his own, but his body wouldn't heal. Blood pumped and pushed at the wounds, soaking his clothing and sliding down his body.

But he kept going. The asshole killed Trent. The fuckers were going after others in their clan and the Redby pack.

The next swing caught his face, claws barely missing his eye, but the bastard might as well have taken it. Blood filled his vision.

He couldn't see, couldn't meet the threats to him, to his Itan. He stepped forward and...

"I tripped over Trent's body." He knew his friend was dead. Knew it in his heart. But still he tripped over his friend and immediately felt guilt. What if he'd hurt the bear, what if he'd...

Right. Trent was dead.

"He was gone, but I did. Tripped and fell." Isaac remembered the fall. Even through his bloody haze, he met the bear's stare. Expect it wasn't a stare, was it?

"What about after?"

After. "After was worse."

Kira nuzzled him, easing closer and pressing her face to his neck. He lowered his head, buried his nose in her hair and breathed deeply. He was surrounded by her, filled with her, and it gave him the courage to continue. Even Ebenezer joined in the soothing touches, the dog hopping onto the couch and cuddling next to him.

"We treated them on the fly, Ty. You went back to the house. It was right. You needed to get Parker back and save Mia. But you didn't see."

Bears didn't whine, they didn't cry out in pain. No, they silently eased toward death. Funny how wolves were the same.

"Do you know it was a hyena that saved us?" He released a flat laugh. "Fucking assholes hurt us, nearly killed us, but one of their own told me how to help the males dying around me."

At the time, the hyena's hands shook as he dumped the baking soda into the water, stirring the container to mix everything together. He didn't bother testing it on himself. He had patients who needed him. Patients who were closer to death than he was and they were more important.

"I managed to shift my hand to claws. Fuck, it hurt. The bear was trying to heal everything while I'm trying to heal everyone else and... it nearly brought me to my knees." He took a calming breath. His bear fought him, scratched and scraped at him for revealing their vulnerability with their mate nearby. It didn't want to risk her turning them away if she knew how weak they were. "But I did it. I wrapped a paw around that male's neck and watched him pour the mix over Lochlan. He was," he shuddered. Lochlan was so, so young. "At that point, he couldn't get any worse. I was on the edge of losing him. Losing the boy in the middle of hyena territory, surrounded by their stench and lying in the middle of the fucking street."

He took a calming breath, but it did nothing for the bear. It twitched and stretched inside him, hating him for reliving the pain of that day. Not the physical agony. It could tolerate that without a problem.

But recalling the faces...

Faces…

"It saved Lochlan. And Steven. And Jack. And…"

"When did you treat yourself?"

Him? Isaac barked out a mirthless laugh. "It was over by then, I think. You had Parker back. You'd already taken care of Mia's uncle and Keen called me in a panic because you weren't healing. I told him how to take care of you and then I collapsed." He huffed out a breath. "I finished dousing Callen and watched for healing. He was the last one. I managed to hang on and make sure he was improving and then I just fell over."

He was done. Out of it, ready to die because of the pain. Fuck, the *pain*, had him ready to slit his wrists.

"How'd you survive? Who treated you?"

"All of them. They…"

At the time, each twitch brought him more pain, each jarring movement sent agony down his spine. Why wouldn't they let him die in peace? He saved who he could and now it was his turn. *Leave me be.*

Isaac was sure he'd yelled those words, roared them at the top of his lungs, but no one listened. They'd run out of baking soda. He knew that. The males remaining upright went from home to home, announcing the impending purge of hyenas while also demanding baking soda. Strange, yet necessary.

Only one thing neutralized the acid.

It'd be funny if he weren't dying.

But he was. So it wasn't.

Kira nestled closer, Ebenezer pressing against him as well, and the two of them gave him strength.

"They found two boxes at the end of the block. Men who'd been at death's door five minutes ago hunted for me and then refused to let me die." He'd never forget the stinging stench of his own blood mixed with the aromas in the hyena household. "Even a few wolves helped. They busted down a few doors, elbowed a path into the house and dropped me in a fucking bathtub smaller than a toilet. But I was in there." The men were working so fast, hands shaking from their own healing. In a rush to slice his clothes away, they added to his wounds. He never told a soul and he wouldn't start now. "Tore my clothes off and drenched me in baking soda. They said I was a red powdered sugar cookie."

"I thought it had to be diluted…"

Isaac ran his hand along Kira's spine, recalling the way she'd mixed and poured the liquid on him. "I was barely conscious and they just coated me in the stuff and turned the shower on low. It had a detachable head, so they'd dump a bunch and then added water. They were…"

Screaming at him to live. Roaring at him and telling him they'd bring his ass back to life and gut him if he didn't wake the fuck up.

"When they realized I'd live, they hauled me home."

Another wave of quiet, the silence broken by the occasional sniffle from Kira, and he pressed a gentle kiss to the top of her head. He'd soothe her, cradle and kiss her once he ended his call.

"Where was I?" Ty's words were barely audible.

"With Mia. As you should have been. Both of you were healing and needed each other." He'd never begrudged his brother the events of those days. Ty had been half-crazed when poisoned and then even worse when healed and had to deal with an injured mate and the Southeast Itan invading the clan den. Ty couldn't have dealt with Isaac's wounds on top of it all.

"Isaac…"

"It's fine. I'm alive and so are most of the men I treated." He'd never forgive the hyenas for those lives. Never. Unfortunately, Ty already visited vengeance on the males responsible for all that pain.

"Was there ever a time I wasn't a self-absorbed asshole?"

Isaac grinned. Well, almost. The pain of the past still rode him hard, but he managed half a grin. "Yeah, I think you were five."

"Fuck you."

They were back on even ground, tugging themselves out of the tar pit of agony and back to the present. "Nah, I'll let Mia take care of that."

Ty snorted and a pregnant pause stretched between them. "I'm glad you didn't die."

Isaac sighed. "Yeah, me too. If I had… If I had, I never would have met Kira, and damn, Ty, she's worth living for."

*

Kira had come looking for him, lasting all of a minute in her empty house alone. Vanessa's attack left her on edge and

201

uneasy in her own home. She figured she'd just wait for Isaac at his place.

It wasn't because she was a big scared-y mole or anything.

And then... he broke her heart. He shattered and stomped on it and ground it into the dirt, his words spearing her with the truth that lived in every syllable.

More than anything she wanted to pick his heart up, dust it off, and put it back together. She could do it too. She *would* do it.

She listened as the call ended, Ty murmuring in Isaac's ear and Isaac's soft responses until it was only the two of them making sounds in the large house. She didn't say a word and neither did he. They simply sat, their breaths perfectly matched.

His lips remained pressed to her skin, his gentle kisses eventually making their way to her forehead. "What are you doing here?"

I wanted to be with you.

I was scared without you.

"Ebenezer Hopplestopple doesn't like my house anymore."

It was close to the truth. If she substituted Ebie with her it'd be the full truth.

She refused to tell him so.

"No?" Isaac reached out and rubbed her dog, scratching behind his ear, which had the pup's leg twitching. "That's okay. I like Ebenezer Fiffleflam in my house." He gave her forehead another soft kiss and she tilted her head back, offering him her

202

mouth. He brushed his lips over hers. "I like Kira Kolanowski, KK to her friends, in my house, too."

"You forgot—" She was gonna tell him what he forgot, but then his lips really were there. His lips and tongue and his taste invaded her mouth until her entire world revolved around Isaac, his body, his touch, his flavors...

She was a big ball of Isaac-loving mush.

Without the loving and with the extra mush.

He pulled away as quickly as he'd darted forward. "I didn't forget the rest of it because, whether it pisses you off or not, you won't have anyone being mean to you again. Next time you talk to your friend Zoey, you tell her I've got this." The kiss was gentle and sweet. "I've got you."

Yup, extra, *extra* mush.

"That's... You can't say things like that and expect me not to melt." She sighed. Stupid man with his stupid sexy words.

"If you melt, I'll just put you in a cup and pop you back in the fridge. You'll be back to—"

Kira elbowed him. "Way to stomp on the cuteness." She wriggled in his grasp, pushing so she could climb from his ungrateful lap. "C'mon, Ebenezer Clipcrabapple."

Isaac just chuckled and tightened his hold, tugging her back onto his lap. "Your dog is gonna end up with a complex. Today dog bones, tomorrow doggie therapy."

She froze and slowly panned her attention to him. "That's a thing now? Really?"

And if it was a thing, should she send Ebie? She didn't think talking things out hurt anyone, hell, she had a therapist before she left town. A werewolf therapist, which meant Kira couldn't talk about why she was actually *in* therapy, but still…

"You're adorable and I'd tell you I loved you if it didn't scare the shit out of me, but no, it's not a thing. I mean, there are behaviorists that specialize in pets with… You know, never mind."

"Oh." She froze and he did the same. When she spoke, she didn't address his animal behaviorist rant. "I'd tell you I care about you a lot, but it's been a handful of days, right? Like, two. Two is fast. Really fast. Even for shifters, it's fast, right?"

Kira reached for his face, hands stroking his skin and exploring his expression. She could see some of his movements this close, but her palms would tell her more.

He smiled. He was smiling big, bright, and wide and… "Ty mated within a day or two. Same with Van. I think Keen was within twenty-four hours." Isaac nuzzled her palm, his scruff scratching her fingers. "I'd say we're behind."

"I'd say you're crazy."

"Uh-huh."

"Why don't I feel like you're agreeing with me?"

"Dunno." He shrugged. "Still hungry?" He gripped her hips as if he were ready to lift her from his lap.

That wasn't happening. "Slow your roll and back that truck up." Isaac froze. "Just an FYI, two weeks is fast."

"Okay." He nodded, his scent told her he didn't agree.

"I mean it."

"Of course you do."

He was humoring her, the bastard.

Kira tried to sound stern. "I'm really super serious here."

"Right."

She had obviously failed.

Kira didn't whine, didn't plead, didn't even joke. She merely said his name. "Isaac?"

He relaxed back against the couch and squeezed her gently. "Yeah?"

"It really is… I mean… It's just…"

"Hush." He stroked her arm, sliding over her skin until he got to her hand. He entwined his fingers with hers and she let him, enjoying the comfort of his touch. "I need you to know that I'm here. I want you. I'm ready for you."

Kira swallowed past the growing lump in her throat. "What about leaving? Moving? You have plans and—"

"And now I have you. That's all that matters to me." He stroked her palm with his thumb. "I wanted to die that day. I wanted them to let me die in the middle of the goddamned street and I would have been thankful that the pain ended. I didn't fight for my family. I didn't fight to see my parents again. I didn't care about anything but the end to my torment. But you, Kira Kolanowski, KK to your friends… I would have come back from hell for you. And because of the pain, I'd smile."

chapter **twelve**

Waiting had never been Isaac's strong suit. Not when he was a kid, not when he'd been in school, and sure as hell not when he waited to sink his teeth into Kira.

And yet… he was waiting.

He sighed and leaned against the side of his car, waiting for the woman of the hour to come strolling out, that mangy dog in tow. As much as he bitched about Ebenezer, he'd become used to the pup. They'd come to a half-assed agreement. Ebie promised not to piss in Isaac's house or car and Isaac agreed not to take the dog on a one-way walk into the forest.

He glanced at his watch and noted the time. He also noted that Kira still hadn't emerged. With a sigh, he crossed his arms over his chest and settled in for a long wait. She still had a good ten minutes, but if his female in-laws were anything to go by, he'd be waiting a while.

Then the creak of dry hinges announced the opening of her front door and he smiled. Apparently he *wouldn't* be waiting a while. The dog emerged with a happy bark, tripping over himself as he bounded down the stairs and raced to the gate. Kira followed him, her tinkling laugh filling the air, and he couldn't help but smile.

The gate rang when she swung it wide and the moment Ebenezer was free, he raced toward Isaac, nails scraping on the sidewalk in his mad rush. He caught the dog with ease, scratching and petting as Kira approached. She walked toward him without a hint of hesitation. She was still uneasy in strange situations, but now he was faced with the cool and confident woman he'd slowly come to care for. Or not-so-slowly.

She neared him, a handful of feet separating their bodies, and he pushed Ebenezer aside. Opening his arms wide, he gathered her close the second she was within reach. The aroma of blueberries and sensual woman crept into him. He moaned and buried his face against her hair. So damned sweet and seductive.

"Hey," he mumbled into her neck.

He lapped at her skin, teeth aching with the need to shift his position a few inches and then sink into her warm flesh. His cock hardened at the thought, thickening and lengthening in an instant.

Kira wiggled, shimmying her hips, and he swallowed his groan.

She enjoyed torturing him way too much and he didn't want her to ever stop.

"Hey," she murmured, tilting her head to the side and granting him better access.

Just… damn.

"Hey," he spoke into her shoulder, letting his tongue flick out for a taste of her sweetness. It burst across his tongue, filling his mouth and he ached for more. But he wouldn't because they were *taking their time*.

Isaac was ready for the time to be over now.

He let his bear out the tiniest bit and his fangs lengthened and sharpened. With his method of torment exposed, he scraped it along her neck, tracking the delicate line of her throat and then venturing to her shoulder.

Kira whined and pressed closer, pushing to her tiptoes as if she couldn't get close enough. Well, he couldn't get enough of her, so they were on the same page.

He suckled the skin, scratching her and then laving away any hint of sting he may have left behind. She shivered in his arms and the seductive scent of her arousal came to him. Her musky hints of sweetness filled the air and he was desperate to drop to his knees and see if she tasted as good as she smelled.

He hoped so.

He also hoped he'd get a chance to discover the truth. Soon.

Someone nearby cleared their throat, but Isaac wasn't too concerned. He didn't scent any strangers—maybe a hint of Mrs. Laurie from across the street—and Ebenezer didn't seem worried. That meant he could keep kissing on Kira until she told him to stop.

"Ahem." The thump of a cane on the concrete *was* a familiar sound and that voice actually *was* Mrs. Laurie from across the street. The woman was a hundred if she was a day and she always got into everyone's business. It'd been helpful when Mia lived in the house and was attacked by her crazed cousin.

Now it was just annoying.

With a sigh, Isaac eased his lips from Kira's shoulder and pasted on a smile. When Kira would have pulled away, he kept her in place by squeezing her hips. It was bad enough he got caught making out on the street. He *knew* the old woman would be on the phone with his mother the moment they left. The last thing he needed was Mrs. Laurie *also* telling his mom that he'd been rock hard.

"Good afternoon, Mrs. Laurie." He coughed and swallowed hard, doing his best to banish the arousal from his voice.

Kira groaned and pressed her forehead to his chest. Yeah, he knew the feeling. With the woman's appearance, away went all prospects of sex. Not that they were headed in that direction. Yet.

He hoped it'd be soon though. Hell, if it meant solidifying their mating, he'd consult a Magic 8 ball and be done with it.

Mrs. Laurie tapped her cane on the sidewalk. "Is that your girl, there? Kiki or something? Turn around, girl."

Kira released a low, almost inaudible groan and slowly turned in his embrace. He let her move, but wasn't letting her go.

"It's Kira, Mrs. Laurie."

The old woman harrumphed. "No making babies on the streets, miss. Don't think I didn't see that."

Kira's whole body warmed and his bear rushed forward. Ancient woman or not, no one was going to embarrass his mate.

He tried to keep the growl from his voice when he replied. "Mrs. Laurie, I don't think—"

His mate's soft hand on his forearm had him quieting. "Of course, Mrs. Laurie. You know, I meant to come by your home the other day." Kira sounded sugary sweet. "I wanted to ask your opinion on growing tomatoes."

His neighbor preened and off the women went, chatting about vegetables and which fertilizer worked best and what type of weather Grayslake had during the seasons and…

Isaac closed his eyes and breathed deeply. He accepted his mate was a mole, which meant she was *very* into gardening. He normally listened to her chatter, especially since they were working together to rebuild her garden, but now she was delving into the topic with others. Others who were as equally passionate about carrots, and then there was mention of some weird carrot serial killer carnivorous wererabbit in Jamesburg.

He didn't even wanna think about that. He just quietly helped her rebuild her steel carrot shield thing and went on his way. He hadn't had the strength to ask questions.

He readily admitted he was afraid of the answers.

They'd moved on to the best *time of day* to plant and Isaac tried really hard not to groan. What did it matter? Seeds went in the ground. There. Done. In, whatever, a few weeks they'd have food. Or at least, the beginnings of food.

211

He wished his mate was a solid carnivore. Then he could just hunt for her like a normal couple.

Then again, he was pretty happy with their non-normal relationship.

The slow roll of an approaching SUV drew his attention, had him looking over Kira's and Mrs. Laurie's heads and watching traffic. The vehicle was all black, windows tinted so dark he couldn't see into the truck, but he didn't have a good feeling about the driver. It was too slow, almost easing to a full stop when they crept past, and he kept his bear's focus on it, trying to see the driver.

Unease assaulted him, digging its claws into his mind and taking up residence. His bear snarled and roared, desperate to rush to the SUV and take it apart piece by piece. Logically, he didn't know if a threat lingered inside the truck. That didn't keep the bear from wanting to bathe in the blood of the occupants. It was just… something inside him said the vehicle was bad news.

"Isaac?" Kira's delicate hand tugging on his shirt tore his attention from the vehicle and back to his mate.

He dropped his gaze to her shining blue eyes and wide smile. "I promised Mrs. Laurie we'd stop by the store for her on our way home."

"Of course," he murmured. He didn't want to bother with another stop, but if it made her happy, he'd shop for the old lady.

"Perfect." Mrs. Laurie clapped. "Now, dear, I made you a list. You must buy exactly two and one eighth pounds of…"

He tuned out their chatter once again until his world centered on the feel of Kira pressed against him. She was so damned soft and sweet. He wasn't sure he'd ever get enough of her touch. Then again, it didn't matter. He'd have his entire life to enjoy her. Day in and day out, she was his.

Even better was the fact that he was hers.

Ebenezer nudged Isaac's hand with his cold nose and shifted in place, his weight easing from side to side as he whined.

"What's up, boy?" He kept his voice low, not wanting to interrupt the women. He also didn't want Mrs. Laurie turning her non-stop talking on him.

Another near-silent whine and the dog glanced toward the street.

The now-familiar black SUV gently rolled by. This time the passenger window lowered, sliding into the door until the driver was revealed in all his wicked glory. He had short hair that shined in the low light, as if greasy and needing to be washed. His body was thin, almost emaciated and wiry, and his gaunt face matched.

The man needed a deer or two.

He also wasn't anyone Isaac recognized. He couldn't claim to know everyone in town, but as the town's only doctor and clan Healer, he knew pretty much everyone. Even if he met them in passing for a flu shot. He knew everybody.

So, in addition to a big dose of protein, the guy needed his ass kicked. The bear was insanely protective of Kira and the male's look was anything but welcoming.

213

No, it was evil, predatory, and filled with deadly intent.

And it wasn't focused on Isaac or Mrs. Laurie. No, it was all for his Kira.

Oh well, the bastard would have to get over it. He wasn't getting anywhere near his mate. Ever.

"Is that okay, Isaac?" Kira's words caught some of his attention, but he kept his gaze on the SUV still making its way past them.

His fingers itched, the bear more than ready to pounce on the male if he stopped and got out of the vehicle. The desire to crush the perceived threat pummeled him. He didn't have a logical reason for the need to murder the man. It was simply a pulsing drive to kill the interloper.

Already the bear imagined ways to destroy him.

"Isaac?" Concern coated Kira's question and he forced himself to pay attention.

"Sorry," he shook his head. "I missed that. What's okay?"

"Going to the plant nursery on our way home?"

Home. Our way home. The hopeful part inside him kinda hoped she saw his house as home. Or hell, hers as long as he was inside.

Then the rest weaseled into his brain.

Plant nursery.

"Of course. I think you mentioned you wanted to grab a few things for yourself, too. Right?" He prayed she wouldn't ask him to remind *her* about what she needed because there was no way in hell he'd know.

He readily admitted he was a horrible mate and sort of glazed over when she started talking about which spade was better.

They looked the same!

Though, he would never say *that* again.

Kira and Mrs. Laurie went back to chatting, gabbing about garden hoses—God save him—and he hunted for that SUV again. The one that had rolled to a stop in the middle of the street, right in front of Isaac's driveway. The glare the driver leveled was enough to send a tingle down his spine and his bear rushed forward. It was ready to defend, ready to kill, and all thoughts of symmetrical rows of dirt were forgotten.

Isaac nudged Kira aside, ignoring her small moue of distress, and strode toward the stopped vehicle. The man might be parked on a public road, but as far as Isaac was concerned, the air the stranger breathed belonged to Isaac and this asshole was polluting it. The fucker could go somewhere else.

The driver's attention yanked from Kira to Isaac and those eyes widened. The hate was overrun with snippets of fear and Isaac smiled, exposing his quickly lengthening fangs. The asshole thought he could come to Isaac's house and get away with that? Hell no.

Blue eyes met his, and the male's skin paled. The closer he got, the better he saw the interloper, the weak chin, delicate nose and thin column of his neck.

Tires squealed and the SUV suddenly lurched forward, burnt rubber filling the air, the vehicle leaving a trail of black lines on the asphalt.

"Isaac? Who was that?" Kira called to him.

"Nobody. Nobody at all. We about ready?" He forced a smile to his lips, pretending their visitor didn't concern him. Yeah, he knew she could scent his moods, but he hoped she'd think his unease was due to Mrs. Laurie's continued presence and not a stranger lurking nearby.

"Sure." She reached for him and he entwined his fingers with hers. "We just have to make four extra stops instead of two and…"

Kira kept going, explaining all the different places they had to go instead of *just* grabbing a late lunch and then coming home for a quiet night in front of the TV. He'd been hoping it'd be the TV in his bedroom—or hers.

Now, it didn't seem likely.

Then again, that might be a good thing. They could swing by Ty's, too. Maybe chat about that driver.

"I'll let you two young people get on now." Mrs. Laurie's voice wavered and she slowly turned her aging body, carefully making her way across the street to her own house.

He kept watch, making sure she was safely inside before he refocused on Kira. "Hey, you about ready? Are we buying Mrs. Laurie the world?"

Kira smiled widely, feigning happiness, but it didn't quite reach her eyes.

216

"Kira?" He cupped her cheek, enjoying the feel of her skin beneath his palm. "You okay?"

"Yeah," she nodded. "Just wondering why you felt the need to lie."

"I…"

Wasn't lying.

Of course, saying that would be yet another lie.

"A lie stings your nose, you know that. Kinda tweaks it a little. The stronger the lie, the sharper the hurt. So, what's wrong?"

"If I don't tell you, will it make you mad and make you think I'm trying to wrap you in bubble wrap and hide you from the world?" He winced even as he said the words, but it was better to know now before he said anything.

"Pretty much." She patted his chest, teasing smile in place. Another that didn't reach her eyes. "You tell me and then I'll tell you what my nose says."

She tapped said nose that was lightly tipped at the end, thin and adorable.

"I saw…"

And he finished her sentence with a description and explanation, watching her expressions for any hint of recognition. He knew her family was filled with assholes and deadly bastards.

"The car was local, the driver was not."

Kira's voice didn't waver or tremble, but she did cling to his shirt, fisting the fabric.

"Who was he?"

"I don't know, but I know where he came from…"

chapter **thirteen**

The male's scent stuck to Kira, tickling the back of her mind, but not truly settling in and giving her the man's identity. There was no doubt he came from Kira's home pack, but the rest lingered just out of reach. It was there and then it was gone before she could catch it. It didn't even feel like a lost memory. No, it was more like it was purposefully hidden. But how?

After the encounter, Isaac made a call to Ty, giving him what information they had. Which wasn't much in all honesty. She could one hundred percent tell the stranger wasn't from the Redby pack.

Her old home was filled with the scents of the desert, dry air, and searing heat and it clung to the driver like a second skin. No, it wasn't someone local.

Ty promised to look into it and now they were off for their afternoon of unplanned shopping and eventually dinner. Of course, shopping meant a lot of shuttling back and forth between the stores and home.

The word had her heart stuttering, the idea that she thought of Isaac's as home. Well, really, wherever they were together—his house, or hers—was home.

That said a lot.

Kira padded into the home improvement store, the bright orange garish against the industrial exposed walls and high ceilings. The place echoed, voices overlapping, as man after man strode past. Most were dressed in torn, well-worn jeans and paint-splattered shirts. No matter where she went, the chain store always attracted the same type of males. Hardworking, gritty, strong.

She reached for a cart, only to have her action bypassed by Isaac. "I got this, you lead and I'll follow."

Kira grinned. "You're gonna regret saying that. I've got you as my eyes now. Just *wait* until we get to plumbing."

She ignored Isaac's frown and set off into the store. The shelves went sky high, seeming to touch the massive ceiling and she was thankful for the large signs announcing the different sections. Even *she* could read them.

"We're supposed to go to Gardening," Isaac called to her and she waved a distracted hand.

"I know. Just a minute, though."

Isaac huffed and she ignored him.

Ignored him through plumbing.

And then through electrical.

Again when they got to tile… Well, at least until she hunted a man in orange.

Then he was all about being present. Stupid possessive males.

Yeah, she complained about it almost as much as she liked it. No one had ever cared about her. No one ever glared at a male for getting too close or growled when another reached for her elbow to guide her.

"Hi," she smiled at the store employee. "I'm trying to glue down some pennies and I need—"

"Pennies?" Both men spoke at once.

"Yes, pennies. You see, in my bedroom—"

"Why are we gluing pennies in our bedroom?" If she weren't annoyed with Isaac for interrupting, she'd kiss him for calling it "we" and "our" instead of "your."

She turned toward him and frowned. "I listened to this DIY show and the couple took sixty thousand pennies and glued them to the floor and then they—"

"You want to glue pennies to the floor?" She got them speaking in stereo.

"Yes. You glue them down and then you lay grout and *then* you put down clear epoxy." She smiled. She could imagine the gleaming floor, sparking with the burnished hues. She'd never seen one in person, but she could imagine the gorgeous color. She and her mother didn't just share a species, but the DIY home improvement gene, as well. At least, that's what she'd been told. Kira couldn't wait to get to the DI part of her Y.

The employee squirmed, giving her the impression he was uncomfortable and confused. Yes, he was definitely confused. How could he not know of the penny floor?

"Kira, how are you going to do that?"

She sighed. "I just explained it. The pennies? The glue? Grout and epoxy?"

"You're blind." Skepticism was clear in his voice.

"Only a little bit of a lot of a bit. My fingers work." She raised her hand and wiggled said fingers.

"Kira, you can't exactly—"

"Blind?" The employee cut in. "Guy, why you letting her out like this? This isn't place for a blind chick, man. Not with all this shit going on here. Ma'am, we have a website. Why don't you have someone help you order—"

She winced. Oh, wrong thing to say. *Here comes big bad bear.*

"Order?" Oh, Isaac's voice was way too calm.

She didn't care about other people's opinions, but if there was one thing she'd learned from spending time with Isaac, it was that he didn't allow *anyone* to talk shit about her eyesight. There was no brushing her off or giving alternatives that meant she didn't get to do things like everyone else in the world.

Kira and Isaac could bicker all they wanted, but woe to the man—or woman—who said a word.

There was no getting around the male grumbling and roaring. Now she just kept an eye on him and made sure blood wasn't spilled.

222

"Look, Depot Giant is a large place and you've got a ton of contractors coming in and out of here. Most of them are in a hurry. We don't want the blind chick getting in the way." The employee held up his hands in surrender. "Let her buy her penny shit from home."

Oh, he shouldn't have said that *getting in the way* part.

Isaac seemed to grow before her eyes, his shoulders flexing and then expanding.

She stepped forward, reaching for Isaac, and gently laid her hand on his lightly furred forearm. So not good. "Isaac? It's not a big deal. You can help me do some research online."

Instead of letting her lead him away, he gently snared her hand and turned back to her, brushing a kiss across the back before encouraging her to grasp the cart once again.

"Of course, it's a big deal. My *mate*," he glared at the employee, "wants to shop and she's gonna. In fact, he's going to be our personal shopper."

The male blustered, frustration and anger hitting her in the face, but another scent blew over her. One that was wholly bear and filled with the natural aromas of Isaac's clan.

"Isn't that right, Ash?" Isaac raised his voice.

A larger man stepped forward, sidling up to the employee, and she saw he wore one of the store's garish shirts. The newcomer was easily Isaac's size, maybe a hint larger, and was one hundred percent werebear. A wave of strength mixed with a hint of menace came to her on the cool store air.

"What's right? Is Larry helping you with everything you need?" The stranger looked to Larry. "Larry, are you helping one of my best friends and his wife with everything they need?"

"Of course, sir," Larry stammered. "Everything they need. In fact, your friend just asked me to stay with him while he's here, and of course, I'll make sure they have what they need."

Kira sighed. There went their afternoon of DIY shopping. Now she'd be stuck with a stranger picking out her supplies instead of the fun of discovery with Isaac.

But instead of complaining, she pasted a smile on her face. "That's wonderful. I'd appreciate any help you can give me."

The two werebears were satisfied and damned happy with themselves. Larry seemed like he'd piss himself any moment. And Kira merely grabbed their cart and headed toward Appliances. Maybe a new stove would soothe her annoyance. One of those induction jobbers. It'd boil water in less than a minute. Yeah, that sounded good. Nice and sleek and…

"Kira?" Damn, he found her. Though, in all honesty, she hadn't gone very far.

She'd only reached the opposite end of the aisle. Well, it was a long-assed aisle, but still, only one aisle. She turned toward Isaac, pasting a faux smile on her face. She could endure this. Make it through the shopping trip and then they'd hash this out in private.

"Yeah, I'm heading to—"

"*Kira!*" His voice echoed off the concrete walls, bouncing back from the metal paneled ceiling, and struck her in the chest.

Wait. No, that was a forklift.

Or the forks on a forklift? She wondered what those were called. Huh.

And hey, it wasn't really her chest. It was more like her shoulder.

And it didn't go *in* her shoulder or anything.

It kinda bounced off. Well, she bounced off it and stumbled right into one of the shelves, and a shit-ton of caulk rained down on her, whacking her in the head and scattering all over the polished concrete floors.

The forklift kept going, plowing into the shelving opposite her. The mile-high metal teetered with the force of the collision, creaking and groaning before slowly tilting under the power.

The heavy pounding of feet on the smooth flooring rushed to her, Isaac stopping at her side while Ash leapt over her and into the seat of the lift. Jerky Larry was on his heels and Ash roared at the employee to secure the other customers and clear the aisles.

Everyone needed to get the fuck *out* of his goddamned store, motherfucker.

Kira wondered how much Ash would owe the swear jar.

For a moment Larry didn't move, but Ash's roar shoved the guy into motion.

Larry's shock smacked her. Apparently the man's werebear boss wasn't much of a curser.

High-pitched screams—from *men*—and loud bellows surrounded her, customers and employees scattering to do as Ash ordered.

All the while, someone yanked at her shirt, tugging and pulling, shaking her with the effort. Kira slowly turned her gaze from the large machine onto a trembling Ebenezer and then to a very angry Isaac. Very angry. The emotion attacked her with vicious stabs, sinking into her blood, and she reached for him. Hand trembling, she stroked his arm, his shoulder, his face.

"Hey, what's got you worried? I'm fine."

He didn't look at her. Nope, kept grumbling and growling as he tugged. "Got hurt… Bastard… Gut him like a deer."

She rolled her eyes. Okay, admittedly, her shoulder hurt like hell and she was ninety-nine percent sure she broke something, but she was still breathing.

"I'm fine, Isaac."

He prodded a particularly tender spot and she turned her attention to her injury. Well, at least she wasn't bleeding. Her skin was a nice shade of purple, slowly easing to a hue so dark it was almost black. But, good news was the blood remained on the *inside* not the *outside*. Always a plus.

She was tempted to remind him of that fact, but he was still growling. She'd hold back that little tidbit for later.

Another round of falling caulk surrounded her, causing Isaac to snarl at the offending products, baring his fangs while more of his brown fur coated his cheeks.

He was threatening caulk. *Caulk.*

226

"Isaac, hush." She stroked his neck, squeezing him. One last tube whacked her in the head and she caught it. She glanced at the tube and then shoved it in Isaac's field of vision. "Hey, is this the glue I need?"

Isaac sighed and finally looked at her. She didn't need to see him to sense his pain. "You're not gonna let me worry, are you?"

"Not so much, no. Am I bleeding? Am I gonna die?"

He growled.

"I'll take that as a no, then. So, help me up and get me home. You can set my shoulder or collarbone or whatever. I may or may not have broken something. And then—"

"You broke *something?*"

"You yell a lot, did you know that?" She peered up at him and almost smiled when Ebenezer's bark came on the heels of her question.

"I— You— You can't—"

Kira rubbed her thumb over his pulse point, noting it slowed beneath her touch. "I can. I'm fine and I wanna go home."

"You broke something," he snarled.

"But that doesn't change the fact I wanna go home. I'm a," she lowered her voice to a whisper, "shifter, Isaac. I'll heal."

"You're stubborn."

"You wouldn't want me any other way." She grinned.

227

"Pain in my ass."

"Yup." She wasn't about to deny it.

"Fine," he huffed. "I'll take you home."

"Not yet, you won't. I need to interview you." Ty called to them and they both sighed. The Itan stomped toward them, his steps louder than any other's. The moment he was within earshot, he spoke again. "I'm not so sure this was an accident."

Well, goody.

* * *

Isaac cuddled his rage to his chest through Ty's questioning, holding it tight as he prodded Kira's bruise while his brother threw inquiry after inquiry at them.

The answers were always the same. Wandered through the store. Talked to Larry, spoke with Ash, Kira wandered away, and then the rampaging forklift.

Now that they were free, he was able to embrace some of his anger and vent his boiling fury.

Soon anyway. The moment he got to a secluded spot and out of earshot of his interfering family. Hell, maybe even when he got away from Kira. She'd endured and experienced so much anger in her life, so much violence. She didn't deserve to be pummeled by his.

And Isaac was very much on the violence train at the moment.

"You doing okay over there?" He didn't look at her as he sped past home after home. They were traveling through town, ready

228

to swing by Keen's house to drop her off before racing away once again.

"Yup." She quickly agreed.

In his periphery, he watched her poke and prod her injury.

"You should leave it alone. Let your mole do the work," he grumped.

"Eh, she's almost done. We were lucky it wasn't broken. Otherwise we would have had to re-break it." So matter-of-fact. As if healing those types of injuries were common.

He supposed, for Kira, they were.

But, wait… she'd only been hit an hour ago…

"Almost done?" He rolled the vehicle to a stop at a red light and turned toward her. "How is she almost done? It takes hours…"

Kira shrugged. "We've had a lot of practice over the years. I may not look like much, I'm pretty vulnerable and weak to most people, but when it comes to healing." Another shrug. "My mole and I got this."

They got this.

"How close to done?"

"It's still a little yellow-green, but that'll be gone in fifteen minutes or so. She gets lazy at the end. But it doesn't hurt anymore."

Knowing she was nearly healed didn't appease the bear. No, if anything, it angered the beast even more. She wouldn't have to be so adept at healing if she were kept safe. Now she was forced to use those hard won abilities to recover from a wound taken while she was in *his* presence and under *his* protection.

Dammit.

He reminded himself that she was fine now. Almost healed. *Fine.*

"Okay. I'm gonna drop you at Keen's house and then I'll be back in an hour or so." Or several hours. At the moment, his bear wanted to shift and hunt the driver of the forklift. Which... he wasn't allowed to do. Ty, as his Itan and not his brother, forbade him from hunting the driver. They didn't have much, just a lingering scent and store video, but Isaac figured it was enough for the bear to chase.

It needed *something* to do. It was hunt or fuck.

Since he wasn't about to maul his wounded mate—a mate who he hadn't actually mated—going for a run was the answer.

He'd go to clan lands, shift, get his fur on and then return for Kira.

There, he had a plan.

"Keen's? Why are you taking me to Keen's? What's wrong with my house?" Confusion filled her tone and he couldn't blame her.

That didn't mean he changed his mind. "I'm on edge, Kira. It wasn't an accident and we don't know who tried to hurt you."

"They did hurt me," she grinned. "They didn't kill me. I'm harder to murder than that."

Isaac closed his eyes and prayed for control. "You think that's funny?"

"I can laugh or I can cry. I am *not* a pretty crier."

Yeah, the bear was about to bust free at any moment. She must have sensed it because then she was there, leaning toward him as she stroked his skin. "Hey, I'm good. Remember that. It was scary as hell, and I know you don't want to hear this, but I mean it when I say I'm harder to kill than that. We both know this."

He did know. He did. That didn't make the fury lessen.

"My point is, the bear is angry and I need to go for a run. It can't do that if it's worried about you. Out of my brothers, the entire clan, Keen is the strongest. Just… stay back if he goes furry. He won't hurt you directly, but if body parts go flying…"

"You're not serious?"

Isaac shrugged. "I haven't seen it myself but—"

"Not about him tearing people apart. I mean you think I'll actually let you leave me? When you're like this, you think I'll happily go to Keen's while you ride off into the fur-lined sunset?" She shook her head. "Not happening. If you want to run, I'll go with you."

"Kira, he wants to run, but he won't leave you."

"So," she shrugged. "Take me with you."

"Take you with me." He stared at her dumbfounded.

"Yeah, I've ridden Zoey's back before. It's hard to balance on her shoulders, but you're wider." She shrugged.

231

"You rode a wolf? I know they're strong but I didn't think they carried humans."

"Oh," she shook her head. "I was shifted at the time."

Oh. Of course. Because that made so much more sense.

chapter **fourteen**

This made so much more sense when they were in the car. Conceptually... Shift, crawl onto bear's back, go for run.

Reality was: oh my fuck, that's a big bear.

Also, how the hell was she gonna climb onto his back after she shifted?

Because... big.

Big bear.

Hot guy, then big bear.

Hot guy... had she mentioned she hated being a little bit of a lot of a bit blind.

She'd stared, hell, he'd invited the staring, but she just got big swaths of tanned skin filling her vision. He'd also invited touching, but she held off. She sensed his bear truly riding the line of control and he needed to vent his rage before they got to naked touching. They hadn't yet and their first time didn't need to be when he was ready to murder someone.

So, no naked touching.

Then he'd become the Big Bear of Doom.

"Uh, Isaac?" she called out to the massive furry ball of brown.

The bear looked toward her, swinging his large head around until he stared at Kira.

"I'm not sure how this is gonna work. You see, with Zoey…" She eyed the distance between the ground and his shoulders. Hell, even if he lay down, it'd be a climb for her mole.

Isaac snorted—as much as a bear could snort—and padded toward her. He filled her vision, just as his scent washed over her. She was surrounded by him, his power and strength, and a sense of soothing peace draped her shoulders.

A large, wet nose nudged her arm, wiggling until her elbow rested on his snout. He kept going, nudging her until she got the idea. Sorta.

"You want me to pet you?" At least, that's what Ebenezer did when he wanted pets. A nose wiggle, a head butt, and then she found her hand on his back and scratching between his shoulders. "Now, you want pets?"

Isaac huffed and glared.

"Okay, got it. Not the point." She nodded and he rumbled, but didn't stop with the nudging and pushing until she stood at his side.

He lowered to his stomach, lumbering to the ground and then he stared at her, black eyes locked on her blue orbs.

"Great. What am I supposed to do now?"

He nudged her more.

"Fine, we'll play twenty questions." She dropped her head back and rolled her shoulders. "Animal, mineral, or vegetable?"

Isaac growled.

"Pain in my ass. Look," she sighed, "I can't do this as a mole, so if I'm coming with you, the only option left is me staying human and riding you like a pony. And I know some shifters are very particular about that. Especially ponies."

Isaac rolled his eyes and then glared at his back.

"Oh. Well. Why didn't you say so?" She sniffed and stared at his back. After a few minutes, he grumbled, she glared some more. "What? I gotta figure out how to do this. It's not like I—" Isaac rolled toward her and it became a game of over or under. She could crawl atop him or get squished.

She chose crawling.

It took a few grunts from both of them and then she was atop her mate.

Her mate.

Her mate.

She was slowly easing toward that truth, both her human half and mole accepting the situation. He was her mate. There was still so much pain and problems to work through, but their relationship couldn't be denied.

She just hadn't worked up the nerve to say the words aloud. Though Isaac had no problem telling one and all that she belonged to him. She once offered to tattoo his name on her forehead.

He didn't say no and she had no doubt that he knew of shifter-friendly tattoo ink.

Isaac padded toward the forest, the trees seeming to welcome them into their home. He slowly increased his speed, dodging obstacles as he raced farther. The scents of earth combined with the crisp edge of growing life sank into her bones. Kira's mole chittered and whined, aching to be set free, but it also knew they couldn't keep pace with Isaac in his shifted form.

So, they'd wait until they were home in their little patch of land. Well, two patches. Ever since Vanessa's attack, Isaac tore down the fence that separated their yards and quickly dug up any underground obstacles that would have kept Kira away.

Her mate thought of everything.

The wind whipped her hair, Isaac going faster and faster. Trees became a blur—more of a blur—the deeper they went.

She enjoyed the rocking motion of his racing strides, moving with him, swaying in time with his galloping strides. It lulled and excited her in equal measures, soothing and yet thrilling to have such a powerful male caring for her. The mole reveled in the attention and affection that came from Isaac.

Kira wasn't going to consider that it might be more than affection. Not today. Not yet.

Eventually their dashing pace slowed, Isaac lessening from a headlong rush to a gentle lope and finally a slow walk. His chest heaved, lungs and ribs expanding with each inhale. It didn't take long to realize why he'd slowed and it lay spread before her in its wondrous glory.

A lake, large and placid and bigger than she'd ever seen. The soothing presence of water crept into her, the crisp scent infusing her with a new calm and some of Isaac's tension eased as well.

He carefully lowered himself and she slid from his back, but didn't step away. She needed to remain connected to him, needed his continued touch. The frantic race to this secluded spot had her aching for the feel of his skin on hers, but she'd settle for his furred body for now.

Only now didn't last that long. No, beneath her hand, his body trembled and the first snap of bone stung her ears. It was followed by another, and then another still. Kira's transformation was different, she went from big to small, fighting to shorten muscle and bone into a tiny mole-shape. Isaac went from comparatively small to massive. He'd stretched to become the bear and now it was time for the metaphorical rubber band to snap back into place.

The shift wasn't pretty. It wasn't sexy or gorgeous or arousing. It just… was. And times like now, when she couldn't see the stretch of skin over bone or the way Isaac's face returned to its human shape, she was thankful for her semi-blindness.

The details were lost to her and she wasn't sad about that fact.

Then he was human shaped. Human shaped and *naked*.

She was back to hating her blurred vision. Dammit.

Isaac stretched his arms above him, groaning with the pull, and then let them drop to his side. "That felt good. You okay?"

If she could touch all that bare skin, she'd be wonderful. Instead of saying what she felt, she merely cleared her throat. "Yeah. Fine. It was fun."

He held out his hand, beckoning for her.

She wondered if he forgot he was naked.

"C'mere. The bear was thrilled you came along. Even if it took you *forever* to get the point." He grinned, his pure happiness coating Kira in its warmth.

"I'll give you *forever*," she grumbled. "You realize you're naked, right? I mean, the naked with the nakedness?"

More joy struck her in the chest. "I was hoping you wouldn't notice and I'd get to hold you. If it makes you uncomfortable…"

Unease filled his voice and he dropped his arm, taking a small step back.

Oh, hell no. She could deal with a lot of things, but letting her mate feel like she didn't want him was not one of them.

"If you're good, so am I." She padded forward, too intent on him to notice the uneven ground and then down she went like a tree. She had half a mind to yell "timber" but she was too busy attempting to fall gracefully.

It didn't work. She was sure she looked like a flailing, spastic idiot as she waved her arms and yelled. The ground raced up to meet her and she squeezed her eyes against her impending doom.

But Isaac snatched her mid-air, arms encircling her waist and then a quick toss had her cradled in his arms and he had an apology on his lips. "I'm sorry. I completely spaced. Are you okay? I shouldn't have stopped here, I should have—"

"For a strong, dominant bear you sure do apologize a lot."

That had him freezing in place. "What?"

"I said—"

"I heard what you said."

She felt his glare, but pushed on. "I like you, a lot, Isaac." *Holy shit, a lot.* "But you can't spend your life tripping over yourself for me. I'm gonna fall. That's life." She shrugged. "I'd prefer not to, but you can't be responsible for everything. The sun and moon do not rise and fall outta your asshole. Life goes on no matter how many times you catch me or how many times I fall." She reached up and traced his scar. He'd gotten better the more time they spent together. He no longer flinched and jerked away from her touch. "You can't live and die for everyone else, Isaac. You are not responsible for anyone else's happiness. Sometimes you gotta worry about you and not everyone else."

His face tensed, the area around his eyes tightening.

"You're glaring at me, aren't you?"

"Yes, because what started as a 'don't worry about me' turned into an after school special about my scars and how I need to heal."

239

Kira winced. "Dammit, I was being subtle."

"No, you really weren't."

She stuck out her tongue and blew a raspberry. "Pft. Bite me, furball."

"Like you're not a little furry, and just point out the place, baby. I'm all about biting you." His voice dropped, all seductive and sexy, and biting was at the forefront of her thoughts.

All over her mind. The whole thing was coated in a big blanket of biting and tasting and claiming.

Isaac breathed deeply and released a bear-ish purr. Yeah, bears didn't purr. That sound belonged cats, but she wasn't about to tell his animal that. "You like that idea?"

"I don't know what you're talking about. Because we discussed this. This is going fast."

"Three weeks is fast?" he countered, sex filling every syllable and Kira's pink bits were getting very interested. Very.

Okay, it had been three weeks. Really only one though since the first couple were spent apart. But still, if she counted them, then it didn't sound *as* bad.

And since it didn't sound *as* bad, she didn't feel any bit of bad about being aroused by him. By his scent, the feel of his skin and the sound of his voice.

Though, at the moment, skin was winning out in the "what's causing arousal" department. Like, by a lot.

She let her touch wander, stroking his cheeks, his neck, and his shoulders. Specifically where his neck and shoulder met. Her

240

bite wouldn't be as blatant as Isaac's on her flesh, but it would be unmistakable.

Her mouth watered, the mole anticipating the taste of his blood on her tongue. It'd slide over her taste buds and soothe the growing ache for him. She'd be filled with him as he slid into her pussy and his tastes consumed her.

Isaac's scents would sink into every part of her body, making his aroma a permanent part of her body.

She couldn't wait. Didn't want to wait.

Kira took a quick glance around them, noting the wide expanse of gray and assumed the ground was lined with rocks. Great. She was all for nature-laced boinking, but she was not getting a boulder up the ass.

She wanted Isaac, just not that much. Unless he was on the bottom…

"Kira, whatever you're thinking, you need to stop. Now." The words were growled by the bear and weren't the smooth baritone of Isaac's human half.

"I was just wondering where we could get horizontal."

A shudder wracked him and he breathed deeply, only to release the air in a heaving gust. "God, you want me."

It wasn't a question, but she felt compelled to answer anyway. "Yes." She nodded. "It's…" She let her head rest on his shoulder. "You're mine. I know it. You know it. I don't know why we're fighting the inevitable."

"I didn't wanna rush you." Brown fur tickled her cheek.

"Thank you for that, but we've been dancing around this. We've kissed and maybe we should have gone past first base once or twice—or ever—before hitting a home run, but it's time for you to score. Or me. Someone is scoring and I expect a lot of applause when we're done."

Oh, a lot of fur came out to play then and when she lifted her head and focused on Isaac, she gulped. Yeah, lots of hair going on there. Wow.

"Mine." He bared his teeth, opening his mouth and exposing ever-lengthening fangs. "*Mine.*"

She trembled. Not in fear—maybe a little fear—but there was a whole lotta desire pumping through her veins.

"Yours," she whispered. All his.

That had his bear pushing farther forward, stretching his skin. His shoulders seemed to expand.

"Kira," he rumbled her name. "Need, Kira."

"C'mon, Isaac." She wiggled, encouraging him to lower her to the ground. Then she carefully eased away, slowly backing and putting space between them. "C'mon."

The farther she got, the more of him was exposed. The dark fur on his chest turned the tanned flesh brown. She followed the line of hair down his body, tracing the fur's path until she got to the juncture of his thighs. Big or small, short or long?

She almost snorted. She'd never heard of a shifter being small *or* short in that department. The males were built like Greek gods with cocks to match. Why would a woman voluntarily get with a furball unless there were perks?

242

His trim hips would fit snugly between her thighs. Mmm… Thighs. His were nice and thick, coated in muscles that he'd use as he thrust into her. Her pussy ached in anticipation, warming and heating with desire.

Yes, he'd fill her, take her, and then mate her. If she were lucky, it'd be all at once.

Kira continued easing away from him, slowly making her way toward where they emerged from the forest. There had to be some sort of path there. Maybe by the time she got there, he'd shift bac—

With a squeak, she tumbled, arms flailing (damn, she did a lot of that) and she tipped backwards. Isaac rushed to her, arms outstretched as if to halt her fall, but it was a tree that saved her from another sprawling flop.

"*Kira.*" He snarled her name, but not in a sexy-times kind of way. No, it was more of a yell than anything.

Yells were not sexy at *all*.

Then he was there, his body aligned with hers from head to toe and his warmth surrounded her. It crept into her, rekindling her doused desire. The near fall sent her need flying, but now, with his slightly-furry skin against hers, she was ready to pick up where they'd left off-ish.

Kira didn't want to mate in the middle of God's nowhere, but making out just a little was okay. Maybe a kiss, or five, before they were once again locked in his classic car.

"I'm okay." She had his attention, now she just needed to keep it. "Stop worrying and kiss me for a minute."

He sneered, hands stroking her, fingers petting her body as if he were searching for any injuries. Distraction seemed like a good idea. For him, not her. She was already thinking of something other than the hard, rough bark at her back.

Particularly the thick hardness pressed against her hip. It was long and big, and she figured it'd probably fill her oh so well.

She couldn't wait to find out. But first, distraction.

"I'm fine, Isaac." She petted his chest. "Just kiss me and then you can take me home and we'll mate."

Another growl, one that ended when his lips met hers in a passionate meeting of mouths. He dominated her, shoving his tongue forward and stroking her. She licked and tasted in return, savoring each tasty morsel that he relinquished. Teeth nibbled and tugged before he delved back into their kiss once again. It quickly went for simmering passion to roaring heat and desperate need.

Need. Yes, need. She needed him to touch her, fill her, possess and claim her.

Her pussy heated further, clenching in time with his suckles and strokes. She knew her panties were growing damper by the second, her body preparing for him. Her mole chittered and chatted, excited about finally claiming the male that belonged to them.

Isaac released her mouth, but didn't cease his kisses and caresses. No, he simply changed location. He traveled over her cheek and then down to her neck, nudging her until she tilted her head to the side to grant him better access. He licked and lapped her skin, as if he couldn't get enough of her flavors.

"S'good." His hands roamed her body, lips and fangs doing delicious things to her skin while he stroked her, sending her need spiraling higher.

He flexed his hips and she rocked hers in return, reveling in the shudder that wracked his body.

Yes. She did that. Kira Kolanowski had big, bad Isaac Abrams trembling and snarling.

Go team Kira!

Those large hands reached around and cupped her ass, squeezing the globes and pulling her firmly against him. He lifted her ever so slightly, fully aligning their bodies, and she quaked with the new sensations.

"Isaac," she gasped.

He rumbled in response, rocking his hips against her once more. He pressed his face to her neck, chest expanding when he breathed and then he released the air with a deep growl. "Y'smell so damn good, Kira." He licked her skin. "Need you."

"Yes." Screw it. Bark burn was worth whatever Isaac had in mind.

It was as if her single word released the floodgates of his passion. His hands stroked and touched her everywhere. His touch brought every nerve flaring to life, her body aching for more of him with each breath.

They both panted, fighting for air as they continued their caresses.

His hands slid beneath her top, gliding over her, his rough calluses scratching and scraping her skin. The delicious sensations had her moaning for more, and he gave it.

More touching. More stroking. More kisses. More... nakedness?

Somewhere between sucking on her neck and cupping her breasts, Isaac managed to unsnap her shorts and nudge the material until they pooled around her ankles.

The man was a drug and she was addicted.

She also wanted whatever he had going on downtown. His lips left her neck, traveling lower and tracing the upper curve of her breasts before they disappeared altogether.

Kira whimpered, aching for his mouth, but he was gone. Gone down and down and... on his knees before her. Oh, that was a pretty, blurry sight.

"Isaac?" The ground was rocky. Wasn't that why they weren't getting horizontal? "The rocks..."

"Hush and lift your foot."

"Naked times are indoor times and..." She didn't really want to finish her thought since once she stepped out of her shorts, he tugged on her panties next. Then that traitorous scrap of cloth was gone, leaving her bare from the waist down.

Bare with a bear kneeling between her legs.

She would have snorted if he hadn't chosen that moment to lean forward and bury his nose between her thighs.

Then she didn't give a damn if she scared the birds with her cries. Not when his tongue snaked out and lapped at her slit. Or when he parted the folds and licked her swollen clit. Definitely not when he sucked on the bundle of nerves.

Kira reached down and sifted her fingers through his hair, fisting the strands as he continued to pleasure her. He kneaded and gripped her hips, pulling her tighter against his mouth and she didn't have the energy to fight. Not when he did that thing with his tongue. And *oh*, that thing too… And could tongues really *do* that?

Apparently, because Isaac did. He did it once, twice, and then again.

Then his fingers filled her, two pushing deep into her heat, giving her a hint of a stretch while it also consumed her with pleasure. The gentle thrust of his digits was joined by the soft suckle of her clit, and Kira found herself merely riding the surge of bliss. She let him do as he desired, gifting her with wave after wave of joy.

He stroked her sheath, flicked and teased her clit, all the while growling and rumbling. The vibrations added to the pleasure until she felt as if she'd burst from the sensations.

She trembled and shook, overwhelmed by his attentions, but she refused to let him stop. Hell no, he better not stop. She'd go feral mole on him if he even hinted at slowing.

Kira tested his hold, experimentally rocking her hips and that earned her a snarl in response. Not one of those "don't fucking move" sounds. It was more along the lines of "do it again."

So she did.

And again.

And again.

Because damn, it felt so fucking good.

She held him steady and took what she needed. She opened herself to him, gently riding his hand as she sought her release. Yes, she'd come soon, body responding to his attentions with a final release.

Super, super soon.

Isaac scraped one of his sharpened fangs over her clit, the hint of pain adding to the gathering pleasure and she couldn't keep her voice contained.

"Isaac!" He did it again, drawing more from her. "Oh, God, Isaac!"

He moaned and continued his torment. Any second now, she'd burst and shatter into a million pieces.

Any… second… now…

His fingers disappeared for hardly a moment and then they were back. Or rather, three were back, stretching and filling her. They touched and stroked, reaching and pressing against her nerves. He curled his digits, pressing against that internal bundle of nerves. He rubbed in time with his tongue lapping at her clit and that was all she needed.

Her back arched without conscious thought, body tensing and trembling with the pure pleasure that assaulted her veins. Her pussy clenched and tightened around him, rhythmically milking his invasion. The feelings raced over her nerves, and still he didn't relent.

No, it went on and on, torturing her from inside out and she wasn't sure how much more she could take. But Isaac wouldn't stop, wouldn't relent in his attentions and she realized she could take a lot.

Muscles no longer responded to her, instead, they simply jerked and twitched at random. Shudders consumed her just as Isaac consumed her. There was no lessening, no pause or easing.

"Isaac," she whimpered, begging for more and pleading with him to stop at the same time.

Her legs were slowly revolting, deciding they didn't want to support her pleasure-drenched ass any longer. She was about a second from collapsing all over him. While she had no doubt he could support her weight, flopping on top of him in a sated heap was not sexy. At all.

"*Isaac*," she tried again.

He licked her clit, that tongue torturing her, and eased back. That hand continued pummeling her with the bliss, but it slowly eased toward manageable.

She could breathe. "Oh, shit." She realized she still panted. "That was…"

"Delicious."

"I'll take your wor—" Kira's voice cracked when his fingers retreated and then pushed into her. "Oh, that's nice."

Isaac released a cocky chuckle and she couldn't even tell him to shut the hell up. Not when he had every right to be proud of himself.

Her world had officially been rocked. She couldn't wait to actually mate him.

Hell, she'd probably die. Cause of Death: Overwhelming Orgasms.

Here Lies Kira Kolanowski, Beloved Friend, Devoted Mate, Lover of the Big O.

That was perfect.

Slowly he slid his fingers free, and she swallowed her whine. They wouldn't get to the mating part if they didn't leave the forest.

Right. She knew that.

Isaac leaned his forehead against her hip, his hands digging into her skin and adding a small sting to the remaining tendrils of pleasure. Her pussy clenched, aching to be filled with more than his fingers, and she wondered when they'd get on to that part of the program.

With the remnants of her release waning, she realized the tree was a little scratchy on her butt. Eh, she could tolerate a little tree burn. It'd be so worth it.

He nuzzled her, rubbing his lightly furred cheek over her heated flesh and it sent another tremble through her. She twitched, involuntarily pushing into his touch. Her body wanted more and Kira admitted the rest of her wanted him, too.

His warm tongue lapped at her, tracing her hipbone before gently suckling her skin as if he couldn't get enough of her taste. Well, she'd be the same if he let *her* taste *him*.

Now, please.

"Isaac?" She sifted her fingers through his hair, enjoying the short brown strands tickling her palm.

"Hmm?"

She tugged on his locks. "Isaac?"

He nibbled her hip. "Hmm?"

There had better be more to this program.

"I want to finish. Do you want to finish? I mean, only if you want to. I…"

She was such a walking, talking, half-blind baby. A big one. Huge even.

Isaac lifted his head, midnight gaze clashing with hers. "Oh, I do." He shook his head. "Just not here. God, I want to claim you, but not against a tree or on rock-strewn ground. You deserve a bed."

A bed would be wonderful. Soft and bouncy and… *Mmm… bouncing.*

"So, how fast can we get home?" She grinned.

"How fast can you get dressed?"

It turned out, very fast.

251

chapter **fifteen**

Isaac kept it together during the mad dash through the forest and back to his Chevy. He'd managed to pull the bear forward so he could shift. It'd resisted with every tug, urging and pushing Isaac-the-human to claim Kira, but he'd finally won and shoved the animal in its mental cage.

He'd even remained in control after shifting back and getting dressed though he did thump his cock a good half-dozen times so he could get it back in his jeans. It'd been a tight fit, his dick wanted to stay ready for her, but he'd managed.

Now they were roaring down the road and back to his house—or her house, he didn't care—so he could finally have her, finally chain her to him with an unbreakable bond.

The bear was on board with that plan.

Drive. Fuck. Claim. *Mine.*

Four words that rounded out what needed to happen. Yeah, he'd need at least a week to properly tie her to him. Maybe two weeks. Two weeks could be good. Or three. He wondered if the town could remain healthy for three fucking weeks.

"So…" Kira drew the word out, lips forming an O that had him thinking of her mouth on him and his dick pulsed.

She shouldn't speak. Especially if that mouth created the perfect shape and… He wasn't gonna make it home without blowing. He just needed to accept he was going to come in his jeans like a fucking teen. So. Embarrassing.

On the other hand, it'd take the edge off so he didn't embarrass himself when he got inside her.

"You know I want you."

He groaned and thumped his cock.

Apparently she ignored the sound because she kept going. "But we still have one tiny issue to discuss."

Discuss? *Now?* Discussions? *Now?*

Isaac gripped the steering wheel tightly, knuckles going white, and he was suddenly very thankful he'd swapped it out with one that had a titanium core. Nothing else would hold up under a shifter's strength. And amazingly enough, most men tended to become overwhelmed with emotion while driving. He wasn't sure if it was due to traffic or the person sitting in the passenger seat that smelled like sex, sweetness, and blueberries. The person who was all female and curves and sex… Lots of sex…

Yup, his dick twitched, his balls drew up tight, and his release lurked on the horizon.

"We never talked about the future." Kira turned toward him in her seat, the new position bringing her shirt even tighter across her breasts. He could only see her in his periphery—he *was* trying to keep his eyes on the road—but what he saw had him groaning.

He should have wrapped her in a blanket so she wouldn't tempt him to pull over and take her on the side of the road.

Unless she was into that. Then it'd be okay.

"What," he cleared his throat and fought not to stare. "What about the future?"

"Really?" She huffed. "When I met you, you were in the middle of packing. You were moving out of Grayslake. Then last week, you were suddenly *un*packed. You haven't dug out any boxes, but we haven't talked about this. You obviously had a plan and now you're not following through? Why? Because of me?" She paused a moment, her gaze unwavering. "Couples talk about these things, Isaac. It's the big hippo in the room and we're not acknowledging it. We," she hesitated, "we should figure this out before we finish our mating. Don't you think? Do you want me to follow you? What about your family? Where were you moving? Why? There's no ignoring it any longer."

His first instinct was to roar. The bear saw her wavering as a denial, and it refused to be brushed aside for something as small as where their den would be located. Nothing mattered but her. His whole life revolved around making her happy.

Why hadn't they addressed it? Because it was a non-issue. Kira was happy in Grayslake so that's where they'd stay. There, problem solved.

Instead of launching into that and starting a big conversation that would last longer than he'd like, he attacked one part of her statement.

"Hippo? Not elephant?" There, that didn't sound too strained.

"Well, yeah." She snorted. "Hippos kill more people than elephants, lions, and crocodiles combined. *Combined.*"

"But the idiom is about the size of the animal." He glanced at her, eyebrow raised.

"Well, yeah. Except, you're avoiding some big thing you wanna avoid. A hippo is more likely to kill me than an elephant so my motivation to avoid the hippos is a gabillion times larger. Smaller package, immeasurable likelihood of death. Big teeth. Huge. Large enough for even me to see."

Then she shrugged like it was the most normal thing in the world.

"How do you know this?" His dick slowly lessened in size as his curiosity was once again captured by his mate.

"Well, I designed this software that—"

"You design software? How did I not know that?" The weight of her glare rested heavily on his shoulders.

"Because we haven't gotten around to some of the difficult topics. Such as why you want to leave, what I do, and how hard it would be to uproot my new life in Grayslake because you're moving away due to the unshared reasons." Oh, her voice sounded way too close to the tone Trista used with Keen when he did something stupid.

And there went the remnants of his erection. "I'm sure we would have gotten around to talking about those things."

After he'd had his fill of her body and was able to take a five-minute break from consuming her.

"Isaac." She didn't say his name with a snap or snarl or even a gasp of pleasure—that would have been surprising as hell. No, it was a gasp, a high-pitched rapid inhale that had him focusing on her and then following the direction of her gaze.

A woman sat on Kira's front steps, huddled in a large jacket, curled in on herself in an attempt to be as small as possible. No, she wasn't even on the steps, she practically plastered herself against Kira's house, scrambling backwards as he pulled into the driveway.

"Kira?"

"Zoey," she breathed out, all air seeming to leave his mate.

"How can you tell—"

"I've been looking at Zoey since I was five. I know the shape of my best friend." She yanked on the door handle and tumbled from the vehicle, feet barely hitting the concrete before she was racing around the SUV.

Isaac was right behind her, racing on Kira's heels and his bear was ready to tear the woman apart if she was a threat to his mate. The female had dark hair, almost black, with pale skin. All the scents of her condition struck him as he neared. Sick. Hurting. Injured.

"Zoey?"

257

The woman raised her head, green eyes meeting his for a bare moment before focusing on Kira.

"KK…" A sob escaped Zoey's throat, the sound hoarse and broken.

Isaac took a step forward and got his better look. He spied the bruising around Zoey's throat, the darkness that mottled her face and the wounds that peeked from beneath her shirt.

His movement had the small woman looking at him again, her body forming an even smaller ball. Kira glanced at him, a broken expression coating her features and he recognized the tears glistening in her eyes. There was a yearning, a plea, and it wasn't for his body so they could finish their mating. No, it was his mate begging him to help her best friend.

That was something he could do.

Isaac lowered to a squat, nearly putting himself at eye level with their visitor. "Zoey? I'm Isaac. I'm the clan's Healer and Kira's mate." A suspicious look met his, and he continued. "It looks like you could use some help. Why don't we go into Kira's house and take a look at your wounds?"

He used the same tone he often used on frightened cubs. Ask them questions, let them decide for themselves, but encourage them toward his own goals. If they felt like the choice was theirs, they were more apt to remain calm and allow him to do his job.

"KK?" The name was barely a whisper, but Kira was quick to help.

"C'mon, Zoey-bear. Isaac is a good guy and he *is* my mate."

"You smell the same. You didn't finish," the woman murmured.

"We don't talk about my boinking and I don't talk about the dildos in your bedside table. That was the agreement. Now, have I ever steered you wrong? Let's go." Kira was all business. Making orders while he usually quietly begged a patient to let him help.

Zoey snorted. "Steered me wrong? You remember that time…" The words ended with a choked sob, the sound lingering between a laugh and growing tears. "It's gone. You left and he needed someone else and everything's gone. He destroyed my apartment…" The small female leaned away from the house's siding, bracing her hands on the weathered porch, and toward Kira. His mate was quick to gather the female close, holding her as she vented her sorrow and heartache.

Kira froze, her entire body going still, and a then a tremble consumed her. "Does he know where you are, Zoey?"

Isaac thought back to the male in the SUV, the one cruising by ever so slowly. Kira hadn't recognized the male's scent, but that didn't mean someone from her pack hadn't discovered her.

Alpha Asshole or her brother. Which?

The woman shook her head, the move frantic and uncoordinated. "No, I wouldn't… I wouldn't…"

"Kira?" He murmured his mate's name, drawing her attention. "Inside your house or mine? If it's yours, I have to get my bag."

She furrowed her brow. He had some supplies at her place in the off chance someone was careless and she was injured again, but nothing that'd help with the damage he noted. He tilted his head at Zoey and then traced the line of the scar on his face. Zoey's wound hardly peeked above the neckline, but it was easily recognizable to his unhindered gaze. Kira smelled blood and pain, Isaac *saw* the blood and pain.

And his beast was driven to fix it, to remove the battered, haunted look from this woman's features.

"Zoey?" Kira's voice was soft and sweet. "We're going inside now and Isaac is going to get some medicine."

"Kira…"

"Hush. It's what's happening. How many times did you patch me up, huh?" Kira didn't wait for an answer. "So, now I'll do the same. Besides, Ebie is excited to see you. You know he loves his Auntie Zoey."

That got a chuckle out the woman, the sound ending on a groan. "Wolves aren't aunts to dogs. It's insulting."

"Well, you can kick my ass about it later. Inside you go." Kira pushed to her feet and reached for the woman.

Isaac was there, ignoring the female's flinch when he got her upright. It took a few minutes of shuffling, moaning, and gasping, but eventually he got Kira's best friend into the living room and resting on the couch. He turned away from Zoey, anxious to get his supplies and assess the extent of her injuries. On his way past Kira, he paused and pressed a soft kiss to her forehead. He drew in a lungful of her scent, holding it close as he told the bear to keep Kira in mind as he helped her friend. The animal needed to remain calm, not just for Zoey, but for his mate as well.

Rage had no place in healing.

"I'll be right back," he murmured against her warm skin and then strode from the room. Whispers followed him, but he didn't pause to listen to the females' conversation. Kira would share what she discovered when they had a moment alone.

That didn't mean he wouldn't inform his Itan.

The coincidences were adding up, and together they didn't seem like coincidences any longer.

Kira's father and brother created and sold the poison that'd not only harmed her but was sold to the hyenas who ultimately used it on the Grayslake clan as well.

Then there was Vanessa's attack followed by a strange male shooting hate-filled glances during a slow drive past the house.

Too many problems, not enough answers.

But he'd have them. Soon.

Not bothering with a phone call, he whipped out his cell phone and shot off a quick message to his brothers.

Research Zoey. Black hair, green eyes. Wolf. Part of Kira's old pack. Sustained injuries similar to Kira. May be trouble.

Tucking the phone into his pocket, he vaulted up the stairs and quickly unlocked his door. It took no time to tear through the house and gather what he needed. Even less time to return to Kira's and quietly make his way into the living room.

The moment he entered, he slid to a staggering stop. "Sweet Jesus."

Kira's shining gaze met his, the tears making tracks down her cheeks, and the pain in her heart was unmistakable.

The pain wracking Zoey was equally obvious.

While he'd hurried, he had taken long enough for Kira to grab a pair of scissors and use them on Zoey's clothes, slicing and peeling the fabric away from her friend's body.

Zoey met his gaze, a stricken look covering her features as soon as she recognized him. With her purple-hued face paled and fear sinking into her, Isaac was quick to push all hint of disgust and anger away.

His patient didn't need to be bombarded with *his* feelings. She had enough of her own.

What he could focus on was his job. Not only was this a person who needed his help, it was Kira's best friend, the one person she'd leaned on over the years.

Isaac couldn't let her suffer any longer than necessary.

Zoey eased away from his mate, reaching for the tattered remains of her shirt and attempting to cover herself.

"Zoey, wha—"

"Kira," he murmured and she turned to him, pain etched in her features. "Why don't you get a mix of the neutralizer going?"

The agony deepened and then his mate seemed to shove it aside, a new strength filling her. "I can do that. Yeah," she nodded. "I'll do that."

Zoey reached for his mate, trembling hand stilling Kira's retreat. "Wait…"

"Isaac will take care of you," Kira nudged her friend's hand away. "Let him."

Then his mate didn't give her best friend a choice, she strode past Isaac, leaving him alone with a battered and injured she-wolf.

With slow, careful movements, he padded to the couch and lowered himself to the coffee table, easing his bag to the floor between his legs. Zoey still clung to the remnants of her shirt, but he slowly reached for her and brushed them aside. Blood was caked to her pale skin, hiding most of the wounds he knew lingered on her body.

A bowl of pink water sat on the floor, a rag suspended in the fluid and he reached for it, wringing out the washcloth before picking up where his mate left off.

And as he did so, he spoke. It soothed patients to hear what he was doing, who he was, anything to fill the silence with something other than painful gasps.

"Kira got most of this off you, let's wipe away the rest and see what we have," he murmured, gently dragging the fabric over her skin. More bruising appeared as well as a few healing wounds marring her stomach. A few were more swollen than he'd like, not truly healing, but merely covered by new skin. He'd have to cut into those. Slice them open, drain them and then treat the resulting damage.

"Not too bad," he lied. He always lied even if his patient could scent the untruth.

Zoey chuckled and then moaned. "Nice try."

"It's part of the job. Clean, patch, and lie. Can't do right by you without all the steps."

He touched another spot, hiding his emotional pain when yet another injury was exposed.

Zoey hissed and then sucked in a sharp breath. "Fuck that hurts. I don't know how she did this. God, years of this. It just..."

Isaac clung to his control, wrapping the bear tightly when it threatened to burst free. "It just what?"

"It just became normal after a while and I didn't... Selfish bitch, party of one."

He flicked a glance to her face, watching the expressions and trying to look past the woman's agony. "It's hard to know something's wrong if you don't know what's right."

"Yeah." She twitched away from him and a tear escaped her eye.

"He, he used that stuff on me and wouldn't give me... And I couldn't stop..." Zoey turned her head enough to stare into his eyes, to lay her life at his feet and beg without thought. "Am I gonna die? I don't... I don't want all this pain. I want it to not hurt. Can you make it not hurt before I... Please."

It was as if the searing asphalt was beneath his knees once again, sinking past his jeans and burning his skin as he knelt beside yet another clan member, yet another male fighting past the agony to beg for death.

Males, men he'd admired and learned from, surrounded him again, watching him fight for life after life. He wasn't losing

264

another, he wouldn't. One was too many and he was already missing two.

Sorrow, the agony of the past and the helplessness of the present, overlaid each other. They crept into his heart and grasped the fear that lingered there. They tied together in roiling knots, stretching and growing and filling him with the pain until he couldn't *breathe*.

"Please." Her voice was thin, barely above a whisper.

"You're not dying, Zoey. It would piss Kira off, and I wanna get laid someday."

Zoey chuckled and then groaned, hand moving toward the darkest part of her body. That's where he'd start. The pain had to be the worst there, so he'd discover the source and begin his healing.

The soft shuffle of feet on wood drew his gaze to Kira hovering in the doorway, pitcher in hand. One that was familiar to him and he hated that it'd serve the same purpose as when he'd been injured.

"C'mere, baby. Help me patch up Zoey-bear." He put a teasing smile on his lips, keeping the mood as light as possible while one woman's heart broke before his gaze and the other crept closer to death with every breath.

"Gonna kick her ass for saying that," Zoey mumbled.

"You and what army?" Kira shot back as she approached, brushing her tears away before finally stopping beside him.

"You gotta sleep at some point, dirt eater."

Isaac pushed their bickering from his mind, their chatter distant as he carefully worked on Zoey. Occasionally she'd gasp or a hoarse cry would burst past her lips, but a few shots of local anesthetic had her suffering through his treatments. He couldn't take care of everything in his makeshift hospital, but it'd be enough while his assistant swung by the clinic, grabbed what he needed and brought it to Kira's.

Minutes turned into an hour and then it eased toward a second before he finally took a break. Zoey passed out at some point, the stress of her injuries and pain sending her into unconsciousness. It was a blessing and a curse, but it meant his bear didn't have to roar at every sound she made. The animal was ready to destroy the male who'd hurt Zoey, which in turn upset his mate. Zoey's attacker was dead. He just didn't know it yet.

Just as he finished cleaning another of the woman's wounds, a knock at the door snagged his attention from his patient. Kira sat beside him on the coffee table, always there to hand him what he needed or take away soaked gauze.

"I think that's Flynn. Hold this."

"I can—"

"Not while whoever did this to Zoey is still out there."

"It's not like he's dumb enough to knock."

Crazy tended to go hand-in-hand with stupid, so he wouldn't put it past the fucker.

When he got to the front door, he looked through the peephole and was relieved to see his assistant, a large box cradled in his arms. Isaac tugged the door open and held it wide. "Just through there. Our patient is on the couch."

Flynn strode past him, all business when presented with a problem, but before he crossed the living room's threshold, he froze in place.

A pale-faced male slowly turned to Isaac. "Healer?"

Isaac furrowed his brow. "What's wrong? Do you have a problem treating another wolf? Or is it my mate you take issue with?" He couldn't suppress the growl. The bear was furious on both women's behalf. How dare anyone—

"No, Healer, never. I just wasn't aware he had… No one knows… I mean… I thought… Is Alpha Bennett back?"

His rising anger gave way to confusion. "What are you talking about?"

The Redby pack's ex-Alpha had almost gotten Keen's mate killed. Hell, in reality, he'd actually *tried* to murder Trista. Too bad for him that 1) killing her outside the planned challenge was illegal and 2) Trista was the Southeast Itan's niece. Terrence had not been a happy, deadly werebear.

Reid Bennett had fucked up and was then taken into custody. No one had heard from him—nor asked about him—since. All anyone did know was that the Southeast Itan hadn't killed the werewolf.

"That's… She's related to him. No lie, Healer. I don't know her, but she scents like a sister. A close cousin at least." Flynn's eyes widened. "Oh shit, you didn't know that, did you?" The young wolf dropped the box, sending it clattering to the ground and waking Zoey. "I'm so outta here if she's gonna die. I like breathing."

"Isaac?" Worry tinged his mate's voice and the expression on Zoey's face was even more shattered.

"Nothing, baby. Flynn's grip slipped. Let me go through this with him in the kitchen and we'll be right back," he assured Kira, waiting for the tension to ease before he grabbed the discarded box in one hand and snared the wolf by the back of his neck with the other.

It took them no time to get to Kira's kitchen and the moment they crossed the threshold he sat the box on the counter and rounded on his assistant. "Speak."

"I-I-I-I didn't know. I don't know. She smells like... But the Southeast Itan... And he never said... She just smells like..."

Between the blood and the emotions surrounding the females, Isaac wasn't surprised he'd missed the telltale aromas that clung to Zoey. Now that he thought about it, he did notice how similar she smelled to the banished alpha wolf.

God, just what he needed. Couldn't anyone in their family find a mate without all the drama?

"I don't care if she's the devil incarnate, she's hurt. So we're going in there to help my mate's best friend. Zoey is her pack mate and soul sister. She will not die." With that, Isaac snatched the box once again, needing to keep up the ruse, and marched from the room.

Of course, in the silence of the house, it was easy to hear Flynn's words. "Hell no she won't die. Reid would kill us."

When Isaac stepped into the living room, Kira's worried gaze was on his as she sat beside her friend; Reid was the least of his worries. No, if something happened to Zoey, it wasn't Reid who would come after him, it was Kira.

And that was scary as hell.

∗ ∗ ∗

Short of magically transferring his strength to Zoey, the woman was healed. She still remained on Kira's couch, bandaged and out cold, but Isaac didn't think she was in any danger of dying.

At least, not anymore. Goddamned Carvrix got way too close to her heart for Isaac's comfort. And then her lungs…

He hoped the woman's wolf was a strong little bitch.

Hands now free of blood and patched up from working with the poison, he rested on Kira's front porch, rocking in the swing with his mate at his side. Murmurs crept from inside, sneaking past the thin glass windows. Cars lined the street, almost a dozen and the number grew by the minute. He watched yet another slowly cruise by, the driver obviously hunting for a space.

Damn the house was gonna get crowded.

Kira sighed and rested her head on his chest, snuggling even closer. "Thank you," she whispered.

He returned with equally soft words. "For what?"

"Saving her. She…" His mate sniffled.

Pressing a kiss to her head, he wrapped his arm around her and tugged her closer. "Hush. Everything's fine. She'll recover. She
269

won't be happy for a while, healing is a bitch, but she'll be okay."

Kira nodded. "I know, but I was so scared."

So was I.

But he didn't say the words. Speaking them aloud wouldn't do anything but ratchet up her unease and that was the last thing he wanted.

Instead, he enjoyed the cool breeze, the rhythmic squeak of the swing, and the feel of his mate in his arms.

A large SUV screeched to a stop in the middle of the street, double parking and blocking most of the traffic. Isaac wondered when Ty would finally get word. Mrs. Laurie had already visited and then scampered back to her home to spread the gossip she'd gleaned from Kira. He would have told her to keep it quiet until they could speak with the clan's Itan, but with the confusion of Zoey's recovery and all the wolves… it just hadn't happened yet.

Ty strode through the gate surrounding Kira's front yard. They'd finally just propped the thing open so they wouldn't have to listen to the bell jingle every thirty seconds.

The clan's Itan bounded up the stairs, murder in his eyes, and swung his attention to Isaac.

He didn't bother getting up. Sure, his mate stiffened in his arms, but a gentle rub had her relaxing once again.

"Isaac." His brother's voice was calm. Too calm. That meant the man's bear was good and pissed.

270

"Itan." It was best to fall back on protocol when Ty got his back up. He had to remind the male that not only was he a bear, he was *the* bear and meant to protect his members.

Not rip them to shreds.

A door slamming deep within Kira's home drew Ty's attention for a moment, and the male glared at the front door as if he could see through the panel.

"Would you like to tell me why I have half the Redby pack in my territory?"

"Not really." That earned *him* a glare and he huffed. "Kira's best friend from her old pack showed up. Her father or brother—maybe both— decided Zoey was a good substitute for testing out their toxins. She managed to make it here, but it was close for a while, Ty." Too damned close.

"That doesn't answer—"

Isaac held up a hand. "I called Flynn to fetch supplies from the clinic, and as you know, he's a wolf like Zoey. So when he brought what I needed, he not only recognized her as a wolf, but also as Reid Bennett's sister. Possibly cousin, but Flynn seemed positive she's the male's sister."

"Fuck. I didn't even know he had a sister." Ty bit off the word and then clenched his jaw, muscles of his neck bulging. "You know what that bastard did."

Reid had nearly killed Trista because of something her father had done to Reid's family. It didn't matter that the Hyena Alpha who'd caused his family so much pain nearly did as much damage to Trista. Reid had wanted the blood debt paid.

One of the few things that'd saved Trista and Keen from Reid was Van.

They'd also managed to capture Reid. Alive. No one was sure what the Southeast Itan did with the alpha wolf, but they'd never spoken of him again.

Until now.

"I know what he did, but that has nothing to do with Zoey," he countered. "Just as whatever Trista's father did was not Trista's fault. We don't hold that against her."

The "anymore" was implied.

"And the pack is here because…"

Isaac shrugged, nearly dislodging Kira. He brushed a kiss across her head with a murmured "sorry" before answering Ty. "Because, even though he was more than a little psychotic, they still respect the man. He held them together for a long time. Right, wrong, or indifferent, that pack is loyal to Reid Bennett and she's his family. She needs help. The pack is ready to give it to her however they can."

"Can they help her on their land? Having this many here makes me uneasy." Ty's chest expanded, stretching the man's shirt.

"No, she's Kira's best friend and that makes her family, which makes her clan." He wasn't going to address the fact that he pulled that idea outta his ass. "Besides, their interim alpha will be here soon. Right now, they're crowding around her and giving what comfort they can. You'll probably find more wolves than humans in the living room. Once he arrives, I figure you two can negotiate the number they leave behind."

Ty took another deep breath, the low snap of string telling Isaac that his brother's clothes were quickly losing the battle with his size. "There doesn't need to be a negotiation. They leave. Done."

"You know we have that treaty with them. Boyne Falls is neutral territory since the fight with the hyenas and you even let a dozen wolves or so work in Grayslake. It'd be a show of good faith if you let a few stay." Isaac remained intent on his brother. "Plus, it makes my mate happy. And if my mate is happy…"

He let the words trail off and the tension in Ty deflated like a balloon.

"Then my mate is happy because the family should be happy."

"And one chink in the chain…" He continued Mia's favorite message.

"Ruins the links and it's harder to fix what was broken than to never have broken it in the first place," Ty grumbled. "Fine. I'll speak with the alpha and we'll figure something out."

Isaac glanced at Kira, noting her even breathing and slack mouth. "It's good to have them anyway, Ty. Who knows if her family followed or tracked her. I'm damned thankful I was able to patch her up, but on the off chance Kira's father or brother show up…"

"Yeah." Ty nodded. "Do they know what happened to her? What they're up against?"

"No. Not right now. You know what I know. I realize you found out about all of this in a roundabout way, but I *had* intended on telling you. I figured you and the alpha could disperse the information as you desired."

"Gee, thanks," he drawled.

Isaac grunted, sounding so like their father it was ridiculous.

Another vehicle roared down the street, fully blocking the road when it rolled to a stop beside Ty's SUV. A large male climbed out, power and authority trailing in his wake. He exuded dominance in the overwhelming way of alpha wolves. Bears, for all their deadly ferocity, were more circumspect. They were slower to anger, but quick to destroy.

Wolves, dominant wolves, went balls to the wall one hundred percent of the time.

Kira shivered, body trembling and then she gasped, jerking away from Isaac. "Wha—" the male's booted foot stomped on the first stair and she startled, jumping in her seat. "What's... Who?"

Isaac tugged her close. "Just Ty and the Redby alpha. I've got you. You're safe."

The male finished his heavy trudging up the steps and stopped beside Ty, curling his lip at their Itan.

Yeah, mistake.

Ty returned the expression only, instead of a couple inches of fang, Ty revealed four and released a rolling, rumbling growl for good measure.

Which, of course—*of course*—had his mate off the swing and across the porch before he could blink. She was a streak of brown hair and curves and he raced after her. His little mole was wading into fang and claw fight with itty-bitty teeth.

She didn't seem to care. Nope, she pushed her way between the two men and *she* snarled at *them*.

"What do you two think you're doing?" She nudged Ty and elbowed the alpha. "My very best friend in the whole world is dying inside—" She wasn't dying and Kira knew that, but he didn't want to ruin her tirade. "And you two are snarling at each other. You're about to fight and cause more drama. Not here. This is my porch, darn it."

She stomped her foot, and he needed to remind her not to do that in public. It made her breasts bounce and it'd drawn the attention of other males. He'd hate to have to kill every man in town.

"Kira, you're in Grayslake. As the Itan, I don't need anyone's permission to—"

"When you're holding my wolves hostage, I have every right to—"

Ty and the wolf spoke over each other and Kira stomped her adorable, tit bouncing foot again. "*I* am not yet mated to Isaac which means *I* am not part of the clan which means *I* don't have to let anyone in if I don't want to."

Ty glared at Isaac. "I could get a warrant."

"To stand on my porch?"

Isaac hoped his brother realized how stupid that sounded. By Ty's blush, he figured she'd accomplished her goal. Now she rounded on the alpha.

"And *you*. I don't know where you learned your manners, but you don't come barging into someone's home and—"

"I'm on your porch." The male pushed the words through wolfen teeth and his tone had both Isaac and Ty snarling at him. Which caused the wolf to snarl and they were back where they started.

Except then the front door opened and Flynn stuck his head out. "Alpha," he tipped his head at the wolf and then looked to Ty. "And Itan. With all due respect, can you please keep it down? Our Alpha Bitch is resting and she's been through a lot already."

With that, the door swung shut and silence reigned in his wake.

The wolf trembled but Isaac didn't delude himself that it was due to fear. Nope, the male was filled to the brim with anger. "The pack does not have an Alpha Bitch."

Ty grinned, eyes sparkling. "You do now. I got a mole. You got an Alpha Bitch. I'm not sure which of us came out ahead, but I'm thinking it's me. Have fun keeping her in line."

Kira spoke up. "No one is keeping anyone in line. Zoey is staying here, with me." His mate turned to Ty. "She doesn't cause any trouble and she's really sweet and I know she could be an asset to the clan."

Isaac tugged her close, desperate to soothe away the growing panic in his mate. At the same time, he glared at Ty and urged the man to agree already.

"Her name is Zoey?" the wolf spoke.

"Yes." Isaac didn't know much else, but he knew *that*.

"And she is Reid Bennett's long lost sister?" The alpha's lips formed a grim line.

"Yes. At least, Flynn thinks so."

"He'd know. Reid's still doing time with Terrence, but when he finds out... I'm not sure how long anyone can keep him away from her."

Isaac agreed and Ty didn't look too happy with the prospect of having the unstable, homicidal male in his territory once again.

The alpha closed his eyes and breathed deeply, once, twice, and on the third time, yellowed eyes met Isaac's. "Is there only one wolf in there that doesn't belong to the Redby pack? Is that the female? Zoey?"

Isaac nodded. "Yes, I recognized the others as belonging to you. There's just Zoey."

The alpha drew in more of the scent and then turned to Ty. "Itan, I'm asking for your hospitality from Alpha to Itan. I have need of your clan's protection and care."

Ty looked as confused as Isaac felt. The Alpha's words were ceremonial and exacting, a quote from the laws themselves.

Ty voiced the question spinning through Isaac's mind. "Why?"

The wolf's body seemed to grow in size, nearing Ty's width and breadth while gray fur peppered his skin. "Because you do not just have an injured wolf on clan lands. Nor is she simply a member of the ex-alpha's family. Your Zoey is not yours. She is *mine*."

"Oh, shit snacks." A familiar feminine voice—*Zoey*—cut through the ensuing silence, drawing their attention to the bandaged and battered woman standing in the doorway. "With a side of fries and a strawberry shake."

chapter **sixteen**

Kira peeked through Isaac's drapes, nudging them aside enough to spy on the house next door. *Her* house next door. The house she was currently not residing in so Zoey could spend wolfy time with the local pack. It hurt her a little, stinging her heart, even though it shouldn't. Back at home, her best friend often did werewolf things that didn't involve an itty-bitty weremole.

But they weren't with their old pack anymore, and Zoey didn't even *have* a pack. Now Kira was the woman's pack and why…

Why was she alone again?

Her mate encircled her waist with his arms, the warmth of his chest sinking into her and heating the skin that'd cooled without him. He surrounded her with his care, attention, and protection.

Maybe she wasn't entirely alone.

A wolf trotted between Isaac's and Kira's homes, the silver fur gleaming in the lessened light. Its nose hovered over the ground, obviously sniffing and hunting for a scent that didn't belong. Finally it huffed out a breath and moved along, searching for any other threats.

Damp lips brushed her neck, Isaac nuzzling her throat and more of his flavors sunk into her. "She's going to be fine, you know," he murmured against her skin.

"No, I know." And she did know. Mostly. "I just worry."

"You know how wolves are. You know they'll protect and care for her. Especially if..."

Especially if the alpha, Bates, was Zoey's mate. Considering that werewolves found their mates by scent alone, she didn't have much of a doubt. Especially after they'd all traipsed into the house and she'd witnessed her best friend's reaction to the male. She wasn't going to say Zoey was drooling but... Kira had handed over a tissue or two.

That was the only reason she'd left her home and let the wolves overrun the place.

Most packs weren't like Kira's. Most alphas cared for their pack and protected them. There was no violence outside of challenges. They did not allow one wolf to pick on weaker wolves. Bates assured Zoey *and* Kira that was the case in Redby.

The alpha had not been happy having to justify his treatment of his pack to a *mole*. He almost put voice to the words, but Ty and Isaac stepped forward, their massive bodies backing her up.

When all was said and done, when all assurances were given and accepted, and a handful of calls were made to check Bates' references (that annoyed the hell out of him), they left Zoey to the care of the pack. Isaac and Kira retreated to his home to spend the night, promising one and all, Kira would be back first thing in the morning to check on her best friend.

Bates looked pissed off that she didn't trust him while the others stared at Kira as something akin to a ghost. They couldn't believe she existed. She was prey who'd lived with wolves and survived. Not only survived, but she'd become *best friends* with another wolf.

Kira didn't want to know what happened to other prey shifters. At all. Flynn tried to assure her they were merely run out of Redby, but she'd also heard murmurings about the now-dead beta Morgan and what he'd done…

No matter what, she was here and Zoey was there, and they had a long night stretching before them.

"Kira?" Isaac whispered into her ear.

"What? Sorry. I was thinking about Zoey and Bates and what their mating would mean." *To me.* She didn't add that part. "Bates is only the temporary alpha. I worry…"

"Bates may seem like a mean and gruff male, but even the meanest are putty in their mate's hands. If Zoey wants to stay, I imagine he'll figure out a way to make that happen. Even if it means taking over a small patch of nowhere in Georgia."

Isaac seemed so sure and solid, and Kira let herself feel a small ray of hope.

"Now, c'mon. I wanna shower, and I think you could use a good soak in the tub." He nibbled her earlobe. "It's got jets and I'm sure it's big enough for two."

"Jets?" She tilted her head and gave him more room.

"Uh-huh. Zoey is safe, you're safe, there are—knock on wood—no dangers hanging over our head. At least not immediately. I know they're still out there, but we're surrounded by wolves. I figure we can relax enough to finish what we started." He ended the sentence with a low, husky whisper that traveled straight to her core.

"Finish…" He captured her earlobe and tugged, forcing a whimper past her lips.

"If you're willing. Only if you're willing, Kira. No matter what, you're mine. Today or two weeks from now, I'll eventually make you mine."

His. She wanted to be his more than she could say. Now it was time to make it a reality. Was she ready?

Yes. No question, no hesitation. The answer was yes.

She wanted to be Isaac's.

Even more, she wanted Isaac to be hers.

"Yes," she slowly turned in his arms, meeting his gaze as she clutched his shoulders. "Yes."

"Yeah?" A grin teased his lips.

"Yeah."

That grin spread to a blinding smile, one that was accentuated by lengthened fangs and deep, midnight eyes. The bear had come out to play, probably encouraged by Kira's acceptance of their claim.

"C'mon then." He stepped out of her embrace and extended his arm, hand open and waiting for her.

There was no hesitation when she reached for him and slid her palm over his. She twined her fingers with Isaac's and easily followed him as he led her through the house. The sounds of the home followed them, the shift and creak of the old walls and aged floors. The steps whined as Isaac and Kira climbed, but it did nothing to bank the growing arousal.

The closer they came to his room, the higher her need climbed. She'd felt his mouth on her, but now he'd be everywhere, he'd touch everywhere, he'd... see everywhere.

Would it disgust him? She'd already felt his scarring and she couldn't care less.

Would he be the same way? He hadn't said a word about her marred flesh after their almost love making in the forest, but she didn't think he'd truly had a moment to look, either.

Now he would.

Kira's heart stuttered, fluttering with the prospect of being bare and revealing all. She knew that he was her mate, that they were meant to be together forever, but... But lifelong insecurities were very hard to banish. Hell, these weren't even lifelong. They were about ten years old.

They stepped onto the landing, padding toward their destination, when Isaac stopped. She nearly tripped, tumbling into him, but he caught her with ease.

"Isaac? Wha—?"

He whirled and grasped her by her forearms. "We don't have to do this."

"Huh?" She wrinkled her brow. "I thought you wanted… Did you not want…? But…"

"I can scent your emotions just as you can discern mine. I know what I'm smelling, Kira, and it isn't an overwhelming wave of need for me." His voice was rough, the bear's growl making it rumble even more.

"You scent… You don't think I want you?" She shook her head and sighed. Still holding his hand, she strode past him and tugged *him* along.

"Kira." Another growl followed by a snarl.

"No, you don't get to drive this train anymore." She returned his gruff tone and kept walking. When his steps slowed, she yanked harder. "I am the captain of this ship to Matetastic Island. Let's go."

"I thought we were on a train." She heard Isaac's suppressed chuckle and released a small, relieved sigh. Laughing was better than backpedaling. She managed to get him through the bedroom door before he slowed once again. "Kira, I know what you said, but I also know what I scented."

Kira swallowed her groan and released him, turning as she did so. "God, you're going to make me be unsexy and blurt this all out aren't you."

"I don't—"

She held up a hand, silencing him. "You know how you didn't want me touching your face? Because of your scars? You were

284

afraid I'd turn away from you like everyone else." She asked the questions, but didn't give him a chance to interrupt. "Well, that emotion and self-consciousness isn't reserved just for you."

Okay, time for the hard parts. She could do this. It was like a Band-Aid.

Though, really, that saying didn't really work since if a Band-Aid was left on a person's skin for a while, it sorta dug its heels in. Then when it was yanked off, it wasn't a quickly banished pain. No, it lingered with icky, sticky residue and bright red, itchy skin in its wake.

She tossed the twisting thoughts aside and realized Isaac still stared at her. She wondered how long she'd debated the Band-Aid analogy.

"Right, you're not the only one who gets to have a pity party." He opened his mouth as if to interrupt, but she kept on trucking. "Women have rejected you because of your scars. They were idiots as far as I'm concerned, but it happened. Now, you seem to be okay with me being a little bit blind." She ignored his snort. "But," she squeezed her eyes shut tight. "But what about when you see *my* scars? I don't even know what they look like, but I've felt them and they're not pretty, Isaac."

Kira ignored the sting in her eyes. "I mean, I was half-naked in the forest, but I doubt you were all that focused on anything but my vagina."

"Oh, baby." The words were whispered and then she was in his arms, cradled against his chest as he carried her to his bedroom.

He didn't release her immediately, didn't lower her feet to the ground. No, he strode right to the bed and gently laid her on the soft surface.

"Isaac, you're the one who started this topic, you need to—"

"I need to show you that you have no reason to worry about how I feel for you." His fingers went to the button of her shorts and she covered his.

"Wait a minute. Naked isn't gonna—"

"Fix this? Of course it will." He stared down at her and the full weight of his emotions slammed into her. Was this what love smelled like? It was new, unfamiliar, and it sure as hell better not be new cologne. "Because, while you saw nothing but my face, I saw so much more of you. Lemme show you," his murmured plea struck her heart and she nodded.

The snap of her shorts was followed by the lowering of her zipper and then, once again, she was naked from the waist down before him. She wondered when she'd get to see, er feel, him naked.

Oh, wait, at his urgings she was now fully naked. The cool air bathed her heated skin, chilling her, but doing nothing to ease her growing need for him.

"Isaac?" Unease assaulted her. He saw it all now. Every lumpy curve and dip, every twisted inch of her skin. From the thin lines to the wide swaths, they were all bared.

He whipped his shirt over his head, the fabric covering his tanned body suddenly gone. Then his jeans were gone, leaving her with a large expanse of tanned skin filling her vision.

286

Isaac went into motion once more, easing her to the center of the bed and then knelt between her spread thighs.

"You don't think I see you, Kira? That I'd be disgusted by your body?" He shook his head. "No way. Because, even as I knelt on the rocky ground, I saw you."

He leaned over her, propping his weight on one arm as he reached for her chest. He traced the top curve of her breast with one finger. He'd kissed her there. Kissed and sucked and nibbled… He drew that digit down her body in… a… straight… line…

She'd been so caught up in the passion, in the heat, that she hadn't even realized that…

"You kissed them all," she whispered.

"I kissed every one I could find." He leaned down, tongue lapping at that spot. "I made love to every part of you I could reach. Because I want you as my mate, Kira. Not just the good parts. Everyone loves toys that are new and shiny and perfect. And then the moment they get dented, they're tossed aside." He cupped her cheek with his free hand, forcing her to focus on him entirely. "Someone tossed away something perfect and I'm picking you up. You're mine, bruises, scars, and oddly named dog. All mine."

She grinned at him, loving him a little more with every breath. "Talking about the dog when we're naked is not sexy."

"No more talking," he whispered the words a moment before he captured her lips.

It wasn't the fast and furious meeting they'd shared in the forest. No, this was a soft, sweet seduction.

And Kira was very, very ready to be seduced. A lot. Times two.

*

Isaac had never tasted something so sweet in his life. She was delicious berries and pure woman, and he couldn't wait to see if every inch of her tasted the same. He delved into her mouth, tracing her tongue and sucking lightly, swallowing her moans.

His cock pulsed and ached and his bear demanded he claim Kira already, but Isaac was going to take his time. They'd only have one shot at this and he refused to be rushed.

Fast and furious could be saved for round two.

He lapped at her skin, following the lines that marred her body. Back in the forest, when he'd first brushed his lips over her breast, he'd nearly gone into a rage. The line was wide and had obviously gone deep. It was puffed and raised against her smooth flesh. It'd been painful and he did his best to kiss away the past.

He repeated the process now as he did then. Lick, kiss, suckle, and then nuzzle. He wanted to banish them all, wanted to draw out the pain and replace it with pleasure. She would know nothing but happiness and freedom now. She would never again be afraid of what the world held. Not with him at her side.

Each touch was a promise. A promise for the future.

He loved every inch of her body. He began at her collar, tracing the thin, pale lines. Probably a razor blade. The remnants were too small to be a wolf's claw. Maybe a knife? The instrument did not matter.

The next was the largest and one that'd nearly sent him over the edge in the forest. He traced the top edge and then continued following the path between her breasts. He paused a moment to kiss one large globe and then the other, flicking her nipples before moving on. He wanted her aroused and needy by the time he finished exploring her.

Wait, her nipples were like ripe strawberries and he went back for another taste of those hardened nubs.

He was rewarded with a low gasp followed by a soft whine. "*Isaac.*"

He fought his grin and repeated the caresses, bringing one into his mouth, sucking hard and flicking the nub with his tongue. She fisted his strands as she arched her back, pushing deeper into his mouth, and he gave her exactly what she desired.

She ached for more and he was resolved to give her whatever she desired.

Kira rocked her hips, lifting them from the bed and he gripped her side, stilling her movements. At her pleading whine, he released the nipple he'd tormented. "Let me love you, Kira. You can do it your way next time. It's my turn, right now."

She narrowed those clear blue eyes. "Does your turn include mating bites and orgasms?"

Isaac grinned and then bit her breast, tightening his grip until a tremble overtook her. He loved that she got off on that tiny hint of pain and he couldn't wait to see what else she enjoyed.

"Yes."

She grinned and twirled her hand at him. "Carry on, then."

He chuckled and nipped her breast, loving when her grin morphed into a wide smile. "I'll carry something on."

Kira didn't have much else to say because then he focused on the task of making his mate writhe, scream, and moan.

All the while, his cock throbbed. Each time he pressed his lips to her skin, it pulsed. Nibbles had that part of him twitching and long licks sent a shudder down his spine.

His bear roared at him, demanding he take Kira and claim her. She was ripe and ready to belong to them.

Isaac didn't deny the animal's assertions. He just wasn't prepared to give up his feast. Despite the beast and his aching shaft, he wanted to draw out the sensations of her body beneath his.

She wasn't a hurried snack. She was a lush, delicious meal.

And he would take his time.

He continued working his way down her body, his heart aching when he got to a mass of twisted flesh below her right breast. His eyes stung as he washed the past away with his care.

"God, Kira." He rubbed his cheek against the marks, coating her in his scent so any male who got close would know if they threatened her, if they hurt her, they'd die.

Not sexy, but true.

Her hands were soft, the touch light, when she stroked his head. "It doesn't matter, Isaac. Not anymore."

He nodded, scruff chafing her soft skin. "I know."

It didn't. Nothing beyond them mattered any longer.

He moved on, memorizing every blemished spot. Each one made him love her more. Each one had him desperate to see her family dead at his feet. Based on the condition of her body, he figured God would give him a pass.

Isaac continued his journey south, exploring Kira, learning her. He didn't just map her body, he memorized what his touches brought from her lips. He tucked her responses away for future use. Someday he'd drive her to release without touching her pussy, without entering her. Words and whispered kisses would get her there.

Definitely not today.

He crossed her stomach, tracing the long line that spanned her from chest to hipbone. It was long, thick, and deep as hell. It'd hurt, it'd burned her from inside out, and it had probably come close to killing her.

His bear roared at the idea, at the mere thought of someone ending his beautiful Kira's life.

It wasn't until she tugged on his hair and forced his head away from her that he realized he was growling.

"It's over. Done. No one else will get near me ever again."

Isaac swallowed the sounds pouring from his throat and shoved the bear back into its cage. "They won't," he promised.

"Then forget them all, Isaac. They don't exist anymore. You and me? We're it. Nothing else matters." Her smile was sweet, her eyes glazed with passion and the scent of her arousal wrapped around him like a needy cloak.

His mate wanted him to discard the past?

He would do anything to have Kira in his life, including forgetting about the males who'd nearly ended hers.

Isaac nuzzled her hip and then rubbed his cheek against her inner thigh, enjoying the smooth flesh against his face. Once again, her musk surrounded him and drew him toward heaven. She was so sweet and delicious on his tongue and he wanted more.

He lapped at her slit, gathering the moisture waiting for him and swallowed, enjoying the salty sweetness. Again he licked her, gathering more, enjoying every hint of her. Her gasps and moans told him he was doing something right, her body reacting to him and telling him he was on the road to satisfaction.

The road to hell is paved with good intentions.

The road to happiness is paved with hardness.

Isaac figured the men or women who originally wrote those words had never tasted Kira. Her pussy was the road to happiness and hell.

She rocked against his lips, giving him more of her and he took it gladly, breathing her in as he tasted her. She begged and pleaded, but he didn't listen. He was too busy devouring her.

Of course, that was about the time she nearly yanked the hair out of his head.

He released his treat and raised his head. "Kira?"

"Oh my God, will you mate me already!" Her face was flushed red, sweat dappling her brows and her chest heaved as she fought for breath.

"But..." He still had to explore her legs. And feet. Her toes really were adorable and he wasn't even a feet kinda guy.

"Isaac, if you don't get your cock and teeth in me in a second, I will tie you to this bed and take what I want."

All right then.

*

Kira was gonna kill him if he didn't get the show on the road. Yes, she admitted things were very touching and wonderful and emotional as he fought to rid her of her past. Yada yada already.

She wanted to be *his*.

When he didn't respond, she opened her mouth to repeat her demand. He wanted her, she wanted him, she just needed him to do his duty.

With a growl, he crawled up her body and then shifted to his knees between her spread thighs. She couldn't depend on her sight to guide her. All she had was her nose. And even with only that part doing its job, she knew every emotion that coursed through him.

He wanted her. He was attracted to her. He... loved her.

He was also ready to burst if he didn't take her. The edge of his release lingered and she wanted him buried deep before he succumbed to pleasure.

Kira spread her thighs wider, exposing herself to his gaze. "Please."

One word had him gripping her hip with one hand while the other encircled his cock. A shift of muscle had the blunted tip pressed against her opening and she shuddered with the connection. He was hot, heavy, and thick, and about to be inside her.

Yes, yes, and yes again.

He rubbed that tip along her slit, teasing her with the heated pressure, until she thought she'd go insane. Up and down and up again, each pass nudging her clit and sending sparks of pleasure down her spine. She was ready, willing, and able as soon as he got inside her.

Her teeth ached in anticipation, waiting and ready to lengthen and pierce his shoulder. The mole was more than onboard with that plan.

Hell, it was waving pom-poms and doing its own version of a weremole dance.

Isaac froze and his heavy gaze landed on her. "Are you sure, Kira?"

Doubt still lingered inside him and that was unacceptable.

She pushed herself up, resting her weight on one arm as she reached for him. He shifted as if to move away, but she captured him. It didn't take a strong grip or a rough yank. No, it was nothing more than her palm against the rough side of his face. Her fingers teased the scarring, the rough line drawing her touch.

"I want you to be mine, Isaac Abrams. You haven't given me a chance to explore your body, but I bet it's in better shape than my own. How about we both quit worrying we're not enough for the other? Accept that I'm not lying to you and claim me already."

Isaac rushed forward, pushing her back and his cock was there again. Only this time, he wasn't teasing or caressing. No, he pushed into her, spreading her with his thickness as he slowly consumed her. He stroked her inner walls with his length, rubbing against nerves ready to sing for him.

"Yes," she hissed and arched, rocking into his gentle thrust.

Of course, it wasn't long before they were less than gentle. They turned into deep, forceful thrusts that rocked the bed and sent it thumping against the wall. A sensuous retreat and then a forceful advance, emptying and filling her in equal measure. With each one she gasped, with each one he groaned, and with each one they reached for their peak.

When they came, they'd also claim, the pleasure overriding any hints of pain.

She was ready. More than ready.

Kira worked with him, panting and heaving in an effort to race to the edge. She planted her feet on the mattress, using the leverage to meet his every thrust. Their bodies collided with an echoing slap of skin on skin, the sounds warring with their panting breaths, moans, and groans. It was sweaty and sexy and dirty all in one.

Sex wasn't pretty, but damn, it felt good.

Kira's fingers ached, her nails burning with her mole's need to assert itself.

Isaac could not bang an itty-bitty weremole. Just… ew.

So she held it back, kept it at bay, but did allow the animal to sharpen Kira's teeth. She would need them soon.

*

Oh, fuck, soon.

Isaac was gonna blow at any moment. She was hot, slick seduction and he was ready to lose himself to her. She moved with him, fought for release at his side, and he ached to fill her with his cum. Any moment now they'd bind themselves to one another and then she could never get away.

He would never be alone. He would have a family. He would have a life that didn't make him afraid to smile.

Because Kira didn't give a damn about his scars and she—*his mate*—was the only one who mattered.

He leaned over her, blanketing her body with his and groaned with the feel of her damp skin aligned with his body. Damn, her arousal, her sweat, her scent… they all called to the bear.

The ache in his bones and the stinging of his gums told him the bear was ready to answer its mate's call.

Yes. Yes. Yes.

As he lowered, she tilted her head to the side, baring her slim neck to him and his mouth watered at what was to come. Her blood would flow over his tongue, his would fill her mouth and then they'd be one.

296

His hips continued their passionate movements, bringing them closer to release, and he reveled in the sensations. His body worked on automatic, allowing Isaac to catalog every feeling that filled him.

Love overrode them all and he was man enough to admit it. At least, to himself.

Kira's sharp nails pricked him, those sharpened tips digging into his skin, and the scent of his own blood reached him. It also reached Kira. She gasped, mouth opened wide, and he spied evidence of her animal's presence. Her teeth were long and sharp, prepared to enter... him.

Now, now, now...

"Isaac," his name came from her lips like a gasping whine. Her pussy clenched down on him, tightening and milking his cock, telling him she was there. She was on the edge and it was up to him to push her over.

He would do so. Gladly.

Letting his control ease, his hips sped, increasing the force of their meetings, sending the bed rocking further. His balls were high and tight against him, prepared to release and fill Kira.

She held her breath, heat squeezing him tight in one fierce fist, and he let that last tendril of restraint snap.

With a roar, he lowered his head and struck, biting deep into her flesh. At the same moment, she echoed his action, sending a bolt of pain down his spine. It joined with the pleasure already pumping through his veins, and then his world exploded.

He came in a rapid series of trembles and twitches, his body's instincts stealing his control. He shook while his bear's roar of approval vibrated through his mind.

Her blood flowed over his tongue, sweet, just like her skin. It was dark and delicious and he knew he'd never get enough. Never, ever enough.

He growled and shifted his hips, pressing them tighter against her as his cock pulsed and filled her with his release. She was his, his mate, his love, and hopefully the mother of his cubs. If he was lucky, he'd already gotten her pregnant. If not, they had all night.

It only took Ty a couple of days. Isaac was determined to begin building his family now.

Slowly Isaac released his hold on her shoulder, easing his teeth free of her abused flesh. He licked and lapped at the large wound. It was another scar to add to her collection, but while the others were created with hate, this one came with love.

She just didn't know it yet.

Another tremble wracked him, his orgasm continuing to play havoc on his body while pleasure still filled his veins. Damn. Good thing he wasn't gonna have to walk anytime soon. He wasn't sure his legs would support him.

Kira removed her teeth and treated him to the same treatment as he'd given her. Gentle, soothing licks were peppered along his shoulder. Minutes ticked past, her tongue bath encouraging his cock to respond, before she finally relaxed against the mattress with a satisfied sigh.

She gave him a sated, sleepy smile, one that had her eyes drifting shut.

He still remained between her thighs, softening cock filling her, and sweat coating them both, but none of that seemed to matter to Kira.

No, it didn't matter because she... A soft snuffle reached him. She fell asleep.

He'd remind her tomorrow that snores were not sexy.

After he stared at her for a while.

Which, if anyone asked, wasn't creepy at all.

chapter seventeen

A happy smile on her lips, Kira padded through Isaac's home toward the back door, her path clear and the layout firm in her mind.

And nary a box in sight. Well, sight-ish.

Isaac's words trickled through her mind, his assurances that if she wanted to remain in Grayslake then that's what'd they do. The Southeast Itan and Healer would be disappointed, but frustrated leaders were nothing compared to an unhappy mate.

That resulted in another round or two of lovemaking and claiming. Okay, it was four rounds and she was really happy her mole was adept at healing. Otherwise, she'd be walking funny.

Her mate's rapid descent reached her, his feet stomping on the aged stairs, and then he hunted her, growing closer and closer. She turned to face him, smile gracing her lips.

"Where do you think you're going?" he grumbled and crowded her, easing closer until her back rested against the door and he was plastered to her front. "Woke up alone." The man practically whined.

Kira slid her hands over his chest and linked her fingers behind his neck. "Going to get clothes."

Isaac leaned down and nuzzled her neck, lapping at her mating mark. "Y'have clothes."

"Your clothes."

"Smell like me," the bear half of him rumbled.

"And I'll smell like you even with my own shorts and t-shirt. I'm not running around half-naked. Especially when I know more bears and wolves will show up today." She pulled away and met his gaze. "I wanna be at Zoey's side and I can't do that in your shirt and boxers. Even with the button in the front, your boxers are kinda drafty."

He grunted and mumbled, "Fine."

"Good." She grinned.

"Gimme a sec and I'll go with you."

Kira rolled her eyes. "It's right next door."

"In a house of males."

"I have your mating bite and I'm sure all of Grayslake can smell you on me."

"Yeah, but all those men. Who knows—"

She huffed. "You said Zoey would be safe with them last night. Both you and Ty assured me the pack wouldn't harm her and would, in fact, protect her with their lives."

Isaac snarled, his acceptance teasing her nose.

She pressed to her tiptoes and brushed a kiss across his lips. "I'll be right back. Start coffee and when I return, we can discuss your reward."

"For making coffee?"

"Uh-huh." She nodded.

And at the same moment, the coffee maker sputtered to life, the rumble of water heating immediately followed by the splatter of the caffeine-laced liquid hitting the bottom of the carafe.

"Let's talk about my reward now."

With a laugh, she nudged him away. "When I get back."

"Five minutes, tops. Or I'll come over and haul you out head down, ass up. And you're taking Ebenezer." Isaac's words were gruff and threatening, but she sensed his teasing. Sticking out her tongue, she nudged him back and slinked from the house, Isaac's voice following her. "Don't stick it out unless you're gonna use it!"

Ebenezer on her heels, the puppy bouncing along after her, Kira easily made her way to her own yard, the path marked with white flagstones. They'd have to pull them up and replace the fence between her house and Isaac's once they began living together, but it was convenient at the moment. She wasn't sure if he'd come to her house or she'd go to his. Either way, the fence had to go back up.

Moving along the marked walkway, her mole remained alert, sniffing and scenting the air with every step she took. Right at the property line, Ebenezer shot past her, racing over the rough lawn. They'd done their best to restore the yard, but it'd take time.

Her dog's snarling barks snatched her attention, Ebie's tone telling her he was upset by more than having to wait for her. No, he was enraged and aggressive like he'd been when Vanessa…

Kira swung her attention toward the pup who was currently snarling at a large male standing on the back porch. An air of menace surrounded him like a black cloak and invaded the surrounding air. The dominance and power encircled him, seeming to create a barrier between him and the rest of the world.

She wasn't close yet, a good forty feet separating them, but she could *feel* his simmering rage. It wasn't a scent or hint of an aroma. No, the feeling crept into her bones, freezing her from inside out.

In her life, she'd been afraid more times than she could count. Her pack was adept at scaring her, at driving her just shy of crazy with terror. She was familiar with the emotion.

This… went very, very far beyond that.

Staring at him, meeting his darkened gaze, she tacked on another *very*.

Ebenezer continued growling, saliva dripping from his fangs as he bared them at the male. Her dog hadn't cared for the interloping wolves, but accepted them into the house once they'd introduced themselves. If she hadn't known he was a true dog, she would have thought he had a little shifter in him.

Now, facing off against this stranger, she knew her little Ebie was all vicious animal.

"You," the male rumbled, his fury seeming to slink across the ground and reach for her with its invisible tendrils, "are either the most stupid or most ballsy bitch I've ever met."

He thumped down the back porch steps slowly, his booted feet colliding with each stair with a booming thud.

Slow. Deadly.

She wanted to back away, wanted to scurry and hide and dig into the dirt where no one could get to her. She could go deep, as could they, but she could go deeper still. And faster. Her little beastie was at home in the earth. Yes, she could sink faster than they could dig.

But she didn't relent. She held fast as the male approached, despite her terror and the adrenaline flooding her veins. Other shifters could taste her fear, she couldn't help that, but she could remain strong beneath the weight of his dominance. She hadn't backed down from Alpha Asshole or his son even when they did everything they could to be rid of her. She wasn't about to relent to this stranger.

Besides, *he* was in *her* territory. Not the other way around.

"So, which is it?" He drew closer. "Stupid or ballsy?"

Kira licked her dry lips, mouth just as parched and unwilling to release any moisture. She should run, race back to Isaac and hide behind his larger, stronger body.

But she knew the fastest way to get caught was to run. It revved a shifter's engines. Got males hot and hungry for the kill. Staying in place was safer. It might be just as painful, but the chance of survival was much, much greater.

"Depends who you ask." She tried for flippant and uncaring, but she wasn't sure she accomplished her goal. And by not sure she meant she definitely didn't.

The stranger ambled closer, his progress slow, but no less deadly. He neared her, less than ten feet separating them, and he breathed deeply before releasing it with a rapid gust. His fight, his rage fled with the exhale. Oh, the menace still clung to him, but it no longer roiled and hunted for a victim. It was as if he banked all that violence with the single action.

"You're Zoey's little pet."

"Pet?"

"Come inside. She's been waiting for you." With that order, he spun on his heel and traveled toward her house only to pause when he hit the steps. He glanced at her and frowned. "Come inside. She's waiting."

The words were filled with a stronger wolf's demand.

"Who the hell are you?" She reached for Ebenczer, the dog's snarls now nothing more than rumbles. She stroked her pup, taking comfort in the smooth fur beneath her fingers.

Hate-lined joy filled the man, bursting from him and nearly bowling her over. "I'm your father's worst nightmare." He stomped up the steps until he stood on the porch. "And Zoey's brother."

She rejoiced at his first statement and overflowed with happiness at his second. Okay, it was fear-tinged happiness, but she still smiled.

Kira leaned down to pat Ebenezer's side, soothing the dog. "C'mon, Ebie. Zoey's inside and you met the wolves, huh? Maybe someone has a cub to play with."

The male snorted. "A pup playing with a *dog*."

A growling male stepped from the house and his scent told her Bates came to her rescue. "That *dog* has helped Zoey's little *pet* more times than either female can recount. He is welcome at any wolf's table including my own."

"What the hell did you do to my pack?" The stranger spat and Kira realized the man before her was Reid Bennett, Zoey's supposed brother and male who'd been banished and taken into custody by the werebear Southeast Itan.

Yeah, staring down an Alpha as strong as Reid probably hadn't been her best idea.

The two males locked in a silent fight for dominance and it was Reid who relented first, leaving Kira and Bates as he stomped into the house.

"You okay?"

"Huh?" Kira shook her head, tearing her attention from the back door. "Oh, yeah, I'm good. He's meaner than Alpha Asshole, but not by much."

Okay, by a lot, but she wasn't about to release that truth and reveal her fear. Then again, the man could smell both the size of her terror and her lie.

He was nice enough not to comment.

"Come on in. Your house is overflowing with pack and you'll see more than a few wolves, but Zoey said you're used to that."

Kira nodded. Most of her old pack simply ignored her and went along with their wolfy business, uncaring of her presence when they shifted. She wished all of them had ignored her.

"Yeah, I'm good."

She climbed to the porch and waited for him to step aside, to either enter her house or give her room to pass. Instead, he stared down at her and for the second time in ten minutes, she locked eyes with an alpha. Maybe that'd been her problem all along. Being unable to see meant she never truly engaged in a visual dominance fight. How could she stare down a male she couldn't truly see?

"Thank you for caring for her." His voice was hoarse.

"What? I didn't…"

"You did. She said you saved her. She would have…" He shook his head.

Kira traced the worst of the wounds she'd sustained over the years, the deep gash between her breasts that ran from the top curve of her breast straight down to her belly button. If they'd waited even another minute, another five minutes… It would have been over for her.

"I didn't do anything she hasn't done for me a million times over." Kira gave him a sad smile. "You don't know what you have with her. She's strong as hell and more vicious than you can imagine when it comes to people she loves. Don't let yesterday fool you. I don't have the story, but knowing Zoey, it took at least three shifter males to tie her down. It wasn't just my brother who did that."

His pure, unadulterated fury poured into her and she forced herself to remain standing. "Five." A hint of pride joined the scents of his anger. "It took five plus your brother to hold her and do that."

Kira nodded. "There you go. There's no one stronger than Zoey."

"There's you."

She adopted a rueful smile. "We'll have to agree to disagree on that one."

Ebenezer whined, nudging her hand, and she tasted the air. Bacon. "All right, pup. We'll see if the wolves will share," she murmured.

"That, we can handle. Most of them will be in the kitchen and I'm sure someone will give him a few slices."

Kira padded past him and into her house. The place was filled with new scents, but beneath them all lurked hers mixed with a bit of Isaac's. Home. It smelled like home and it made her realize that it wasn't a place that made her happy, comfy and safe. It was Isaac. He was home.

Which had her thoughts whirling and wondering and… she'd have to talk with him later. Yes, she'd wanted to find a home outside Alpha Asshole's reach, one where she could be safe, but that didn't mean it *had* to be Grayslake. With Isaac at her side, she could be safe anywhere. Maybe their final decision last night wasn't so final.

The moment they entered the house, Ebenezer trotted toward the kitchen and at the same moment, someone yelled for Bates. The wolf left her with a murmur, telling her Zoey was upstairs.

The wolves in the house barely gave her a glance. She got a delicate sniff from one or two who were shifted, but overall, she was ignored. Which was good since, as much as she wanted to be comfortable around them, she couldn't. Knowing they weren't her old pack and *knowing* they weren't her old pack, were two very different things.

Kira padded down the narrow hallway between the kitchen and entryway. Regardless of her familiarity with the house, she kept her hand trailing over the wall to her right. She brushed her fingertips over the thinning wallpaper and along the trim surrounding the small door that led to the crawlspace beneath the stairs.

She continued on her path, nearing the bottom of the steps.

Of course, like any other time when she had someone other than Isaac or Zoey with her, she tripped. It could have been something as simple as a discarded pile of clothing, an errant shoe, or the stepstool. Again.

Regardless, she went sprawling, knees colliding with the worn wood, heel of her hands striking the ground as she fought to catch herself. At least this time she didn't snap a finger or gouge the hell out of her shin.

Not the stepstool, then. Yippee.

A low snort came from her right, followed by a laugh covered by a cough.

Ass. Holes.

With a groan, she pushed to her knees and took a moment to get the throbbing pain under control.

The rapid patter of feet on the floor above her told her Zoey was coming even before her voice echoed down the stairs. "Kira?"

"Yeah, I'm here."

"On the floor," the speaker snorted.

And then Zoey was there. The Zoey who'd gotten into more fights than Kira could count. To Kira, it was annoying. To anyone else who wasn't used to her friend going from zero to "I will gut you with a spoon" in under two seconds, it was scary as hell.

"Excuse the fuck outta me?" Even a foot shorter than the male, Zoey seemed to loom over him. "I didn't just hear that, did I?" Zoey stepped forward and the wolf stumbled back. "I didn't hear my best friend, my sister, trip on something because you people can't follow a simple goddamned direction. Did I?"

"Uh… Alpha…"

311

"Because I'm pretty goddamned certain I told *everyone* to put their shit back where they got it and if it was clothing, they damned sure weren't going to leave it in the middle of the goddamned floor." Zoey was big on damn. "And I also said I'd tear apart any wolf who didn't do as I asked because I didn't want Kira to get hurt. You know, Kira, the woman whose house you're standing in? The woman who *saved me yesterday?*"

"She's prey, Alpha."

Zoey's rage slammed through Kira and she knew things weren't going to end well unless she could calm her friend. She opened her mouth to speak, to do something to diffuse the situation, but another voice overrode hers.

One that told Kira things just went from bad to a fuck-ton of worse.

Isaac responded to the wolf's pronouncement that she was prey. "And so are you."

Then snarls, grumbles, grunts, and growls filled the air a split-second before the unmistakable sound of shattering glass reached her. Dammit.

Kira flopped to her back, waiting for someone to finally realize she still lay on the ground. Really, she was waiting for Isaac to remember her. It didn't take him long. Shortly after he finished breaking things with someone's body, his face filled her vision.

"Hey." She smiled. She was pretty sure he frowned. "Did you throw a wolf through my window?"

That was the only conclusion she could draw.

"Just a little one."

"A little wolf or a little window?"

Isaac shrugged. "Big wolf, small window. He has a few nice cuts now." He reached for her. "Lemme help you up."

"Aren't you going to do something about the bleeding wolf?" She raised her eyebrows and got another shrug in response.

"Yeah. I'll make sure he rinses off the front porch. Blood really stains."

"Isaac," she sighed.

"He was an ass. Now he will be less of an ass. At least to you."

The power of both Reid and Bates slapped her and then the two massive males were there. And *then* she saw nothing but Isaac's back.

Kira sighed. *Men.*

*

Women. Isaac growled.

He'd allowed her to go to her house and then she was to come right back to him. He'd even allowed for an extra five minutes because she'd probably want to visit with Zoey for a moment. He knew Bates wouldn't allow even Kira to keep Zoey from resting for very long. So when she *still* hadn't returned after what he believed was an appropriate amount of time, he'd gone hunting.

Frustration was his companion as he stomped from his yard to Kira's. That'd quickly blossomed to annoyance when he found a handful of wolves feeding Ebenezer strip after strip of bacon.

Did *they* have to sleep with the farting dog? No. The answer was no.

The annoyance transformed to anger and worry when he scented Reid. Isaac accepted that the male would be allowed to come back to Grayslake to see Zoey, and he had no doubt males loyal to the Southeast Itan lurked nearby, but he didn't like the alpha so close to Kira.

Then he'd heard her stumble, her flesh striking the ground, and worry filled him. Until a fucker chuckled. It was low, almost silent, but there.

Zoey got to the wolf first, ranting at him, but it was Isaac who took out the dirty laundry.

Now, hands a tiny bit scratched, but still ready to tear into any other males who pissed him off, he faced the two alphas.

"Bates," he tipped his head at the interim alpha, but didn't take his gaze from Reid.

The crazy alpha had done enough to their clan, to Isaac's family, and he wasn't about to let the male harm Kira.

Prey or not, she was *his* and he'd tear apart anyone who forgot that fact.

"Isaac." Bates's voice was smooth. "Will the wolf live?"

Isaac shrugged. "I suppose."

Zoey's voice boomed through the house. "As long as your mate doesn't kill him."

Kira cleared her throat. "Just an FYI, that's a possibility. Since she doesn't have to worry about me because I have Isaac...

314

Did I mention she's a balls to the wall kind of girl? I'm pretty sure I did, but just in case. Yeah, she is."

With a curse, Bates stomped toward the living room, only to stop short before leaving them entirely.

"You can't kill him." Him meaning Reid. Dammit.

The alpha gave Isaac that warning before disappearing. His low tones were offset by Zoey's rising voice, but Isaac was sure the alpha would win through whatever means necessary. Zoey and Bates weren't mated yet, but with the scents of arousal surrounding the male… Isaac didn't think it'd be much longer.

Isaac faced off against Reid, staring down the wolf. Because no matter what, a wolf wasn't much against a bear. Well, as long as the wolf fought fair and didn't ambush a bear or hold a gun to his opponent's head.

Like Reid did to Keen and Trista.

Pussy bastard.

He crossed his arms over his chest. "How long are you staying?"

The wolf mirrored Isaac's stance. "As long as Terrence and Ty allow."

So, he'd leave by the afternoon, then.

Reid wasn't done. "Part of my sentence is to make peace with Keen and Trista." The wolf smiled, albeit ruefully. "Funny how I'm tied to those two, huh? Trista's asshole father fucked with my life and now I'm tied to him through her."

Isaac furrowed his brow. "How are you supposed to make peace? You almost killed them, Reid. I'm surprised Terrence let you off your leash."

Reid chuckled. "I wanted Trista's family to disappear because of what her father did to mine."

Isaac nodded. Trista's father had repeatedly beaten and raped Reid's mother before dropping her across the wolf's territory line. There'd been a message carved into the female's skin. The story haunted Isaac's mind and part of him recognized Reid's desire for blood.

"I tried to end their line. Funny how God fucks with you, man." Reid shook his head.

"What are you talking about?"

Reid took a step back and leaned against the wall, giving Isaac a moment to really look at the deadly wolf. Lines of fatigue and worry were etched into his skin, making the male look older than his thirty-four years. "If I want to end the hyena alpha's line, I gotta kill his kids, right? Destroy any lingering evidence of his life."

Isaac growled and Kira pushed closer, reminding him of his need to care for her. He did not like hearing about the wolf wishing for anyone's death.

He froze and shoved the echoing sound down. He couldn't protect her in this house of wolves if he went after Reid. He'd bide his time.

"I'm not going after Trista, Isaac. Or anyone else in your family. I've already given up on revenge. Fucking Terrence is making me do this kumbayah bullshit. Your clan is safe from me. Hell, I feel like the man has my balls in a glass jar. Turned me into a pussy. Talking about my feelings and shit."

Isaac would have laughed at the dominant male's words if he hadn't wanted to avoid a fight. "The point is, had I succeeded, had I continued, I would have had to go after another of Heath Scott's bastards." Reid sighed and stared past Isaac, gaze directed at the living room. "I'd have gone after my own half-sister." The wolf closed his eyes with a sigh. "Life has a way of fucking with you, huh? God damned bastard fathered Zoey. He... My mother..."

Truth lived in those words. A truth that had him following the threads and coming up with a convoluted family tree and more questions than answers.

"In a way, that makes Trista your sister, too." Kira's soft, timid voice broke through the silence and the words had Reid stiffening a bare moment before he relaxed once again.

"Yeah, yeah it does."

"How'd it happen? How'd..."

How'd the wolf's mother give birth to Zoey and no one knew?

Reid shrugged. "I can only assume my father made Zoey disappear. My mother obviously carried her to term, but I know the kind of bastard my father was. He let Mom carry her but wouldn't let her keep the baby. Sometimes I'm glad the old bastard is dead."

"That's..." Isaac shook his head, having a hard time wrapping his mind around the concept.

If something similar happened to Kira, would he do the same? He'd like to say no, but to condemn a child to the type of pack that'd hurt Kira so badly… he couldn't do it.

"What's next then? That pack is so fucked. Plus it's tied into Redby and even Grayslake."

Reid shrugged. "They die."

That was the alpha Isaac remembered.

"You can't kill an entire pack," Kira snapped, stepping behind him before he could stop her.

The wolf snorted. "Of course I can."

Isaac believed the male.

"You…" Kira's attention shifted to him, then Reid, and back again. "He can't mean to go after Alpha Asshole."

"I'm pretty sure he does." Isaac grinned at his mate. Her shock was kinda cute.

"But… He's just one…"

Reid's chuckle was filled with menace. "Sweetheart, while every other baby was fed milk, I was raised on blood and pain. A few wolves aren't much."

"You can't take on the whole pack." She tried again and Isaac draped an arm across her shoulders, giving her arm a reassuring squeeze.

"Not the whole pack. I think a few will probably run. I'll let Terrence's men take them out."

"Terrence?" Isaac quirked his brow.

"Yeah, the regional alpha is less than thrilled with me. Told Terrence that he could kill me or let me into a werebear clan; I wasn't staying with any wolf pack and I wasn't allowed to go lone wolf. I'm 'unstable.' So I'm officially a bear now. When I can stop trying to kill his guards and merely make 'em bleed a little, he wants to give me a werebear clan." Reid shrugged. "Can you believe that? Wolf leading bears? It's bullshit, but I'm still breathing. So what the fuck ever."

Apparently Kira wasn't done. "How can you take on a whole pack? You had that woman with you and you still lost against Keen and Trista. There are *a lot* of wolves."

Isaac tightened his hold, ready to shove his mate behind him. He really needed to talk with her about how she should converse with crazies.

"Oh, that was rage. Pure emotion. Made me sloppy." The words were matter of fact, as if he'd come to terms with his failure and attempting to kill an innocent woman was no big deal. "I boiled over with it. I had my chance and I wanted it. I leapt too soon. Now though…" Reid met his gaze and then turned his attention to Kira.

A rumbled growl formed in his chest, but he pushed it down. So far, the ex-alpha had been calm and almost cordial. There was no reason to destroy Kira's home by shifting and going to battle. Yet.

"Now, it's more of a simmer." The wolf turned his head, looking past him, and Isaac glanced back to find Zoey curled against Bates on the couch. "When something's simmering, it can go one of two ways. It can calm and relax, settle into its flavors, or it can boil, foam and roll over the edge, destroying

319

whatever it touches." Reid focused on Isaac. "With Terrence's therapy bullshit, I'm a simmer. Ready. Waiting. I've got death on my left shoulder and pain on the right. Both of them are more than ready to tear into that pack just as soon as someone tells me what I need to know."

"What do you need to know?" Kira's voice broke the widening silence.

"Which one of 'em should die first."

chapter eighteen

Kira sat sideways across Isaac's lap, head on his shoulder as she snuggled close. Her best friend adopted a similar position with her new mate. Well, mate but not. Zoey was still recovering and the two of them hadn't "sealed the deal" quite yet.

Based on the woman's snuggles and happy sighs, Kira didn't imagine it'd be much longer. Not if Zoey and Bates had their way.

Reid on the other hand... If he got what he wished for most, it'd probably mean Bates' head on a platter. He'd taken his new job as big brother a little too seriously.

Staring at the massive male, Kira wondered if the ex-alpha's therapy really had done anything for him.

"I'm sure you told Bates, but walk me through it." Reid's voice was hoarse, from this inner wolf, emotion, or both.

Zoey sighed, but recounted her story, bringing their small group with her as she relived the last few days.

Days. *Days.* Zoey traveled across the country, Carve tearing her apart, for *days.*

Kira wasn't sure how the woman had survived.

"Mitchell was pissed. I mean *pissed,* and Kira wasn't there and she's…" Zoey hesitated, so Kira picked up the slack.

"I'm his favorite victim. His favorite pet."

Two things happened at once. Isaac gave her a reassuring squeeze, but it was Reid's reaction that shook her. He shot her a look that contained both rage and regret.

"And Mitchell is?" Reid jotted the name down and kept his attention on her.

"My brother." Kira grimaced.

The ex-alpha's movement ceased. "Brother?"

"Yes."

"Which makes…" His voice trailed off, but the question was there.

"Which makes Alpha Clarke my father." She jerked her head in a stiff nod.

"He condoned your brother…" Disgust filled his features.

Kira shrugged. "I'm prey amongst wolves. I mean, how strong can an alpha be if he sired a *mole.* He probably would have been happy to see me gone."

Why can't you just die? Mitchell yelled those same words more than once.

322

"It's the biggest reason I left. I kept working up the nerve to run and finally Zoey…" Kira looked to her friend, the woman who'd helped her flee the pack and suffered because of it. "I wish I would have stayed."

Her best friend was quick to shake her head. "No. Never wish for that. They would have done it at some point. We just managed to get you out first."

"Zoey? What else?" Reid's attention went to his half-sister.

"I think…" Zoey focused on Kira. "I think he found you. When you left and he couldn't locate you for a few days, he was pissed. When I told him you were gone, he was enraged. Like, oh my God furious. Then he was suddenly happy. At least, for a little while. Then he got pissy again. That's when he came after me." Her friend nibbled her lip. "Did something happen? Did you see anyone following you?"

A wolf on the other side of the room snorted at Zoey's choice in words. Isaac tensed beneath her, hands tightening as if to move her aside. Dammit, he'd already shattered one window in her home.

Before Isaac had a chance to hunt and kill the offending male, Reid pushed to his feet. He rose slowly, body unfolding from her small chair with unhurried care. With the same speed, he turned toward the source of the snort and moved forward. The crowd parted for him, eventually revealing a single male cowering against the wall.

"A-A-A-Alpha Bennett—"

Reid didn't give the male a chance to utter more than his name. Nope, because then the wolf was up and out. As in, Reid literally lifted the large werewolf over his head and threw him across the room. And right out the window.

Dammit.

Reid brushed off his hands, sliding one against the other as if touching the male dirtied him, and then carefully returned to his seat.

"Continue."

"Um…" Continue? As if he hadn't just tossed another wolf without breaking a sweat? Wow. That's all she had. Wow. "There was," Kira furrowed her brow. "The only thing that's really happened was Vanessa." She shrugged. "I mean, I was bitchy and she was sort of 'I'll kill you now, you she-whore' back."

Zoey narrowed her eyes at Kira. At least, that's what she imagined. The scents from her best friend indicated Kira must have had "idiot" tattooed on her forehead at some point. "Vanessa? You said a bear gave you a hard time, but Isaac's brother took care of things. You forgot to mention *killing* to me, KK."

She winced and nodded. "Well, I hypothetically, may or may not have, kinda sorta stretched the truth a tiny bit."

"Kinda? Like you're a little bit blind?" Zoey snapped, Isaac chuckled and Bates released a censoring whisper. "What?" Annoyance and disbelief filled the woman. "It's not like no one knows she has trouble seeing. It's like Isaac's scar. Just because you don't talk about it doesn't mean it's not *there*. Keeping quiet doesn't magically make it disappear. And if you think I'm wrong, you're stupid and a fat head and I don't wanna mate with you anymore."

324

Bates' growl was clear, as was Zoey's answering snarl, and then Reid joined the party.

Kira snapped her fingers at Zoey. "Hey, puppy, chill the fuck out."

Silence met her statement and she suddenly realized what she'd said. The first word wasn't a big deal, neither were the last few. It was that whole middle part that gave her pause.

"Puppy?" Reid's voice was smooth.

"Puppy?" Bates' was right behind Reid's.

"Fuck you, you blind rat. I am not above setting traps in your garden, bitch."

"Rat?" Good Lord, now Isaac was growling.

"For the love of fur, everyone needs to take a breath before I bite all of you." Kira snarled and they all quieted. She wanted to believe it was because she'd frightened them. In reality, she knew it was because *prey* threatened a handful of *predators*.

Whatever. They weren't talking, so she called it a win.

Kira huffed. "Yes, Vanessa was a tiny bit deadly and destroyed the garden while chasing me."

In truth, she was more upset by the garden than the bear trying to stomp her to death.

"That's why it looks like a cat's sandbox... I'd wondered. Your garden is your one good thing." Zoey's voice was soft and quiet.

It was. Out of every shitty thing in her life, the garden was her haven. At least, it had been.

"Yeah." She cleared her throat, pushing down the growing knot. "So, she came after me, but Isaac intervened. She had Carve on her claws."

"What kind?" Zoey's question overrode the men's inquiries.

"Weapons grade."

"Dammit." Her best friend hissed. "So that's why he was happy."

"You think she got it from…"

"Yup."

"Small words for the slow ones in the class," Reid drawled.

Kira put the meaning behind her exchange with Zoey into words. "He went from pissed to happy to pissed again. Which probably coincides with him realizing I was gone, then finding me along with someone who'd happily see me dead—Vanessa. When she failed, he was angry again and took it out on Zoey. Until then, he'd kept his playing focused on me." Tears stung her eyes and she blinked them back. "I'm so sorry he turned on you. I thought he might try to follow me, but we never imagined…"

Zoey's touch was familiar and soothing as she stroked Kira's hand. "Hush. I'm fine now and we're in a good place, huh? You have your Isaac and I have a new pack. A good pack. We're all right."

"You have me, too," Bates grumbled.

Reid spoke up. "That doesn't explain away everything though. Like why was a half-hyena wolf from the south sent to them? Why did that pack then send weapons grade Carvrix to her home hyena pack?" The wolf shook his head. "Why are Kira's father and brother so intent on killing her? They followed and probably sent this she-bear after her, but why? Did anything else happen?"

Kira glanced at Isaac. "The forklift?"

Isaac gave her a flat look. "The male from your Arizona pack *and* the forklift."

"Male from our pack?" Zoey spoke up and everyone ignored Bates' growl that the Arizona pack was in Grayslake. "Forklift."

Kira told the story of the strange male she didn't recognize and the incident at the home improvement store.

"Questions, but no answers," Isaac murmured.

Reid pushed up from his seat and towered over them all. "Oh, there will be answers." The weight of the man's gaze settled on Kira, heavy and oppressive. "How many times did you endure pain from him?"

Kira shook her head and chuckled. "When didn't I?"

Zoey drew their attention. "Before you were eighteen, that's when." Kira furrowed her brow, trying to think back. "Remember? He hated you, but Alpha kept Mitchell in check. After your birthday, when the pack recognized you were an adult…"

Now she remembered. Remembered the first searing wave of pain, the first mark Mitchell burned into her skin. It wasn't the deepest, not by far, but it was the one she could recall with startling clarity. Her first taste of Carve. Her first, but not her last.

"Yeah," she shoved back the emotions crowding her throat. "Yeah, I remember."

She just didn't want to.

*

Isaac would never let her go again. Not with the heavy weight of danger looming before them. Especially not when the truth of her past was laid at his feet.

He'd been a whiny bitch about a couple of scars marring his body and face. There were many, but they'd emerged in one massive sweep. Well, two. Regardless. Fight and it was done. Nothing lingered besides the stigma of his injuries.

Yet Kira. Dear God, how had she survived day after day, year after year?

Whispering low, he voiced the question that'd been burning his mind. "Why didn't you leave?"

She sighed and leaned against him, her head resting on his shoulder. The others continued talking, Zoey giving Reid background and insider information about her old pack.

"I was a coward. It wasn't a normal life. I know that. It wasn't normal or right or anything else that said 'this is what you can expect for the rest of your days.' But it was what I had, and fear of the unknown is a very strong motivator to endure. Between that and the lack of destination, I felt stuck." She shrugged and

328

he fought to contain the growing anger inside him. "Zoey got me out."

"Why Grayslake?" Another question. "You said you didn't have a destination…"

"The Alpha's fear. I overheard him talking to someone and he said he'd do what they asked, but didn't want to get pulled into 'Grayslake bullshit.' There was so much fear there. The emotion nearly had me crumbling to my knees. If the town scared him, then I thought I'd be safe here. I didn't know anything beyond that and it was enough for me."

"I'm glad you came." He pressed a kiss to her forehead and drew her scent into his lungs.

"Me, too." She nuzzled his chest.

Reid's hard voice and harsh words had him focusing on the discussion at hand. "I'm fucking going."

"She's my fucking mate." Bates volleyed back and Isaac had to admit, the male had a point.

"She's my fucking sister." Yeah, Reid had a point too.

They kept doing that, snarling and growling at each other while the pack members shuffled and shifted in place in agitation. Hell, if something didn't defuse the situation they'd soon have a whole lotta violence in the middle of Kira's kitchen.

Isaac pulled his lips back and released a harsh whistle, the high-pitched sound snaring the attention of the two alpha wolves. "One thing you need to think about while you're whipping out your dicks and comparing…" Kira and Zoey snorted. Isaac held back the urge to do the same. Barely. "If a wolf takes out the alpha and his son, that man has to take on the job." He raised his eyebrows at Bates. "I imagine Zoey doesn't want to leave Kira or go back to her old pack."

Zoey's murmured "no way" had an immediate effect on Bates. While the male glared at Isaac, Bates also released some of his anger. The wolf realized he wasn't going to be the one to take down the Arizona pack.

"Now," Isaac continued, "if the wolves are killed in a fight with a bear, even if his status as a bear is a technicality and not a physical reality… Well, your territorial alpha is just gonna have to suck it up and find a new alpha for the pack." He focused on Reid. "I don't know anyone crazier and more deadly than you. Feel like killing a couple of crazed wolves?"

Reid nodded. "Yeah, lemme tell Terrence I'll need an extra day."

The wolf was a cocky son of a bitch, but if anyone could destroy a good hunk of that pack, it was Reid.

"You might want to tell him you're about to take out a pack's inner circle." Isaac drawled.

"Eh, I guess I can tell him that, too."

That was one crazy motherfucker.

Reid turned from the table and strode toward the hallway. Every wolf pressed against the wall, making way for the dangerous ex-alpha.

"That is one crazy motherfucker," Kira whispered, echoing Isaac's thoughts. "Do you think he can do it? Isaac, they don't play fair."

"He knows." More than anyone in the world, Reid knew about not playing fair.

At least now it'd be sanctioned. Sort of. Retribution couldn't be denied and between Zoey's and Kira's testimony, he didn't think there'd be trouble. Well, much trouble.

With the dominant wolf's departure, the rest of the crowd broke up, wolves wandering away, leaving them alone once again.

"What now?" Kira voiced the question tumbling through Isaac's mind as well.

"Now, we stay vigilant and keep you two safe." Bates was quick to respond. "As much as I hate to let Reid have all the fun, we'll wait to hear from him and be on the lookout for anyone from your pack or other shifters who might be a threat."

Isaac didn't like the idea that others from his clan would have been swayed by Mitchell's smooth talk and convinced to go after Kira or Zoey.

But it'd happened with Vanessa, hadn't it? An idea planted in a jealous, half-crazed woman's mind and then the she-bear was going after his mate.

"Do we keep them here? Or back to our own dens?" Isaac murmured the question and noticed both women tense.

"We aren't going anywhere." Kira spat the words first and Zoey nodded her agreement.

"We'd be at an advantage on our home turf, baby. I'd have the whole clan to protect you." He rubbed a hand down her back, trying to rid her of tension.

"And we'd have the whole pack," Bates added.

"But we'd be separated," Zoey whispered.

"And we're not stupid. We know how to sit in a house surrounded by a bunch of deadly shifters," Kira huffed and turned her ice-blue gaze on him. "He's already driven me out of one home, I won't let him steal another."

"Kira, baby…" He sighed and pressed his forehead to hers. "You're set on this?"

His bear snarled at the idea that she'd be exposed to danger. Hell, his human side balked at the idea.

"Yes."

"Fine." He took a deep breath and begged his bear to remain calm. "But I'm talking to Ty and having a few guards sent over. He needs to know what's happening and I need you protected."

"I can send over a few wolves," Bates interjected.

"And I appreciate that." He truly did even if he wasn't going to take the man up on his offer. "But—no offense—my bear would feel better with a few men from our clan."

"Fair enough."

That seemed to signal the end of their small meeting. Bates urged Zoey from his lap and Isaac did the same with Kira. While the two women embraced with promises of phone calls and popping over for breakfast, Isaac shook the wolf's hand. With their mates being best friends, he figured he'd be seeing a lot of the male.

When the ladies began planning breakfast, lunch, *and* dinner, he knew "a lot" was an understatement.

It took five tries to get them away from each other, but they finally managed to part the chattering women, and Isaac tugged Kira toward the door while he had his chance. He nudged her outside, smiling when a yipping Ebenezer bounded over to them, tongue lolling and butt shaking.

"Hey, Ebie PiffleWaffle." Kira stroked the pup and Isaac groaned.

"Can't you give the guy a little respect? You already forced Ebenezer on him."

Kira squeezed his hand, the touch trembling as she pulled him to a stop. The pup paused along with them, Ebenezer lapping at her free hand.

"Ebie is…" She shook her head and he realized the dog might just be more than a dog to Kira. "He's hope for me. You know *A Christmas Carol* when Ebenezer Scrooge was hateful and mean? Then he changes and becomes a good person. One who's nice and loving and…" Kira stroked the pup's head and he saw what the animal meant to her.

"I'm sorry, baby."

"I hoped, you know. That maybe they'd love me. That they'd suddenly be better, but they weren't. So he became my promise. I promised to find a place where he could have fun and play and he really is the shittiest guide dog ever, but he's mine and even though I stopped hoping my father and brother would change, I still hunt for happiness with him." She shrugged. "I know his name isn't Ebenezer Pifflewaffle or Hufflesnuffle, but they make me laugh. I missed that the most.

I have hope and laughter with Ebie, but for the first time I have something else."

"What?" He couldn't stop himself from asking.

"A future. Love. Happiness. Everything."

"That's more than one thing." He needed to get the words out while he let her statement run through his mind.

A future. Love. Happiness. Everything.

"Doesn't make it less true."

"No, it doesn't." He licked his lips, mouth suddenly dry. "It's true for me as well."

Smooth Isaac. Real smooth.

Isaac tried again. "Just before you moved in, I told my brother I was leaving town." He ran a finger down his scar. "I didn't think I'd find a mate here. And as I held my niece, he told me I'd miss her, that I'd miss the clan and my family. Then I said I wouldn't have any of my own if I stayed." He cupped her cheek and wiped away her tears with his thumb. "But then I met you and I'm… I'm glad I was wrong."

chapter nineteen

Isaac watched Kira sleep, her body curled toward him, her hair fanned across the pristine white of his pillows. She was beautiful, luscious, and his.

All his.

He couldn't believe his luck, but he'd keep her just the same.

Sounds of the house's occupants stirring drew his attention, his bear straining to listen to the murmurs and clang of pots and pans. The higher-pitched voices belonged to his brothers' mates while their deep baritone offset the ladies.

He hadn't been able to keep them all away. They didn't give a damn about danger. Someone in their family was threatened and they circled the wagons. Isaac just wished they'd circle them outside.

Kira whimpered and wiggled closer to him and he readily gathered her near. Those sweet curves molded to him, cushioning his hardness. Dammit. If he could have convinced his family to stay outside his home, he might have gotten laid last night. Instead, he woke with blue balls. Well, went to sleep with them and simply awoke in the same state.

She rubbed her nose against his chest, nuzzling and snuffling until she finally settled in. Her breathing never slowed into an even rhythm and he knew she'd woken.

He leaned his head toward her and pressed a kiss to the top of her head. "G'morning."

Kira harrumphed. "No, it's really not."

"Why not?"

"Because," a reverberating clang floated from the first floor. "They're all here. I love them, I really do, but they are hell on my ears. And nose. And my organizational skills."

She practically wailed the last part of her sentence and he figured that's what upset her the most. They'd settled into a routine, a way of living, that kept Kira safe and feeling confident in his home.

His family was currently tearing that hard won peace to shreds.

"As soon as Reid takes care of your father and brother, they'll leave."

"Promise?" she grumped.

"I promise. They worry about us." He tugged her closer. "They're just hanging around because they love us too. Even if they don't know how to be quiet to save their lives."

Another clang followed by a low "dammit" and then Mia's ever-present chastising "language."

"At least they left the cubs at home."

Isaac chuckled, remembering his conversation from last night. "It was a near thing. Parker tried to smuggle Sophia and him in a suitcase. Never mind that no one brought anything larger than a duffle bag. Parker thought it'd be a good idea to see how grown up bears dealt with problems." He shook his head. "Mia told him grown up bears went to bed without dessert."

The light sound of his mother's footsteps reached him and Isaac groaned.

"What?" Kira's voice was muffled.

"My mother." The second the word left his mouth, a knock reached them.

"No hanky-panky this morning. We've got things to cuss and discuss."

Now Kira groaned.

His mother still lingered near the door and he called out to her. "Yes, Mom. We'll be down in a second."

Isaac waited until Mom fully retreated and then he whispered to Kira. "We probably have time for a quickie."

"You *do not* have time for a quickie, young man!"

He huffed. "I have just been cock-blocked by my mother."

Annoyed, he rolled from the bed and helped Kira from the depths of the blankets and mattress. He stared at her curved form, wishing he could trace her bare curves with his tongue. Unfortunately, his family was making as much noise as possible, which wasn't conducive to lovemaking.

337

"C'mon, baby. I can at least wash your back," he murmured.

"Nothing more?" Teasing sparkled in her gorgeous eyes.

"Not if I don't want my mother walking in on us."

Kira gasped. "She wouldn't."

"Are you two coming?" Mom's voice echoed up the stairs.

"Yes, she really would."

That had his mate rolling her eyes and sighing before tromping into the bathroom. Isaac was right on her heels, gaze on the sway of her hips and the bounce of her ass. He knew a quickie was out of the question, but his cock still hadn't gotten the memo. He was hard in an instant, more than ready to slide into her wet heat.

Instead, he got to the shower before her. A twist of a knob had the water flowing and he stepped beneath the spray before allowing the liquid to warm. Sometimes a bear had to do what a bear had to do.

Once the water heated and Kira joined him, he fought to keep his touch casual and not arousing. They had to hurry. He needed to think of non-sexy things like his parents having sex.

Isaac glanced at his now soft cock. Yup, that did it.

Before long, they were clean, dry, and dressed. He strode ahead of Kira, eyes scanning their surroundings as he hunted for anything out of place. When he came to an errant end table, he nudged it back. The discarded pillow was tossed onto the couch and he rearranged the coffee table as well.

By the time he made it to the kitchen, he was fuming on Kira's behalf.

He lowered himself into an empty chair and tugged Kira onto his lap, entwining his fingers with hers. Holding hands like this, he was able to feel the unevenness of her digits and the fact that things were out of place enraged him further.

His mother placed a heaping plate of food before him and he felt Kira's twitch of interest. They'd get to eating in a second. First...

"Isaac, you remember how you had me research Zoey? Well, I also looked at—"

Isaac held up a hand for silence. "I love you all, but I'm getting damned tired of repeating myself. And as an FYI, I threw a wolf out of Kira's window for this. Don't think I won't take it out on one of you." He leveled his angry glare on his family.

In all honesty, he knew the women loved Kira, his mother in particular. So it probably wasn't them who'd disregarded his mate's safety. He wouldn't put it past his oblivious brothers though. *Men.*

"I know Mom and Dad taught us to put things back where we found them, but that seems beyond someone in this house. So here it is: if you move furniture, put it back. If you move a pillow, put it back. If you put anything on the floor or out of its original place. Put it the fuck back." Mia didn't chastise him for his cursing and neither did his parents. They must have either realized the depth of his anger or felt the same. When he noticed the glare Mom leveled on Ty, Van, and Keen, he figured it was a bit of both.

339

Isaac untwined his fingers from Kira and raised her hand, making sure she splayed her fingers. The two on the left were bent at odd angles, one a little more pronounced than the others. "I splinted this, but it's still a hint more crooked than it was before. And do you know why she broke her finger? Because someone didn't replace a stepstool."

"Isaac…" Kira murmured, a rebuke in her tone.

"No." He shook his head. "I promised not to treat you like an invalid, like you can't take care of yourself, and I won't. But making sure you're safe in our home is another story."

He stared at his family, gazed on his brothers, and he noted the sheepish expression on their faces. Low "sorrys" reached them, but it was Mia's tear-filled gaze that snared his attention.

"Oh my God, I'm so sorry. I didn't even realize… I didn't mean…"

Kira didn't give him a chance to say a word. No, his mate wiggled from his lap and padded around their small gathering, weaving between chairs before she stood before Mia. His mate drew the Itana into a tight hug. "It's okay. You didn't know and I'm fine. I promise."

Mia sniffled and nodded against Kira's shoulder. "I just…"

"Hush. I'm all healed. That's no reason to get upset."

"But it's *crooked*." Mia practically wailed and Isaac shot a panicked look at Ty. The man looked just as panicked as his brother.

"So? The only one who'd care is Isaac and he doesn't seem to mind. Besides, he doesn't have room to talk in the 'what's uglier' department. Have you seen his face? I think I should get hazard pay or something."

Dead silence reigned and his mate flashed him an impish grin while everyone else in the family stared at Kira and then him.

They worried over his reaction and what they didn't realized was that he no longer gave a flying fuck about anyone else's opinion. Only Kira's. And her teasing proved she didn't care either.

Which just gave him another reason to love her.

And chase her through the house.

With a teasing growl, one that was answered by her wide smile, he leapt from his seat and bolted around his brothers, reaching for his mate.

Giggling, Kira released Mia and dashed away, racing past his parents, and their chuckles followed them to the stairs. She retraced their path and he had no doubt she wouldn't have trouble gaining the stairs. She obviously trusted him as well. She depended on him to put things in order as they made their way to the kitchen.

Kira rounded the banister, eyes shining and smile wide.

Isaac released another snarl, causing her to giggle once again. "I'm gonna get you."

"Isaac! We really need to talk about this!" Keen's voice reached him, but he only cared about the woman currently running from him.

"Later."

"But, it's import—"

The bear thought ripping Keen's head was a good idea. "*Later.*"

Isaac stomped up the stairs, following the patter of Kira's lighter steps. He knew where she'd end up, he just had to pounce once he got there.

Except as he climbed the last few steps he watched Kira slide through the bedroom doorway, bare feet slipping on the smooth wood. Yes, he saw her slide in, then heard a fearful squeak followed by her trying to scramble back into the hallway.

Her panicked gaze met his, her near sightless eyes focusing on him.

He should have listened to his gut and not let her sweet-talk him into staying in his home instead of on clan land. Because there were only two things that would make his fearless Kira panic and tremble.

Her father and her brother.

Isaac vaulted over the last few steps, running over the ground that separated him from Kira. He stopped short when an armed male filled the doorway, his hand buried in his mate's hair.

The man wasn't old enough to be Kira's father, no gray hairs and definitely not enough wrinkles, which meant he faced off with her brother Mitchell.

A brother who looked just like the male who'd driven past his home mere days ago. The male encouraged Vanessa to attack, tortured Zoey, and then tried to end Kira's life at the home improvement store. It'd been a half-assed attempt at best. The man was desperate.

Desperate men, wolves, were dangerous.

The wolf brandished a gun, waving it toward Isaac which had him re-evaluating his next step. He couldn't just rush the male. He didn't just clutch a gun. No, his free hand was buried in his mate's hair. It'd take hardly any effort to point the weapon at Kira or himself and end their lives. He had to play this out. At least, for a little while.

Then later, after the asshole was dead and gone and Isaac's heart began beating again, he'd kick his own ass for being stupid.

"Who are you and what are you doing with my mate?" Isaac tried to keep his voice even, but the words came out with a snarl.

The man tightened his grip on Kira's hair, tugging a moan from her chest. The male did it again, smiling wider and wider with each sound. If he had the patience, he'd pluck every hair from the male's body. That'd be fun. Hair, nails, teeth...

The man, Mitchell, was nearly Isaac's height, but nowhere near his bulk. Thin and wiry like most wolves. Definitely not an alpha then. Those guys were always massive and mean as hell.

His red hair looked like fire and the deep green eyes sparked with fury. Even his skin was pale and pasty white. Nothing like Kira.

If he'd seen the male on the street, a mere glance would have had him disregarding Mitchell as a threat.

He wasn't disregarding the fucker now.

"She's not your mate. She's nothing but a meal ticket and she went and fucked it all up." The man snarled and yanked, dragging Kira into the master bedroom by her hair. "Get in here. Now. We're gonna do this and then I'll get what I want and you bears can go fuck yourselves."

"Mitchell," Kira hissed. "What do you think you're doing?"

Mitchell released Kira and she tensed. Isaac thought she was preparing to fight or run, but no, she was preparing for the strike. The strike of bone on skin that sent her rocking backward.

Isaac's bear roared in displeasure. Someone had hurt their mate. *Thiers.*

He would die. Slowly as long as he got to the male before his brothers did.

Kira straightened and wiped at the corner of her mouth, gathering the droplet of blood that'd pooled on her flesh. "You still hit like a girl."

What the fuck was she doing?

*

What the fuck am I doing?

Staring at Mitchell's tight fist and then the gun he clutched tightly, she wasn't sure. She did know that she needed his attention away from Isaac and on herself. Kira could survive just about anything. Hell, she had over the years. She didn't think she could survive losing her mate.

No. She *knew* she couldn't survive losing her mate.

"You stupid bitch." Another strike, this one nearing her eye, but colliding with her cheek. The crunch told her he'd broken something. The pain... well, it didn't give her any sort of clues. *I fucking hurt everywhere, dumbass,* wasn't very informative.

"Yeah, you say that and yet I'm still breathing. Kinda hard to believe you."

Mitchell kicked her, missing her chest and merely colliding with her shoulder. Pain seared her, but nothing broke.

Score one for Kira.

"Why wouldn't you just die? I don't understand. Why?" He almost sounded interested and she was half-ready to tell him.

Then she remembered he really wanted her dead so answering probably wasn't a good idea.

"It seemed like a good idea at the time." Oh yes, Kira, antagonizing the crazy is so much better.

"Damn you!" Another punch, this one colliding with her jaw.

Hey, still nothing broken. She was doing okay so far.

Isaac eased closer, stepping onto the landing and moving forward until ten feet separated them. Of course, that's when Mitchell noticed her mate's approach.

"Back off!" Mitchell waved the gun around. "You stay back. I have something to do and I'm gonna do it *right* this time." Her brother cocked the gun, some revolver that actually had a hammer to tug back. Huh. "I know what I have to do."

Mitchell steadied the weapon and trained it on Isaac. Hell no.

"What do you have to do, Mitch?" She rushed the words past her swollen lips. It came out muffled and slurred, but the man focused on her.

"You want me to tell you? Hell no. I'm not that stupid."

Yes, he really was, she just had to keep him going until... something. God, in a house of bears, someone had to realize a wolf had invaded. Right? Then again, there *was* a massive oak near the house whose branches were long and sturdy and... Dammit. And no one's super-sniffers seemed to be working. Even *she* hadn't scented him. She breathed deep, hunting for the scent that identified him and found... nothing.

"Of course you're not stupid enough to tell me." Another handful of disjointed words. "Hey, how come I didn't sniff you?"

The wolf chuckled. "I did something right when it came to this, at least." Mitchell lowered to a squat, his gaze intent on her. "I tested that on you, too."

He ran the muzzle of the gun along her cheek and rubbed it along the column of her neck. He kept going, toying with the neck of her top and tugging on the material with the metal.

Isaac growled and suddenly the cool gun was gone, once again pointed at her mate. Dammit, why couldn't the man shut the hell up already?

"What'd you test on me?" She spared a glance for Isaac and fought to ignore the man's glare. He could kick her ass later. Like, after he gutted Mitchell and tore him into tiny pieces.

"Carve was just the beginning." Mitchell looked to her once again. "Doupan, Douse, came next. Can't really get them with Carve if you can't get close, yeah? Doesn't have the same effect if it's just an injectable. Gotta get in there." Her brother leaned close, running his nose over her skin, breathing deeply, and she fought the shudder that threatened to overtake her. "We know that, though. Don't we?"

Yeah, she knew. "Yup."

Mitchell's stale breath bathed her, and her stomach lurched, threatening to lose what little it held. Though, if she vomited on him, she bet he'd let her go. And then *of course* when the wonderful idea came to her, her stomach decided to settle.

It settled because cold, hard fear took its place.

The third step creaked. Then the fifth.

Someone was coming upstairs and from the soft patter, she knew it wasn't one of Isaac's brothers or even his father. It was one of the females in the house.

"Isaac, sweetheart?" Meg. His mother was padding up the stairs as if she didn't have a care in the world and she wasn't about to walk into the middle of this shit-storm.

Everyone's attention shifted to the edge of the landing where Meg Abrams would soon appear. Kira held her breath, hoping Isaac could convince the woman to stay downstairs.

"Just a minute, Mom."

"This will only take a second," she called and Kira's heart stopped.

347

No, no, no.

She just found happiness and a family—a non-homicidal family—and she couldn't lose it already.

"*Mom.* You really need to wait." Isaac pushed the words through gritted teeth.

"You're acting as if I haven't seen what you're packing. Albeit, for Kira's sake, I hope it's a little bigger than it was." Meg huffed. "I just need to pass a message along from Keen. They don't think you'll snap at me and it's important apparently. More important than your privacy. So you can go after your brother once we're done."

The eighth step groaned.

"Mrs. Abrams, I really need you to stay downstairs," Kira tried. "I've… Uh…"

That was about the time Margaret Abrams, mother to the four Abrams brothers and ex-Itana, appeared at the top of the stairs. Her sweeping gaze traveled over them and then finally returned to meet Kira's stare.

Oh, shit. This was so not going well.

Especially not when the sweet as pie woman seemed to swell in size, her chest widening and fur slithering over her skin. "Do you want to tell me why you're holding a gun on my daughter? Or why she's all bruised up? Lemme tell you, you've got two seconds before I take you down."

"Which means Little Kira will die in one." Mitchell practically purred the words. "And I know you're not her mother. Her mom is dead. Come to think of it." Her brother wrenched her

348

strands, yanking even harder until she met his stare. "Your daddy is gone, too."

Kira sucked in a harsh breath, fighting for air. "So, you killed Alpha Asshole?"

Best news she'd had all year.

Mitchell raised his free hand, fingers still clutching the gun, and brought the butt down on her cheek. Yup, more crunching. That one was broken.

"*Don't call him that!*" Another strike, another creak of wood that had her brother blindly pointing the gun toward her mate and his mother. "He took care of you for eighteen years, you little bitch whelp. Dad isn't dead. Your *father* is dead."

She wheezed out a chuckle, taunting him with the sound as confusion filled her. "We have the same *father*, Mitchell."

"No." He shook his head. "The beta was your—"

A squeak, which meant someone else had climbed onto the steps. Mother fucker. Did they all want to die?

"The beta was my what, Mitchell?" The pain in her cheek was pulsing through her, but she took comfort in the fact he hadn't coated the gun in Carve. That meant she'd at least make it through the whole ordeal. Though it'd be nice if someone killed her brother before he broke any more bones.

Was it too much to ask for someone to come in behind the man? Really?

The next sound had her blood turning to ice, freezing in place and sending a wave of pure fear through her body. Only, it wasn't a single sound, but several, the rhythmic click clack of Ebenezer's claws on the wood. Once again she remembered she needed to trim them and now he was coming upstairs and then he'd see Mitchell and then—

The growl told her he'd reached the landing, his canine eyes spying Mitchell even if his nose didn't pick up the scent. If Kira hadn't sniffed out the male, there was no way her pup had. If Ebie had scented her brother, he would have gone ape-shit.

There was no love lost between Ebenezer and Mitchell.

Kira pulled against Mitchell's hold, tilting her head until she spied the dog near the banister, right beside Meg. His fur stood on end, hackles raised and fangs bared. The sounds coming from her sweet dog rumbled and vibrated the air, seeping into her bones.

"Ebie, it's okay, boy," she whispered, trying to soothe him before he came to Kira's rescue. He was such a good pup even if he sucked as a guide dog. He'd saved her time after time and the last thing she wanted was for him to be injured.

Ebenezer snarled, seeming to yell at her for being so stupid. Yeah, well, she imagined Isaac would roar at her when things were done. Ebie could get in line.

"Shut *up*, you stupid bitch." Mitchell shook her, which had the dog bolting forward with a bark and snap of his teeth. "And shut that fucking dog up before I kill him."

"Shh… It's okay, Ebenezer." Again she fought to calm him. "Mommy's fine."

Mitchell's growl joined her pup's. "Why couldn't you make this easy like you were supposed to?"

Kira refocused on her brother. "What Mitchell? What was supposed to be easy? Because I'll do what you want."

Now *that* had Isaac snarling and Meg was on his heels.

Mitchell bared his teeth and snarled back at their small gathering before returning to her. "We were flush for eighteen years and then you just had to *die* to keep it all going. But you wouldn't."

"Why'd I have to die?"

God knew her brother had tried often enough over the years. Time and time again he'd told her he wanted her gone, but their father wouldn't let her leave.

"So we," the gun was once again beneath her chin, "could get the money." Ebie barked again, seeming to grow more agitated by the second. "Will you shut that dog up before I kill it?"

Mitchell hit her once again, as if punctuating his demand with a new wave of pain.

A few things happened then.

Isaac roared.

Meg snarled.

And worst of all, Ebenezer leapt. He went from six feet away to flying through the air, his teeth bared, mouth open, and more than ready to take a hunk out of Mitchell.

Only… only he didn't get a chance because that's when her brother turned, pulling the gun from Kira's face, aiming at her dog.

351

His finger tightened on the trigger. A flash of light signaled the striking of the bullet and the high-pitched whimper told her it'd found home in her dog's body.

He shot her pup.

He shot her Ebie.

He shot... Ebenezer fell to the ground and his fur slowly turned a bright red as blood flowed from the wound.

Oh God. She couldn't breathe, she couldn't think, she couldn't... Her gaze remained focused on her dog, Ebie's eyes on hers. Pain filled the air, so much pain. She could shoulder her own agony, but he... He was hers. Her one good thing in a life of hell tinged with the red haze of Mitchell's torture.

He trained the gun on the pup again, muzzle pointed directly at her sweet boy.

No. *No.* Kira could endure a lot, but this... *No.*

With hardly a thought, her mole lent a hand and her human teeth sharpened and lengthened while her nails grew to the wicked points that helped her when she shifted. When molded to her human shape, she went from cute to deadly.

She didn't hesitate. The moment teeth pricked her lower lip, she struck. She snatched his arm, wrapping her fingers around his forearm and tugging him closer. Mouth opened wide, she sank into him, teeth going deep and bringing blood to the surface. It flowed into her mouth, filling her with the coppery fluid. The mole wanted to push it from their stomach, heave the disgusting liquid from their body.

352

But she couldn't. Not yet, anyway. Releasing him meant he could hurt her Ebie again.

So she held on, held on and dug in and refused to release him even when he punched her face or struck her side.

"Fucking bitch!" Mitchell screamed.

Kira ignored him. Ignored his yells and struggles.

He shoved and pulled, fighting to break free, and he did finally succeed. He managed to tear away from her mouth, but *she* managed to take a chunk of flesh with her.

The second he was free, he fought to flee, but she was there, on him, tackling him, and biting him. The gun fell away beneath her assault, his arm no longer able to support the weapon's weight.

That meant everyone was safe. The gun couldn't hurt them and she had a squirming Mitchell beneath her.

Mitchell who'd hurt her.

Mitchell who'd lived to torment her.

Mitchell who'd tried to kill her again and again.

And had succeeded with Ebie.

Kira didn't need the mole's urgings. No, she went after her brother in earnest, biting and tearing, scratching and scraping every bit of flesh she could reach. She ignored his cries and whimpers and the voices that surrounded her.

Nothing mattered but the end of Mitchell. Nothing.

He'd hurt so many… Kira, Zoey, Ebie…

The thoughts had her biting harder, opening her jaws, shifting slightly and then biting again. She wasn't sure how many times her fangs sunk deep or how often her claws found purchase. No, none if it mattered.

Until she was wrenched from Mitchell's trembling body, a thick, strong arm around her waist and a gruff voice filling her ear.

"Enough." The single word held an order she was hard-pressed to deny.

But she was able to. The molten rage pumping through her veins let her override the desire to do as the male said. It let her scratch his arm, kick, and fight to be free and attack the man who'd done so much to her.

"Enough, Kira." This time the man shook her as if *she* were a pup. A pup like Ebenezer who'd been shot and was bleeding. The *asshole needed to die*. A massive hand wrapped around her throat, fingers spanning the front of her neck and squeezing tightly. "Stop."

She froze, waiting to see if she'd be choked by this familiar man.

"That's it. Easy now. You're safe and Isaac is taking care of Ebenezer. I need you calm, Kira." The words rumbled through her, and she let them sink in.

George. George needed her calm because Isaac…

Kira tore her gaze from the bloodied Mitchell and sought Isaac. He sat hunched over Ebie, the dog's body unmoving and her mate's body blocked her view.

She struggled against George's hold, tugging and pushing. "Lemme go." She yanked. "Ebie."

"I'm gonna let you go, but you need to leave Mitchell be, okay?"

She nodded. Okay. She knew they wouldn't let him leave. With luck, someone would finish what she'd started.

The moment George released her, she fell to the ground, feet fighting to find purchase on the blood-slick floor. She ignored the red fluid, ignored the mass of liquid coating her skin and sinking into her clothing. Nothing mattered but getting to Ebenezer.

She slid to a stop beside the dog, sitting opposite Isaac. His hands worked fast over the pup, digging and soaking up blood as it welled from the wound.

"Ebie…" Her hands hovered over his fur, desperate to touch him, but unwilling to taint him with Mitchell's fluid. "I…"

Isaac gave her a snippet of his attention. "Are you hurt?"

"Not enough that it matters." Mitchell was hurt more than she was, but her bruises and breaks were already on their way to being healed.

His gaze traveled over her. "Then go to his head. Let him see you. I've got him comfortable, but calm would be better."

Kira did as he asked, shuffling around so she could meet Ebenezer's gaze. Those eyes still conveyed his pain, but relief seemed to roll through the pup. His tail thumped once, rising from the wet floor before lowering once again.

"That's a good, boy," she whispered. "Everything's okay. It's all gonna be okay."

Kira prayed she wasn't lying.

chapter twenty

Isaac couldn't get his hands to stop shaking. Even now, after the blood had been bathed from Kira's body and Ebenezer slept peacefully in the corner. The trembles remained, sliding through his body in fits and starts that were bound to drive him crazy.

He twitched and jerked, his body desperate to remain active while his mind slowly accepted the events of the last few hours. They spun through him, whirling and twisting until he couldn't get them to stop.

He thought he'd die when Kira bit Mitchell. He knew what she'd do before she went into action, but it hadn't made witnessing the event any less horrifying.

Ebenezer leapt, and the split second after the bullet hit home in the dog's chest, Kira burst into a flurry of movement. It all blew up in a matter of seconds, men rushing forward, his father vaulting past him to get to Kira while yelling at Isaac to look at the dog.

357

He wanted to go to his mate, save his mate, but his father had it under control. If he couldn't trust his father...

Dad stopped Kira, which meant he needed to do everything he could to save Ebie.

Isaac managed to pause the memories and stared at his hands. He'd washed them a dozen times, but he still pictured the blood that'd coated them. His palms and Kira's, but from two different sources.

She'd nearly killed him. Nearly, but not quite. Of course, Isaac didn't think the wolf would last long in Terrence's care. Sure, the Southeast Itan spared Reid's life, but he was pretty sure that wasn't going to happen with Mitchell.

In fact, he imagined Reid would pay the male a visit before all was said and done.

He should be disgusted at himself for valuing life so little. But he wasn't.

Maybe everyone had a little bit of Reid's violence inside them.

The low murmurs of his family drifted to him. He knew they were talking with Terrence's inner circle, the male having flown in the moment he heard of the recent events. The man could travel fast if he needed to. Apparently a private jet came with the title.

Kira slept through his arrival and even now slumbered on the bed. He refused to wake her.

Ebenezer whimpered and twitched, and Isaac strode toward the pup. The dog raised his eyes dilated from the drugs pumping through his veins.

"Hey, buddy." He stroked Ebie's head and scratched behind his ears. "You're okay and so's your mom, yeah? Just be easy." The dog huffed and licked Isaac's hand before laying his head down once again.

"Isaac?"

He rolled to his feet at the sound of Kira's voice and padded toward her. "Right here." He lowered to his knees beside the bed and slid his hand beneath hers, gathering her fingers and holding them tight. "I'm right here."

"Hey," she whispered.

"Hi. You okay?"

Kira nodded. "You showered with me, you know I'm okay."

With his free hand, he brushed aside her errant locks, tucking them behind her ear. "Physically you are. I'm talking about up here." He stroked her temple.

She snagged him before he could retreat and brought his palm to her cheek. "I'm good. A little drained, but good."

The voices downstairs grew in volume and then ebbed low once again. His mom's voice cut through them and he had to smile. The woman could bring the fiercest bears to their knees with one look and a single growled word.

"You look tired," he murmured.

She shrugged. "A lot happened. A lot..." She huffed and blinked rapidly. Isaac pretended not to see the tears shining in her eyes. "A lot changed, huh?"

"Scoot over. Lemme hold you."

She narrowed her eyes. "You could crawl in on the other side."

"I could, but then I'd get stuck with the cold spot. This way it's you, not me."

"That's so wrong. You're making your recovering mate take the cold spot and—"

Isaac froze. "Are you in pain? Are you hurting anywhere?"

The moment stretched out between them and she finally growled. "No, dammit."

"Then scoot."

It took no time to get settled, Isaac nice and warm while Kira snuggled up to him. "See? I had ulterior motives. You get the cool space and then you're forced to wiggle against me." He grinned.

Kira nuzzled his chest. "Would have done that anyway."

He pressed a kiss to her head and breathed deeply, drawing in her sweet scent. Blueberries. The blood that'd covered her from head to toe hadn't diminished or masked her true scent. "I know."

They lay for a while, the silence only shattered by the rumbles from downstairs. Cars rolled past the house, tires rubbing against the asphalt in their travels. Birds in the backyard chatted and squeaked while the wind played in the trees.

And still they remained quiet and calm.

Kira gave him more of her weight, her body half covering him in a curvaceous blanket. He curled his arm around her and stroked her back, enjoying the feel of her bare skin beneath his

360

fingertips. She was soft and sweet, love in a small mole-shaped package.

And he'd almost lost her. God, he'd almost lost her.

She sniffled and then her hands were on him, petting him with gentle touches. "I'm okay. You're okay. Things are good now."

"He…" He trembled. Not in fear. Never in fear. Abrams werebears weren't afraid of some mangy wolf.

Unless he pointed a gun at his mate.

"Isaac?" Her voice was firm and solid. "Look at me." Kira eased to her elbows and he met her gaze. The bruises were gone, the swelling almost disappeared due to her mole's help. "He didn't do anything that hasn't healed already."

Right. She was right. The knowledge did absolutely nothing for his emotions.

"I just got you, Kira. I just found you and—"

"Technically, I found you." A smile teased her lips.

"I'm being deep and loving here." He wished she could see better if only to feel the full weight of his glare.

"I'm sorry. Continue."

"You're ruining this."

"Isaac," her voice was soft and suddenly serious. "You're not the only one who's thankful. You need to understand that. Without you, finding you…" She shook her head. "I don't even want to imagine life without you. You see me and even though you want to tie me to a chair and keep me safe, you let me fuck things up on my own. So, yeah, I just found you and I couldn't live if I lost you."

What a way to take the wind out of a man's sails. "You gonna make fun of me if I tell you that after that mess with the hyenas, I didn't think I'd ever find someone like you? Hell, I'd decided to leave to try and find a mate. Life is lonely when there's no one to share it with." He traced the gentle slope of her nose with his finger. "And then there was you."

"No, I won't make fun of you." She turned her head and nuzzled his palm, her warm breath fanning over his skin. "You know, when you think about it, we're both a little bit broken, huh? But put us together and then we're only a little bumpy and bruised. We fit, Isaac."

God. Damn. She knew how to wreck him.

"I love you, Kira. More than anything in this world."

Her smile was blinding, bright, and filled his soul with happiness. "Love you, too. Ever since that first roar, really. You were so *angry*, and I broke *so* much, but you didn't raise your hand to me, not once."

Anger over her past treatment reared its ugly head, threatening to send him hunting Mitchell and finish the job Kira started. Instead, he took a calming breath and answered her.

"Well, I'm glad I'm the first guy you came across. Otherwise, who knows who you'd be mated to and I would have left without finding you." His bear snarled at the idea and he reminded the animal that she belonged to them. She had their bite on her shoulder and that was forever.

"Now, you'll take me with you. I know we agreed to stay, but Isaac, home is with you. It isn't a house, it's just you." She grinned and he couldn't dredge up the same emotion.

Things were so different now.

"Do you really want to go? I mean, to the Southeast Itan's compound?"

Her smile slowly fled and she furrowed her brow. "You said you wanted to and," she sighed, "I just want to be with you and I want you to be happy. If that's with the Southeast Healer, then it is. If it's here in Grayslake, then it is, though, I do want you to think about moving into my house. I can't," a shudder wracked her and he stroked her back, trying to ease some of the trembles. "I can't stay here anymore."

"But what do you want?"

"No," she shook her head. "We're not gonna be one of those couples who goes back and forth with the 'I wanna do what you wanna do' and then neither of us makes a decision."

He almost grinned at her disgruntled expression. Almost. Honestly, it was a near thing.

"So, you need to settle in and think about this: where do you want to raise our cubs? Here or traveling throughout the territory?"

"I," he sucked in a breath and then released it with a wheeze. "Are you saying…?"

Her pale blue eyes widened. "What? No. *No.* These are hypothetical cubs. At least, I think so. I mean, I'm assuming so." She shook her head. "Focus. If there are hypothetical cubs

363

in the picture, where are they being raised? On a plane traveling all over or here?"

A high-pitched squeal echoed up the stairwell, a stern feminine voice coming right on its heels and then a small, annoyed growl right behind that. Sophia, Mia and Parker.

He'd accepted the job because he was hunting for a family like Ty's and now he'd found it, right where he'd started.

"Here. We'll raise them here."

"Good." She pressed a kiss over his heart. "That's what I want, too. I want to wake up with cubs jumping on our bed and go to sleep exhausted by their very existence. And with luck, we can occasionally pass them off to your parents."

Her smile slipped then, easing from her lips until no hint of happiness lingered. "Mitchell said Alpha Asshole wasn't my father."

Emotions clogged Isaac's throat, but he forced himself to speak. "No, he wasn't."

She didn't react to his words, simply stared through him as if he didn't exist. "He was telling the truth then. Do we know who was? Do I have a family?"

"Yes," he squeezed her and shook her gently until she focused on him. "You have a family. Right here, in this house. You have three brothers, three sisters, two nieces and a nephew. And Kira," he cupped her cheek, "you have two parents who would kill for you. The only reason Mom didn't gut the bastard was because Ty kept her restrained. And let me tell you, she went after Ty with a wooden spoon after everything was said and done. She told him as soon as he was done healing the first bruise, she was going to give him a second just because she could." He traced her cheekbone. "You have a family."

"Then why..."

It'd been hard to listen to, but it was harder to put voice to the words. He wished Keen was nearby. Then he could have his brother tell the convoluted tale again.

Instead, he was alone with an emotionally strained and physically healing mate.

"Your father was the Alpha's beta. He and your mom mated, but the alpha was against inter-species matings." Isaac swallowed the bile that threatened to rise. "Your mother came from a rich family, but she was alone. She'd been an only child to aging parents and everything was left to her. When the alpha heard about this... He ended up named as your guardian in the event something happened to your mom and dad."

Kira's lids fluttered closed and a single tear escaped. "And something happened."

"Yes. Then he became your guardian. He had control of your money until you turned eighteen," he murmured.

She nodded. "That's why it went to hell after my birthday."

"Laws are pretty specific when it comes to switching packs and matings. It's to make sure that someone can't be forced to give up their money or possessions if something happens to them. It used to be easy to snatch a rich shifter, force them to join a pack and then *encourage* them to change their will. After that, their death insured the money went into the pack's accounts. Hell, sometimes the wills were forged. It was just a matter of kidnapping, forging, and killing."

365

"Oh God."

"Until you were eighteen, you kept the alpha and his son flush with cash. Once you crossed the line and the trust went under your control…"

"I didn't even know about it, though. But they had no use for me. Why didn't they just kill me then? Why all the games? Why…"

He knew what she asked. Why had they tortured her? Because that's what they'd done. Year after year, month after month, they'd tortured Kira. He hated the words he had to utter.

"The guidelines in place as part of the trust didn't allow the funds to be passed to the Alpha unless you died of natural causes. Murder and suicide were not acceptable means of termination. It would be remanded to the national pack because your murder or suicide proved your pack wasn't caring for you properly. They wouldn't have deserved the money."

"Termination. That's one way to put it." She snorted. "So, why the constant bouts of Carve, then? That wasn't murder?"

"They would have claimed you were taking part in a medical study. It would have been your choice and it wasn't anyone's fault if you reacted poorly to the drugs."

Kira shook her head and then rested her cheek against his chest. "At least I'm not truly related to them."

"No, you're not."

Silence wrapped around them. Emotion clogged the air, but it wasn't as oppressive as it'd been. Hopefully they could work through the rest of it and then focus on the remainder of their lives. He refused to diminish the fucked up happenings that surrounded them, but he wasn't going to let it rule them.

He'd done enough of that with a single fucking scar, hadn't he?

Isaac reached up and traced the line, remembering more of Keen's words.

"Want the rest?"

She shook her head. "No, but I probably should."

"You know Zoey is the old hyena alpha's daughter and Reid's sister?"

She nodded.

"Zoey was sent to live with Alpha Asshole by Reid's father. They were allies once upon a time and he wanted her gone. Heath—the hyena alpha—discovered her existence and found out that pack mixed and sold Carvrix. In exchange for not starting anything between wolves and hyenas over Zoey, the wolves would give the drug to the hyena pack."

"Which is what scarred you." Her voice was a mix between disgust and surprise.

"Yes."

"Can our lives get any more fucked up?"

Isaac chuckled. "No, I figure at this point, it's all par for the course. None of my brothers mated without a bunch of family drama. We just followed in their footsteps."

Kira growled and it was wrong that he found that sexy. "What about Vanessa? The wolf outside the house?"

367

"Vanessa got Carve from 'some guy' she met. I'm assuming it was Mitchell. We believe it was Mitchell outside the house. After Vanessa, he tortured Zoey and then came here himself after she escaped."

"I just..." She shook her head and he snuggled closer. "I can't believe it all."

Isaac buried his face in her hair. "You don't have to believe anything but the fact that I love you. Everything else is noise."

"You do?"

"I already said it twice now. If I say it three times, it must be true. So, I love y—"

"A-a-a-a-a-a..." The squeaky sounds cut him off, the familiar scream for him rising from the first floor.

Maybe if he was quiet, Sophia would forget him.

"A-a-a-a-a-a..."

Dammit.

"You're being beckoned." A laugh lived in her tone.

"Yeah. I'm rethinking the cub thing right about now. Just as an FYI." Then her whole body shook, curves jiggling and rubbing against his body. The trembles had his cock waking up and noticing the soft body plastered to his. He tucked a finger beneath her chin and forced her gaze to meet his. "I am, however, not opposed to practicing."

Kira's lips met his in a passionate kiss, one that conveyed their love for one another, passing pleasure back and forth in a never-ending wave. He wanted to do this—and more—for the rest of life.

Yes, he loved Kira Kolanowski, KK to her friends and Colon to anyone stupid enough to utter the phrase in his presence. But he still had one secret he might share with her someday.

She may have fallen in love with him at first roar, but he… he fell for her with the first look at her ass. It sure as hell wasn't romantic, so he'd keep it to himself for a while. Maybe forever. Which, coincidentally, was how long he decided to keep her.

the end

If you enjoyed this book, please be totally awesomesauce and leave a review so others may discover it as well. Long review or short, your opinion will help other readers make future purchasing decisions. So, go forth and rate my level-o-awesome!

By the way… below are links to help you hunt up the rest of the Grayslake series:

All Romance eBooks - http://bookbit.ly/grayslakeare

Bookstrand - http://bookbit.ly/grayslakebs

about celia kyle

Ex-dance teacher, former accountant and erstwhile collectible doll salesperson, New York Times and USA Today bestselling author Celia Kyle now writes paranormal romances for readers who:

1) Like super hunky heroes (they generally get furry)
2) Dig beautiful women (who have a few more curves than the average lady)
3) Love laughing in (and out of) bed.

It goes without saying that there's always a happily-ever-after for her characters, even if there are a few road bumps along the way.

Today she lives in Central Florida and writes full-time with the support of her loving husband and two finicky cats.

If you'd like to be notified of new releases, special sales, and get FREE eBooks, subscribe here: http://celiakyle.com/news

You can find Celia online at:
http://celiakyle.com
http://facebook.com/authorceliakyle
http://twitter.com/celiakyle

copyright

CPSIA information can be obtained
at www.ICGtesting.com
Printed in the USA
LVHW092251211219
641379LV00001B/35/P

9 781502 964472